The Monkey Cages

Library of Congress Cataloging-in-Publication Data

Names: Charles, Casey, 1951- author.
Title: The monkey cages / Casey Charles.
Description: Amherst, MA : Lethe Press, 2018.
Identifiers: LCCN 2018010485 | ISBN 9781590216491 (pbk. : alk. paper)
Subjects: LCSH: Gays--Boise--Fiction. z Idaho | Teacher-student
relationships--Fiction. | Gay rights--Fiction. | GSAFD: Historical fiction
Classification: LCC PS3603.H37643 M66 2018 | DDC 813/.6--dc23
LC record available at https://lccn.loc.gov/2018010485

Set in Sabon and Bebas Neue
Cover design: Frankie Dineen
Back Cover Photography: vkbhat and Istockphoto
Interior design: Frankie Dineen

THE
MONKEY
CAGES

Casey Charles

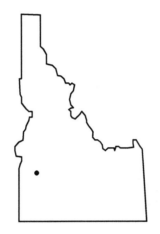

ACKNOWLEDGMENTS

Many thanks to those who have helped me with the development of this novel: Annie Dawid, Carla Hagen, Eric Haas, Jane Smiley, Jacquelyn Mitchard, Jon Jackson, Peter Charles, Steve Berman, and Jerry Wheeler. My thanks as well to Leah Maines and the Abroad Writers' Conference as well as the Jackson Hole Writers Conference.

Excerpts from Robert Anderson's play *Tea and Sympathy* are reproduced with the express permission of the Estate of Robert Anderson and Samuel French, Publisher.

In creating this fiction, I have consulted the following important sources: John Gerassi, *The Boys of Boise: Furor, Vice, and Folly in an American City* (1966, 2001 reprinted by the University of Washington Press); *The Fall of '55* (2005 film, directed and produced by Seth Randal); Gene Franklin Smith, *Boise* USA (a play produced in 2008); William Benemann, *Men in Eden: William Drummond Stewart and Same-Sex Desire in the Rocky Mountain Fur Trade* (2012, University of Nebraska Press).

THE MONKEY CAGES

Casey Charles

PART ONE

To the tune of "Teenager in Love"
by Dion and the Belmonts

1. BOISE BRAVES

He's tightening the laces of his shoulder pads, his freckles and wavy hair tilted down to those dangling white strings, his cup like a Shakespearean codpiece pointing at me from under thick canvas pants, that butt so round, so firm, so fully packed, those calves bare above sharp black cleats, clicking like hooves of a stallion across the locker room floor. Kurt. Perfect Kurt—cool, cocky, full of *sprezzatura*—whatever that means. I just read that word somewhere, but it fits his chiseled chest, his thirty-one-inch waist and rippled stomach, that Charles Atlas build you see on the back of *Superman* comics. He heads toward the field now, toward the sunlight framing his stride in the open doorway, his helmet held like a head below his hips. Above the number six on his Boise Braves jersey, the big letters of our mean and lean linebacker: MCKELLAR.

I'm still leaning over the bench, fumbling with knots, tackled by Kurt's body before our first scrimmage, before I've even suited up. I realize I'm just a skinny second stringer. When and if Coach Williams ever takes pity on me and lets me play, I know I'll get creamed by some bulldog guard while I try to rush the quarterback. Kurt's locker-room sack is a whole different ball game, though. At first, I just chalked it up to envy, jealousy, admiration. I figured every bookworm like me looks up to Kurt, wants his muscle, his hustle, his rugged looks. But why can't I stop staring at him? Why do I put my hand in my pocket when he's undressing, why do I stay hunched over pretending to tie my cleats until he leaves, why do I wake up at night with him on top of me instead of my girlfriend Pam?

We're all soaked in sweat when we head to the showers after practice, after the laps, pushups, mouth guards, and helmets as stuffy as a church in summer. "What are you lookin' at?" Kurt suddenly asks me while we're drying off. It's not really a question—more of a threat.

"Nothing." I turn red as a nectarine, hanging down my head like Tom Dooley, humiliated to be found out, exposed. He smiles smugly, removes the white towel from around his waist, starts patting down his dark patches, checking out my skinny body.

"Don't sweat it, Caddy," he laughs, using my nickname, snapping his towel at me as I pull on my Jockeys, my butt still wet from the shower. Maybe Kurt is okay after all. Maybe he won't declare me a homo in front of the entire team. Maybe he's just teasing, at least nice enough to notice a junior, especially one as insignificant as me. I'm a total string bean, almost six feet tall and not more than one fifty-five on a good day after a coffee milkshake down at Spreckles with my best buddy Freddie Udall, the only person in the world I can talk to. Freddie and I, we bonded freshman year, for better or for worse.

"Excuse me, is this seat taken?" I remember the brainy kid with a pair of Jack Benny glasses asking me almost two years ago during lunch hour. The picnic tables outside were getting full in late April's warmth, everyone in the yard with trays or bag lunches. Freddie carries a black lunch pail that looks like a barn. Me, I've got my Davy Crockett box, bologna and mustard on Wonder bread, a slice of cheddar, an apple I never eat, feeding them to horses on the way to school.

I nod. "Have a seat," I say and pat the place across from me with my hand, my mouth full. Fred sits down with his torpedo full of skim milk or something equally healthy and gross, looking up at me, smiling wryly at his own nerdiness, our knees banging together thoughtlessly. Freddie sports a retro argyle sweater and white shirt with a tie no less. I wear a wide-striped t-shirt, my butchwax buzz cut, my jeans rolled up at the cuff—all the James Dean rage. *Rebel* is at the drive in. It's '53 in the USA. Big round "I Like Ike" buttons have worked their magic, even though my dad voted for Stevenson.

By this time, ten months into high school, we all have a pretty good idea who Udall is. He's one of those kids that ruins the curve, every teacher's pet, the one with the high scores, the unpopular bench warmer who supposedly runs long distance. Us boys from St. Catherine's Elementary already have him pegged. Precious Freddie Udall, home-schooled until Boise High, his mom picking him up in their new woody at precisely three fifteen every afternoon, his dad some big wig at the Idaho First National Bank.

But it doesn't take long for me to feel the intensity of Fred's gaze that noon hour, his white skin and perfectly groomed dark hair, his long mouth, the deliberate chew and swallow of his deviled ham or tuna fish or whatever the heck that thin spread is between the grainy bread.

"You want one?" He hands me a vanilla wafer. I hate those boring cookies, but his hand almost shakes, his offer is so tentative and tender. I have no choice but to accept it.

"Thanks," I say around a mouthful. "You're in Hinton's right?"

"Yea."

"Did you read those poems? The ones by E.E. Cummings?"

"Yea, loved 'Buffalo Bill.' 'Jesus he was a handsome man and what I want to know is how do you like your blue-eyed boy, Mr. Death?'" Freddie knows the whole thing by heart already. That's the way he is.

"Yea, cool stuff."

"You want to be my friend?" he asks me without a hiccup.

Do I what? What kind of kid asks a question like that out of the blue?

"Why not? I kind of hang out with Skip and the guys from Saint Catherine's, but I could be your friend too, I guess. Maybe on the side."

"Those guys hate me. The in-crowd. They call me names all the time. The Momo homo. Jerks." He pauses and looks up at me. "Sorry. I forgot you might be part of that gang, actually."

"Yea, well, I don't know. I'm friends with those guys, you know, but I don't razz people like that, usually."

"You don't need to be my friend." He clasps his thermos to the inside of his lunch box with the neatness of an altar boy. Fred shuts the lid and sits there for a second with his hands on his pail, blinking. "I just thought I'd ask. You seem a little bit different than those jocks."

Jocks is it? What a little shit. I can't believe I let this weirdo sit next to me. It's Mom's fault. Her politeness training is so inbred, I've turned into one of Pavlov's dogs, whoever he is. Sure enough in no time I spot my friends, Trent and Skip and Runt, strutting toward us, perked up by the sight of yours truly, Tommy Cadigan, who can barely figure out a story problem in Mrs. Orcello's math class confabbing with this certifiable dork. I'm in for it now.

"What have we here?" Trent starts in. "If it isn't Little Lord Fauntleroy with Coke-bottle glasses. Hey there, Tommy. What's Miss Udall got to say for herself? Does she still know it all?" He has his hands on Freddie's shoulders, shaking them playfully. Freddie stands up, but Trent put his arms around him.

"Want to dance, little fella?" Trent says, shoving him side to side. "Maybe you and Tommy can go to the social tomorrow."

"Shut up, Trent." I get up and walk over. "Leave him alone."

Trent shoves Freddie around to face him for a fake dance while the kid struggles. Freddie's glasses fly off his face and hit the ground, cracking one of the lenses. I run over and pick them up.

"That was a dirty trick. Lay off him."

Trent lets go, but I figure he's only worried about getting into trouble. He and Skip and Runt scurry away, smirking and laughing. Assholes. Bad bananas when they're together, even if they are my buddies.

"You okay?" I ask Freddie.

"Yea. I got another pair at home. But I can't see much without them. Guess I'll have to be the one-eyed monster for the rest of the day." He sighs. "I'm used to it. The monster part anyway." He picks up his lunch pail, straightens his sweater, and walks off with all due diligence, as my dad the lawyer would say.

"Wait up," I call after him and he stops, refusing to look back. I run after him.

That's how Freddie and me became inseparable—this Catholic boy, son of a Basque mother and Irish father, and Frederick Oren

Udall, scion of that Mormon elder and pillar of the Boise community, Edward Udall.

We're in the living room in our pajamas watching the *Jack LaLanne Show* on the Philco television console one Saturday morning, trying to keep up with Jack's jumping jacks. "I heard he swam from Alcatraz to Fisherman's Wharf handcuffed," I tell Fred.

Freddie shrugs. He's unimpressed by physical prowess. "Those biceps are gross. How can you stand this show? Look at his black jumpsuit with that dumb little high-water belt."

Freddie, none too keen on muscle for muscle's sake, frowns upon my obsession with Kurt McKellar, which he calls hopelessly "prurient." He's already studying vocabulary for the college entrance exam, even though we're still juniors. We are on the floor now, trying to do pushups when Mom comes in with our dog, Coco, the boxer mix who climbs on Fred and licks his face. Freddie is not really an animal person, but ever since the puppy tore a hole in his temple garment under the sprinkler last summer, he and Coco have cultivated a certain rough magic.

"You boys." She shakes her head. "Heavens to Murgatroyd. What time is it? Tommy, would you do me a favor and take Fred upstairs, get dressed, make your bed, and empty the wastebaskets. And don't throw everything in the closet, please. When I get back from the hospital, I want to see that room neat. Chop, chop. And son, turn that idiot box off." Mom about faces and heads out the back door in the kitchen. She's a nurse. She works Saturdays. Actually, she seems to work all the time.

"I just don't understand what you see in him," Fred sighs in disbelief. I'm trying to explain my locker room obsession with Kurt McKellar to him. We're jogging around Julia Davis Park, the big green patch in the middle of Boise, where the library is and where our miserable excuse for a zoo sits. We call it The Monkey Cages, since apes are the main inmates. Fred and I are running in circles, and he as usual is wearing me out until I stop before the playground.

"Just give me a spot. Help me do some of these pull-ups." I'm trying to put on some muscle mass, my reluctant companion laying his hands on my thighs to push me up as I try to reach ten, the magic number. I give up after five chin-ups, huffing and puffing and smiling. "I tell you, Daddy-O, that Kurt is one cool guy with a perfect bod. I see a lot. And want to see some more."

Sweat makes my drenched t-shirt stick to my back. When I try to pull it off, my head gets stuck.

Fred comes over and pushes my noggin out of the cotton. "The trouble is it's not just that I want to be like him, which is never going to happen. It's that I want to be with him, like I have some stupid crush or something. I can hardly keep it in my stupid pants when he's around. I can't believe I'm telling you this, but you're the only one who knows what I'm talking about."

Freddie is my best friend. We've sworn to no secrets between us. That's down in ink somewhere. He's confided in me at weak moments that he's a lot more interested in Gregory Peck and Monty Cliff than Audrey Hepburn, even though he keeps telling me that sex without love is like a car headed down the highway without a driver, whatever that means. We've had our moments, the two of us—the camping trip in the Sawtooths last summer when it started hailing and we got so cold we had to huddle all night, feeling one another up. We've jacked off together a few times on warm summer afternoons, after some cajoling on my part.

It's the boys will be boys thing, we always say after it happens, if we say anything at all. Freddie usually gets all quiet, staring at me in eyes before he sticks his head in some novel like *The Charioteer.* For me it's just kind of fun, a release, a way of sharing with my close buddy the workings of my one-track mind, though with the Kurt thing, the track is starting to feel like the one Casey Jones headed down.

Of course, at school we both claim girlfriends, though Freddie mostly goes steady with his books, finding a date at the last moment for dances. Me, I've been going out with Pam for a while now, taking her to proms and the drive-in, walking downtown for sodas and stuff. But this Kurt crush is giving me second thoughts, more than thoughts actually, giving me some signals about where I'm driving, some green lights that are weird, exciting, dangerous. Could it be that I like guys more than girls? How is that possible?

"I gotta do something. I just gotta. I'm going steady with Pam for Pete's sake." We're walking out of the park now, cooling down. I'm kicking rocks, gesticulating like a mad Basque sheepherder. We're headed down to Spreckles for a shake. Freddie is pensive. He just walks with me slow and intent like a lazy trout that eyes a fly but is not about to be lured by some dumb guy with a pole.

"I wouldn't sweat it too much," he says. "Just hormones. Lust. As the preachers say, just one of the seven deadly sins. Satan has you in his grip, my boy." Freddie's *Crucible* imitation, trying to downplay my dilemma, and, at some level, his own by reverting to a little sarcasm. "What about Pam? She'll straighten you out."

"But I just don't lust after her in the same way. I don't get a woody when we make out at the dances. I like her, sure. I think she's beautiful, but I'm not trying to get into her pants. It's not the same. I love the way she smiles. I like talking to her, but I don't know, the spark just isn't there right now."

"Take Kurt to the prom." Freddie glances at me. He must have expected me to try and throw him into a headlock as he leaps out of my reach while grinning.

I just shake my head. "Thanks for the advice, twerp." I wish I could better explain the absurdity of my sex drive. "Actually, I wanted to invite you, but your dance card is full with what's her name, your little incest-is-best cousin."

We reach the swinging glass doors of Spreckles where I am forced to cool it, my shirt back on but still damp. Mr. Spreckles looks up at us. "Look what the cat dragged in." His green bow tie and white shirt in sync with the décor: olive green booths lining the wall, swivel chairs at the counter with jukeboxes, stainless steel lids for the frozen flavors of ice cream underneath. "If it ain't Mutt and Jeff."

It's Saturday afternoon, hardly a soul in the place except for some post-canasta grandmothers, their dainty fingers maneuvering long spoons in one corner and some kids crawling around a booth beside a frazzled mother Freddie and I are swirling on stools at the counter, reaching in our pockets for nickels and dimes we've raided from the box on my dad's dresser. Fred has been warned of the dangers of sugar cane, but away from the Udall compound, I figure he is about to indulge in some very dark chocolate as he pushes D4 to play his fave, "Maybelline." Mr. Spreckles has already begun working on my coffee shake. And, as usual, the first thing he wants to know is how the football season is proceeding.

"Coach Williams better take the Braves to State again," he says. "I'm counting on you guys."

"He's the best." Mr. Williams, our coach and history teacher, is definitely the coolest prof in the school—*sin duda* as Señora Vargas would say. It's such a rush to see him appear while I'm standing under a hot shower, trying not to watch everybody check everybody else out, so cool to watch him striding around in his khakis and Pumas.

"Nice hustle," Coach invariably says to Kurt or Trent, paying no attention to *moi*, just once in a while giving me a chuck on the shoulder or pat on the butt after a sack, saying "Chin up, Meriwether"—one of his favorite phrases, culled from our endless Meriwether Lewis and Captain Clark fests in history class.

Freddie and I are in American History this year with Marty, as we call him off the record. He can't be over twenty-five, though he always sports a five o'clock shadow on his round face, his dark hair combed across his impressive forearms as he shuffles across the classroom with his hands in his pockets, waiting for one of us to explain the Dred Scott decision or the Missouri Compromise. He is totally boss. Everybody loves him including me, so mesmerized by his presence I sometimes can't hear what he is saying. He's the one making us read *The Crucible*, which is why Freddie tells me it is better to marry than to burn. I'm doing my report on the Salem trials, Fred his on earlier Mormon settlers in Utah and the polygamy controversy. A bit of a history buff, Freddie. A bit of a four-eyed wonk.

"Coach Williams got you boys learnin' about some serious business in this country, I hear."

I love the deep, compelling sound of El's voice. El, or I suppose her parents call her "Elvina," is our fountain friend who sings at the local nightclub downtown. She moved out from San Francisco with her band to play jazz standards at the Gamekeeper inside the old Owyhee Hotel. A tall lady with long fingers, a wide smile, and a husky voice. She's sage.

"Good afternoon, boys." She looks over our heads at Mr. Spreckles, who is trying not to grimace. Eli is one of his best customers, but we can tell he isn't altogether comfortable with a Negro in his shop, not in the "Deep North" as my dad calls our town, but then he's from California and loves to make jokes about our little capitol. Spreckles himself could care less. We've heard his stories about black soldiers he befriended during the war, but he's obviously a little worried about the way Freddie and I eagerly carry our frosted tins over to the booth in the corner to join El for a little dish on the latest.

She is dressed for summer in a brown pleated skirt and a beige blouse, wing-tipped glasses with little jewels in the corners of the frames. Even on a warm Saturday, she is as neat as a pin, though quite a bit larger. She is sitting across from us, looking a little unsure about what to do about these white boys who have glommed on to her. "So what's the scoop? What's that Mr. Williams up to in that history class you been telling me about? It ain't just football over there in that school, is it? Surely, Mr. Fred here isn't runnin' no football." She smiles at Fred in his running shorts.

"We read a couple of sections from the court decision on deseg-regation," Fred says with all seriousness. "We have a test on the Constitution coming up, and we're supposed to write an essay on the meaning of equal protection. Everybody is wondering if they are going to be bussed to different schools, but we don't have any segregation around here. Everybody's white. Indians I guess, and the Army base at Mountain Home. But Boise, I mean, Miss Elvina, you're the first—"

"Call me El by the by, Freddie. And I understand you. Completely. Me and the boys faced a period of adjustment when we moved here from San Fran. Weren't nobody gonna rent a place to three colored jazz singers from California until we hired a certain well-known lawyer to help us get some decent digs. I'm happy to hear your football coach is also an enlightened man. Pleased to know you boys are learning a little about what "justice for all" has come to signify in this country. I admire that man."

"Marty's the best," I say again, at a loss for words.

We fall quiet as Mr. Spreckles approaches with Elvina's Raspberry Rapture—scoops of vanilla and raspberries topped with raspberry sauce. Our conversation turns to the Gamekeeper. El wants us to come by meet her pianist and drummer before the bar opens some afternoon during rehearsals. We are stoked as we scrape the bottom of our glasses for the last of the sweet freeze.

On our way back to the bike rack, we and the day are cooling down, the wind now in the pines, Indian summer sun beginning to fall behind a few scoops of clouds. We're pretty jacked we've been invited to a nightclub, even if it will be during the day.

Freddie, with a rather sheepish grin, turns to me as we reach the park's edge and says, "Maybe you should take Marty Williams to the prom." He takes off across the lawn after he sticks in his needle. I give serious chase, but I can't catch him until he stops and lets me tackle him. I'm on top of the wisecracker, have him pinned on the lawn by the arms, when he looks up at me and says, "Marty's the best," imitating my voice exactly.

2. BABY BUDD

"Handsome is as handsome does," Miss Winfrey reads from her Signet Classic. "What exactly does that statement mean?" She scans our twenty blank and nervous faces from behind her jeweled lenses, a silver chain hanging from the stems, her dark and wavy hair adding relief to a countenance that has nothing to do with the star of *National Velvet*. We are juniors. English with Winfrey is hard. The weekend is over and most of us want desperately to avoid her gaze, slouching behind our desks, bowing our heads toward Melville's novella *Billy Budd*. I had to look up about thirty words in the first ten pages, and none of us are in the mood for this on Monday morning.

Pam speaks up. "Actually, Claggart says, 'handsome is as handsome did too.' So it's in the past tense."

"Thank you, Pam. You're absolutely right. But what prompts Claggart to make this remark? What does Claggart's adage tell us about Billy, about Baby Budd, as Dansker calls him? Mr. Cadigan, can you enlighten us?" I'm in the back row, working on one of my maze doodles, scratching dandruff. She always calls on me. She's seen me trying to write poetry in the library.

"Well, I'm not sure," I stall. "The note says you're only as good-looking as your actions are. Billy's handsome for sure. Everyone kind of worships him. He's completely cool. And he gets his work done pretty well too, so I guess I'm not sure what's going on. And then he makes a mess, which makes him less handsome, I guess, or less perfect."

Miss Winfrey shoots me a stern glare. "Well, Tom, at least you have read the footnotes. That's a start. But what is the catalyst for the Master at Arms's strange comment? Let's start there."

"Billy spills his soup while the ship is rocking, and Claggart is walking by with his stick," Cheryl Nolte, Trent's steady, blurts out without raising her hand. She's an eager beaver, that one.

"Yes, indeed," Miss Winfrey nods. "He taps Billy from behind with his cane and says 'handsomely done.' What else does the narrator tell us about Claggart's sarcasm in this ambiguous scene? What's Claggart's relationship to Baby Budd? Anybody."

"His boss," Skip Johnson volunteers reluctantly.

"Obviously," Fred comments, getting revenge on the guy who likes to call him a pantywaist in the hallways. "But Dansker tells Billy Claggart is down on him. So Claggart is out to get Billy for some reason. There's more going on here than just a sadistic boss."

"Claggart's jealous of Billy," Pam suggests.

"He's the devil. He's wants to ruin the innocent sailor," Cheryl has read the intro.

"'Claggart was about to *ejaculate* something hasty at the sailor,'" I read from a paragraph. I underlined that word the night before, nursing a boner beneath the dining room table, thinking of cleats and whistles, grass stains and white tape, the sickening smell of Ben Gay and BO, the welcome whiff of Coach William's skin bracer. The guys in the back row start smirking as I emphasize the word "ejaculate."

"Yea, the greasy liquid," Trent guffaws from the back.

"Pervert," Skip throws in, referring to Claggart, I hope, and not me. Miss Winfrey is impressed by our participation, but she will brook no chaos in her classroom.

"Mr. Johnson may be on to something," she interrupts, "though his choice of words is unseemly at best. Let's slow down for a minute. Why is Claggart jealous? Something about desire may be a work here, something about repression."

"Claggart is turned on by Billy." I blurt out again, too eager for my own good. "Everybody is. Maybe he wants Billy, but he knows he can't have him, so he's going to get his revenge on the guy who he can't have."

"Whom," Pam corrects me from the front row. Everyone is staring at me now. "Gross," I hear one guy mumble behind me.

"Okay, okay, that's enough," Winfrey tells the snickering class. "Please, some decorum. So we know that Melville's allegory is working on more than one level. I want you to think next time about why Billy may be a sex symbol, why the narrator works attraction so closely into this tragedy." The bell rings, and the class springs up, ready to get the hell out of there after our gross discussion.

"You're disgusting, Cadigan," Skip Johnson says as he brushes past me to join up with his fellow jocks. I'm standing next to Pam, waiting for her to get her stuff together so we can head out. She says she's sorry she corrected me on my grammar in front of the class.

"No big deal," I tell her. "You're probably right. Hell if I know the difference between who and whom or how to diagram some of those sentences Winfrey puts on the board."

"Are you going to Cheryl's skating party on Saturday?"

"First I've heard of it." I feel touchy, put out by the guys giving me grief about Freddie. "I guess I didn't make the cut."

"I can get you in."

I shrug, a little ticked at being snubbed. "No way. Not without an invite. Hey, babe, I gotta go," I say, pointing to the can. "I'll see you in math."

I duck into the bathroom and stand in front of the urinal, trying to squeeze out a few drops, trying to calm down. The door opens as I stand there, my zipper down, my bladder empty, my eyes glued to a palimpsest of graffiti and unmatching paint on the wall. I quickly snap the elastic band of my briefs and fumble with my zipper. Trent Young, our fullback, stands in front of the mirror with his comb, lots of Brylcreem holding his dark hair in a wave on top of his scalp.

"Hey Trent," I say, touching the pimple on my chin as I look in the mirror.

"Cadigan. What's this Billy Budd is beautiful garbage? "And why the hell are you always hanging out with that flit Udall anyway? You ain't going queer on us, are you? You know you're cruisin' for a bruisin', kid. Big time."

"Why's that?"

"You're smart enough." He speaks into the mirror, avoiding my eyes. "Figure it out. By the way, pretty boy, your flag is at half mast." He glances at my pants through the mirror, then turns and swaggers out, slicking down his sideburns with his palms. I look down. My zipper is almost up for crying out loud, but I close it all the way, self-conscious and a little freaked out by his cryptic comments. What's wrong with me anyway? Why can't I keep my mouth—or my zipper—shut?

3. PAR FOR THE COURSE

Freddie and me, we think we're know-it-alls, I guess, getting A minuses in everything but math now at the end of our third year. But the truth is we're also pretty self-conscious, breaking out on our foreheads and under our belts. Speaking of belts, I have managed to rope my sidekick into a little trouble on the golf course tonight. It's Saturday, right before Spring break, and my old friend Bobby Sullivan, who lives on the sixth hole, is home for the weekend from his boarding school. He has a key to his parents' liquor cabinet and has proposed a link-up on the golf course with some of the guys. In spite of Freddie's reluctance, I am looking forward to getting into some trouble with my gang of nogoodniks, most of them jocks except for Bobby.

Bobby's dad works in Washington as a lawyer for some committee on Un-American Activities. He's in the news all the time condemning the United Nations. He's out to get those Reds. The Sullivans have maids and a big colonial behind a hedge that hides the golf course. They've dug a bomb shelter in their yard, a corrugated metal bunker covered with potting soil. The Sullivans are getting ready for the mushroom cloud to hit the Potato State. Our school is also starting to have drills, marching us into some dungeon to simulate a fail-safe scenario. The Red Scare is burning like a forest fire in the Sawtooths, and if Bobby has room in the shelter, I'm headed over to eat Campbell's Tomato Soup until the fallout allows us to emerge with our gas masks into a radiated Idaho. He hasn't invited me exactly, but I know where their bunker is hiding.

Bobby is a pretty hip guy, in with the in crowd, an old friend of mine from the days of tedious church picnics, dry ice, and bingo. Bobby and I used to have a blast chasing each other around print-dressed grandmothers who gambled shamelessly. Nowadays, we don't see much of each other. He's in prep school in California, no doubt off to Hahvahd soon, being one of those smart guys who never studies. I hate kids like that since I'm a bit of a grunt. I spent all summer last year reading five pages of *Quo Vadis* and most of *Lord of the Flies*, but I plowed through Archie comics like there was no tomorrow.

"Live a little, bud. Break out of your shell. Party pooper." I'm still trying to talk monk-man Fred into our Saturday night high jinx, even if he isn't inclined to socialize with a bunch of bullet heads who like to snicker at his nonconformities. He finally surrenders to my prodding, puts his ex-libris bookmark into page three hundred of *Mutiny on the Bounty*, and gets on his bike to follow me to the chi-chi North Side.

"Come on, Udall, don't be a wimp," Kurt McKellar teases, handing Freddie a pack of Salems he's stolen from his mother's cabinet. He follows that up by offering the bottle of Beefeater Gin Bobby has brought. I can't believe Kurt has shown up, hanging out with a bunch of juniors. Must be the Trent and Skip connection. McKellar is definitely boss, in faded blue jeans and that white tee showing off his biceps, even if he is razzing Freddie and struggling to maintain a two-oh so he can graduate.

"I don't smoke or drink," Fred says with his usual unflappable conviction. "I'm sure Tommy will take a puff, however."

"*However*," Trent Young repeats in high-pitched falsetto. "Give me a break, Udall. You know half of us are LDS. Who gives a flying fuck? We're just fooling around." Trent is a bull, a big dude some nice muscles and hair on his chest already. His Dad owns the most popular drive-in around Boise, the Howdy Pardner, where dancing girls perform on the roof Friday nights while his father Al plays piano and Trent flips burgers in the kitchen.

In spite of his flamboyance, Al Young still stays active in the Church of the Latter-Day Saints. He is also one successful businessmen. A lot of Jack Momos hang around this neck of the woods, though Freddie's devout family is not among the rebellious. When the cigs come my way, I light up like an old pro, stifling a cough. It's a warm evening, about six of us lying on the grass hidden from view behind a sand trap. We can see stars and feel the cool turf under our elbows. Talk runs to souped-up Chevys and Sherry Miller's tits. Trent keeps telling us how great she is in bed.

Runt interrupts him. "You're probably a virgin." Runt Ford is a scrappy kid from the other side of the tracks, a sarcastic SOB, always getting suspended, riding around on a seat-less Raleigh he probably stole from the rack outside the monkey cages in the park. He's borderline juvie, and his parents are slobs. My unforgiving mother calls them trailer trash. She's a Basque hardliner, Mom; she came from beret-wearing sheepherders—salt of the earth, poor as dirt but proud as hawks in the hills. She has no tolerance for the slovenly. Anyway, Runt has it tough, but he doesn't make it any easier by being a first-rate asshole.

"Screw you, Ford," Trent says. "Just because you've never even French-kissed a chick. You've probably never even got off."

"Every day. Sometimes twice. I seen him in Algebra playing with it," Skip Johnson says, taking a swig of gin and scratching himself down there.

"Remember when Podkaminer stopped gym class and looked the Runter in the face?" Trent reminds us.

"'Leave it alone. It will grow.'" I quote our teacher, an ex-Marine who would brook no pocket pool in his boring exercise class. Everyone laughs. Runt doesn't seem to care.

Kurt chuckles. "Tommy remembers it well enough. Wonder why." He's staring at me, pleased with his power to turn Caddy red.

"Look, I can never leave Winston alone." Bobby reaches down to put his hand over his crotch. "Horny enough right now. Always am. Even if Mary Wagner won't let me into her panties."

"You guys ever heard of a circle jerk?" Kurt sounds like a seasoned veteran. "Some of us do it in the park while these old guys watch.

They give us some bread for the trouble." I look over at Freddie, who is suddenly frozen, pushing his black lenses farther into his forehead. He raises his eyebrows at me, a gesture that speaks "let's get out of here" in no uncertain terms.

"You queer, man?" I ask Kurt with nervous sarcasm.

He jumps up and pushes me down sits on my stomach, pinning my arms. "What did you say, you little pussy?" He's getting drunk, ready to start a fight but at the same time grinning sheepishly into my eyes.

"Lay off." Bobby raises his voice. "Tom's my buddy. I invited him." Kurt winks at me and rubs his crotch on my stomach before rolling off, shrugging his shoulders. "Just joking around," he says. The rest of the guys are starting to follow Bobby's lead, heels of their hands below their belts.

"I think I better go," Freddie says to me.

"Come on, Udall," Johnson says. "You guys ain't goin' nowhere, you little chickens. We're in this together. No one's going to say anything, especially if everyone swears not to. You guys in?" He turns over on his stomach and looks at the rest of us. Freddie stands up, but Trent grabs his hand and pulls him down into a friendly bear hug.

"Leave him alone. He can just watch if he wants," Bobby orders. It's his party. "Give me the bottle." He takes a hit and hands it to me. The gin burns bitter, but I feel it after three swallows. Light-headed, a little dizzy, a little silly.

"If Mary were here," Bobby moans, undoing his belt buckle and pulling his zipper down. He already has a hard on. I can see it in the dark, rising from his jocks, his pants below his knees. Kurt follows suit, looking at me with that smirk as he takes it out of his faded jeans with holes in the knees, rubbing it against his flat stomach. Before long, all of us except Freddie, have taken off our shirts and slipped down our shorts, Skipper looking around now and again to see if anyone is about to come.

"Yea, man," Kurt says, "Jack it, Tommy. That's it." Freddie is watching me, so I feel almost too embarrassed to get hard, but when

Kurt gets to his knees right next to me and leans back on his heels, I can't help it. We are all going at it, most of us on our backs looking up at the stars.

"It's comin' man," Kurt moans, pressing my arm with his free hand. His touch surprises me as he ejaculates all over his stomach muscles and lets out a low, "Jesus." I come ten seconds later. Everyone else follows suit, relaxing for a still moment.

"Oh, wow," Runt starts in. "That felt so good. I've never done it with anybody but myself before." We all lay in silence for a while, wondering what we are going to do with the mess on our stomachs, our thighs, our hands. Who cares, I think, reeling from the thought that Kurt McKellar actually got off next to me. I glance over at Freddie sheepishly. He sits knees to chest, stoic and unnerved, while the rest of us soak it up and get dressed.

"You guys should come down to the park next weekend and check it out," Kurt announces. "You can earn some extra change and get your rocks off too. It don't mean you're a flit if you fool around for dough. Plus, it's a blast. Lots of the guys are down there Saturdays."

Kurt gets up and adjusts his jeans, giving me another suggestive look. "I gotta go, you guys. See you soon. Hang tight." Kurt staggers off, one foot in the sand trap. The rest of us watch him leave.

Freddie stands up and says to me, "let's go."

After a few "take it easy's," we head back to my house, shuffling across the dark fairway alone together, the moon almost full, dark shadows from pine trees casting omens over manicured grass. Tomorrow in the light of day, no one will notice Salem butts or dried semen around the sand trap as they rake. I'm feeling a little shame-faced but stoked about my wank with Kurt and Bobby, though my exhilaration is dampened as I sense my best friend's more deliberate steps over the cool turf.

"So, why are you such a stick in the mud?" I ask him after we sneak up the stairway and close the door to my bedroom. I turn on the lamp between the two single beds. Freddie is kicking his Buster Browns off, facing me. He's five six in stocking feet, thin and wiry, those thick black-rimmed glasses part of his anatomy. Sure, he looks like a square. Sure, he's breaking out around his big nose. Yes, he's uncompromising in his principles. But he is my best friend and has been for at least two years. I'm not going anywhere without him, regardless of his quirks.

"I guess I think it's impure. I know I'm a prude, but for me sex has to do with love. I probably should have just taken off, but I wasn't going to ditch you. I also wasn't ready to give those guys the opportunity to tie me up. So I just sat there with my knees up watching. Watching you the most. Trying to ignore my boner. Man, that was some kind of prayer circle."

"Gives a whole new meaning to polygamy," I try to joke, slipping off my shorts and sliding under the cool sheets. He may be a milksop, but Fred is the only person in the world I can relate to. My parents are always working—especially Dad with his trials and tennis tournaments. Only time I see him besides dinner is Sunday morning when he cooks scrambled eggs with hot dogs and the two of us read the Sunday *Statesman*, me mostly the funnies, while Mom sleeps in. Summers we wash the DeSoto wagon, squirting each other and Coco, our boxer, with the hose. Dad and I never talk much unless Freddie and I can argue philosophy and politics. Freddie's even developed, in his spare time, his own "world view," as he calls it, the manifesto he has worked out in some marbled notebook somewhere.

"I told you a million times," Fred continues, hopping into bed, "my first law is love, the kind of love Jesus had for John. I can't see flogging my log with some dumb jock as part of what I envision as love or even sex. Call me a sap, but I have to listen to what Jesus speaks to me." He removes his glasses and places them under the lamp, lying on his back and staring at the ceiling while I turn off the light. It's late, but neither of us is about to sleep.

"What happened to the revolution you're so worked up about? I thought you called yourself a rebel with a cause."

"My revelation is not about sex. It's about money and power, about the way money screws everybody up. It's about Orson Pratt and the ideas he brought to the church a hundred years ago with his Consecration. 'An inequality in riches lays the foundation for pride.' That's what he said. 'It's easier for a camel to pass through the eye of a needle than for a rich man to enter the kingdom of God.' There's no way around that statement. Private property is a sin. The house my dad is building in the suburbs is a sin. All the money he makes at the bank needs to be given to the poor. Not just the LDS poor but all the poor. You've heard my speech before."

"So where does sex fit in? Why can't a bunch of guys have fun once in a while? Why does sex always have to do with the ownership of a woman, or ten women, or even a man? Talk about inequality. Tell me again how many wives good old Orson had in his stable?"

"I don't know . . .maybe twelve. You're trying to change the subject. You can get off on Kurt all you want. I'm just telling you in my humble estimation, it's a waste of spirit."

"Didn't you tell me your precious Oren Pratt married a teenager at the ripe old age of…what was it…sixty something? Your precious Pratt can get away with that kind of bullshit while me getting off on McKellar is a mortal sin? Please. Give me a break."

"I'm not condoning Pratt's lust for teenage girls. I'm just interested in his political ideas. Just like you're not concerned with your beloved e.e. cummings's attachment to McCarthy's witch-hunt. I'm not sure how sex fits in yet to my utopia, to tell you the truth. I know women should not be second-class citizens. That much, yes. But for me sex has to do with being close to someone, with sharing. Not with gin and cigarettes at the end of a par four."

"So you think I'm a slut."

"So you think I'm a puritan."

"I don't think tonight was such a big deal. I'm not a complete homo if that's what you're thinking. McKellar is a hot guy. I admit it. I idolize him. So it was neat to be around him for a while. He's a total turn on." I'm silent for a minute after my revelation. "Maybe I am a homo. Jesus, Freddie, don't tell anybody. What if people find out I said that? I'll get creamed. Besides, I'd have to start wearing a ring on my little finger and lisping, like our drama teacher Mel Dir with his pack of Pall Malls. Oh shit."

"Getting drunk and jacking off on a golf course does not a homo make," Freddie tries to assure me. "I wouldn't worry too much. Just because the two of us have fooled around at the river a couple of times doesn't make us certifiable flits. Not yet anyway. For me, McKellar is just a lunkhead with a fat dick. So what? If you want to worship him, that's your deal. If you want to go to the park to make a few bucks to save up for the bike you want to get, fine. I'm not stopping you."

"Yea, sure." I flip over on my other side, my back to him. "You condescending little killjoy. I'm going to sleep." The conversation ends there. I don't want to talk anymore. The gin is wearing off and righteous Freddie is getting on my nerves, especially since deep down I know he is probably right. As usual.

4. THE MONKEY CAGES

Julia Davis Park qualifies as a getaway for me, a place to ride my bike aimlessly when I'm facing the old ennui, like Cole Porter. The park sits down by the river, and the banks are filled with plenty of nooks and crannies for me and my buds to explore once we get sick of tennis or hoops. Tonight it's just me and the coming summer, me fed up with Freddie's proselytizing and Mom and Dad's sarcasm, me and my one-speed Schwinn Cruiser with rusty chain and broken light, me in my shorts and t-shirt letting the back door slam after getting sick of watching *I Love Lucy* reruns.

Don't get me wrong. Freddie is still my best friend, but after the golf course thing, I know I have to discover what's out there on my own. My mom has laid folded pajamas on the end of my bed in order to prevent yet another set of stains on her precious sheets. I've been facing some very deliberate emissions lately, wanking off in a variety of locations. I think mostly about Kurt's body, but sometimes it's for an older, wiser man, a teacher who comes into my head whenever I follow Freddie's manifesto. It's hard not to be horny in these dog days.

And holding hands and cuddling at the drive-in with Pam just isn't doing it for me. She comes from a really strict family that believes in curfews and dress codes, so she won't let me anywhere near her thighs during the drive in's showing of *The Seven Year Itch*, which is probably okay. I'm not sure what I'd do if she did ever give me the green light. I seem to be much more adept at hugging pillows these days.

Who cares? Tonight it's enough to glide under the cool shade of maples, no hands on the bars, in the dusk light near the "zoo," that pathetic set of cages at the east end of the park where a couple of patas monkeys hop along with a rock hyrax, some weaver birds, and a lemur or two. A rather informal affair. As I head past the cages that evening, the lemur starts to craw and croak from a branch, but the rest of the inmates are sacked out.

I look up from the snorting monkey to find McKellar, Johnson, and a couple of other dudes hanging out around the big fountain, bench racing, shooting the shit. They wave me over. I stop, straddle my tilted cruiser, registering the major biceps rising like baseballs from Kurt's arms.

"What's up, Caddy?" Skip asks. My teammates call me Caddy not just because of my golf club days but also in reference to a certain lack of coordination on the gridiron and added value as a bucket boy.

"Not much. Just trying to stay cool."

"Where's freaky Freddie, your sidekick?" Kurt asks.

"Beats me," I reply, refusing like St. Peter to remind McKellar Fred Udall is not a freak, but my best friend. "What you guys doin'?"

"Waitin' for some action," Skip says. "You want in?"

In on what, I'm wondering? A few minutes later, a green Cadillac drives by real slow, the guy staring at us through his rolled down window. Kurt nods at him, slouching back with his legs spread as the fins of the big car sail by. It is definitely a Coupe de Ville; the white top gives it away. Just like Elvis's, but it's not a convertible.

"Looks like we got one on the line," a guy I've never seen before remarks. He sports pegged pants and pointed black boots, and his tight white t-shirt has the requisite cigarettes rolled up in the sleeve. I know a greaser when I see one. They're down near the Y all the time, leaning against a wall outside the bowling alley. This guy is bad news, but the thrill of being with Kurt trumps my flight response. A totally cherry Pontiac Chieftain is next—a two-tone with those signature lines down the hood. There are plenty of those roadsters in Boise. A nervous guy inside glances stealthily at the five of us while Kurt lifts his chin to him.

"Those guys are worth a ten spot for each of us, I bet," Skippy says, glancing at Kurt and the rest of us.

"Depends on what they want," Runt puts in. "I'm not givin' no blowjobs, I don't care how much they pay. They can blow me, but that's it."

I've heard of blowjobs but am not sure what they entail. I'm starting to feel kind of queasy, my heart banging against my ribs while I look at Kurt's sly grin. I'm just about to pedal out of this monkey business when Kurt stands up and walks over to my bike.

"Don't worry, kid," he whispers, putting his hand on my shoulder. "It's fun, no big deal. Just follow me." Out of their cars, the two men emerge from the trees. They are as old as my dad, dressed casual in khakis and plaid sport shirts. The one with the Frank Sinatra fedora looks familiar as far as I can make out in the dark. They won't get too close to us, though, remaining near the grove of junipers and staring. Pegged pants saunters over to them and starts talking. By this time, I'm paralyzed. Kurt's touch keeps me glued. Freddie's assessment of him crosses my mind for a split second, but Kurt's chest, bulging out of his sweatshirt mesmerizes me. I can't help starting to get a boner right in front of everybody.

Our leader shuffles back over, his Elvis hair slicked back with a flip in front, his skin as white as a bleached sheet, sleepy eyes full of that "who gives a flying fuck" attitude that scares me half to death.

"The bald man wants Kurt. The guy with the hat doesn't care. He just wants to get into our pants."

"How much?" Skip asks.

"They have twenty for all of us." There's a pause as we eye the men, and they glare at us. I want out, but it's too late. I'm ape-shit scared and don't like the idea of getting naked in front of some insurance salesman who wants to fondle me.

"I'm taking off," I say. "This is too creepy. You guys can split the bread." Kurt comes over and puts his arm around my neck, a friendly headlock.

"Relax. You can go with me. The more the merrier. The rest of them can handle the Pontiac guy. How about that, Hal?" he looks at our fearless leader.

"Cool."

Kurt and I walk toward the far side of the bandstand, where it backs up against a hedge near the monkey cages. The patas are quiet. The lemur grunts and then quiets down as the man slinks toward us. I watch Kurt pull down his gym shorts and start playing with himself as the guy approaches, falling to his knees and putting Kurt's limp dick into his mouth. Kurt closes his eyes for a second and looks over at me with a smile, moving his hips.

His shaft grows rigid as the man moves his mouth up and down the thickness. I can't believe this is happening in front of me, can't believe Kurt actually likes having this man's mouth around his beautiful cock. It grosses me out, makes me mad, especially when Kurt starts grinning at me and reaching over for my crotch. I panic, feeling sick to my stomach as I watch Kurt put his hand on the guy's half bald head. How can he let this stranger do that to his body? I feel betrayed, afraid, and confused. Turned on and grossed out at the same time. Jealous and angry. Why is Kurt selling himself for sex? Why aren't we doing it together? What am I doing here?

I turn and run, desperate for my bike and the night's breeze. My head down, I run toward my wheels when suddenly I bump into someone in the dark, knocking his hat off just as he's coming around the bandstand. I pick up the fallen fedora, hold it out, and say "sorry, sir," stumbling toward my Schwinn, jumping on and taking off like a bat out of hell. The lemurs are suddenly crying in high-pitched screeches, their ringed tails and yellow eyes coming into my vision, though I can't see their bodies. Not until I'm a block away do I realize whose hat I just held in my hand. I'd seen that face at the dinner table with all his kids and my best friend sitting next to me as his mom passes the coleslaw.

5. MR. U

No way will I tell Fred, at least not until I figure out what to do. Sure, he doesn't take to his Dad's big-bucks agenda, but he still respects him. Edward Udall is an elder in their ward or whatever it's called. He's the vice-president of the biggest bank in town, and he manages a family of seven with the skill of a school principal. He's building a house in Nampa, the growing suburb where the Mormon clan is setting up their community. He wears dark suits and starched white shirts with tie clips and wingtip brogues.

I've stayed at Fred's house loads of times for dinner and always feel kind of like an extra in *Oklahoma*. Hell, they're real nice to me. I get all the mashed potatoes I can eat, and Freddie's mom is always chipper and upbeat in a flowered apron and oven mitt as she brings bacon-topped meatloaf to the table. We all get assigned chores—setting the big chrome-rimmed red table, blue oval placemats with matching water glasses. Freddie leads us in grace, his sisters clearing the white plates, rinsing, loading their dishwasher. It's all too perfect.

I start thinking about one night a while back during dessert, when Fred raised his eyebrows toward me, jiggling his green Jell-O with a fork, murmuring some remark about fossilized pineapple.

"That'll be enough, Fred," Mrs. Udall quickly says.

"Father, may I please be excused?" Sibyl, Fred's little sister asks. Her dad's reply sticks with me.

"Not until you have finished your Brussels sprouts, young lady. The Lord has provided us with this bountiful repast, and we must partake in His plenty." Syb puts her head down and stares at the green globes, little balls resting on her plate, while the rest of us wobble our lime Jell-O. Her fork touches the tender worlds. She's not ready to catapult them into her mouth.

"How about if I eat Freddie's Jell-O instead? He's just playing with it anyway," she suggests.

"That will be enough, child," Mrs. Udall states, her grimace only momentary before her toothy smile returns. She has just had her hair done, and it sports one of those Annette Funicello flips. Quite stylish, I note, her pleated skirt billowing out from a wide patent leather belt. "Fred, have you spoken to Thomas about our new YSA chapter? I'm sure he would love to know about it." Fred looks at his mother blankly, pushing in his frames with his signature index finger.

"A new YMCA?" I stupidly ask.

"Not exactly, young man," Mr. Udall replies, chuckling with an insider's savvy. "The YMCA is not an association to which our family belongs. Fred, why don't you share with Thomas the news of your new vice-presidency?"

Freddie blinks twice and adopts his speech and debate persona. "It appears I have received the unique honor of being elected as the inaugural vice-president of a new chapter of the Young Singles Association of Boise, Idaho. I feel a bit like John Adams, I must say. The association brings young men and women together for social events, including glee clubs, Bible workshops, and bird-watching groups. We hope to serve Hawaiian Punch and Rice Krispy squares if we receive approval from the bishop. We are all very excited, Thomas."

"Fred masks his enthusiasm with sarcasm," Mrs. Udall says to me, "but don't think for a second he's not proud to be a founding member. The YSA provides a healthy and safe place in our ward for teens to undertake the courtship process in preparation for years of happy marriage that lie ahead. Fred will be able to begin his search for the young woman who will bring his family and children into the world. We in LDS feel it important to nurture intercourse between the sexes in an environment free of dubious influences of the likes of that James Dean fellow."

All five of the Udall children smirk and giggle in response to their mother's unfortunate choice of the word "intercourse."

"Now, children," Mr. Udall raises his voice in a tone that sounds like a preacher. "Let's not show disrespect for your mother. She has dedicated her life to raising you. Just as you, Sibyl, will do one day with your own family."

She must have been six or seven. "Not me. I'm going to Africa with Freddie. I want to be a missionary."

"You will learn, child," her father says. "For now, your mission lies before you in the form of four Brussels sprouts."

"Convert the heathens!" Freddie says, "Swallow them whole."

"Frederick, please," his mother states, "don't be insufferable."

After dinner, Freddie and I remove ourselves to the train set in the attic, where we secretly trade baseball cards. He likes Mays, I Stan the Man Musial. Of course we're budding intellectuals, arguing about the Birchers and the Communists, but baseball is also good to us.

While I'm brooding and reminiscing in bed after fleeing the monkey cages, after my run in with the good old boys, I realize I've never really gotten to know Mr. Udall. He's as intimidating as any grown-up I've ever run into, and even more formidable because of his status in the Boise world of big business and big religion. I can't figure the guy out, can't wrap my head around his reason for sneaking down to the park to play with boys. It doesn't make sense given what's at stake for him. I don't even want to think about the why or the how. I just want to bury it, keep my mouth shut. Mr. U probably figures I won't tell anybody because I was down there too. He probably figures I'll take the Fifth. He has to be worried about his son, though. He knows Freddie and I are tight.

Sure, I'm shocked and dismayed, as they say in those penny dreadfuls my mom reads. Who wouldn't be? Mr. Udall doesn't strike me as a crotch groper, but of course I don't strike myself as one either. We're both mesmerized by Kurt, even though I'm now pretty disgusted my linebacker would allow that car salesman or whoever he was to put it down his greedy throat.

Screw McKellar. Slut. Of course, Freddie is right. He always is, but that realization doesn't keep my sheets dry. I have to figure out what to do about that. Maybe good old Mr. Udall has the same problem. We both have the same fire down below even if I'm not an elder in LDS. Hell, I did spend my year or two as a reluctant altar boy, feeling the sweet squeeze of Father Ward as he helped me with my surplice before ten o'clock mass.

Living in a glass house, I can't really stone the hypocrite by divulging his dirty little secret. Plus, I'm no rat. Sorry for the stupid *Dragnet* clichés. I just can't bring myself to ruin his life or, more importantly, to ruin Freddie's. Leave him to his conscience, I think, remembering *Hamlet*. I always wondered about him and Horatio, his best bud, his Freddie. Let sleeping fairies lie, I decide. I'm lying too, after all. I just want to forget it, forget the whole episode, forget McKellar, Hal, Skip, Runt, and the man in his Caddie. I just want to play for Coach, go running with Fred on the levy, cross country ten miles with my best friend—with our shirts off. I want to jump in the river with him, drown all this sex stuff. Please God.

I'm plenty worried about Freddie, though. We've never had secrets between us. We're blood brothers. We cut each other's thumbs in my tree fort and drafted our own Laws of the Land together after studying ancient history with Mr. Gates. Soon after, Fred received his revelation from his own private angel Jonathan, and was full of his vision—his illumination as he calls it.

Fred is big time deep, got to give him that. What a weird kid. One of a kind, all right. He has his own set of ten commandments. "Thou shalt not own property. Thou shalt not build hierarchies. Thou shalt tell the truth." Utopian stuff. Praise Jesus, I don't have to face my best friend until Monday, so I have a day to hone my deception skills. Frankly, I don't know what I am going to do when I see him, but I have time to cogitate, and come summer, which is right around the corner, I'll be working at the hardware store. And Freddie's family is in the process of moving to Nampa, so we'll both be fairly busy. He's not going to be able to ride over to my house anymore once they move. He'll be busy with his YSA group, busy packing boxes, busy criticizing his family's conspicuous consumption.

We are planning to head up to Eagle Lake in a couple of weeks, though, if I can get Dad to loan me the Jeep. Go early before it gets hot, do some trail running, then head for the water somewhere secluded. Mushy PB and J sandwiches. Tang. It'll be fun if Freddie doesn't rattle my cage, doesn't rip my secret out of me.

6. Y ME

The Treasure Valley Y downtown, is, let's face it, a bit seedy. Anyone can go in there, and its stucco, two-story walls are boring and boxy. I joined this summer to swim and get in shape, and most of the guys are there for the same reason. Skip comes once in a while, and so do some other ball players from school. Yes, McKellar shows up, of course, but I keep my distance from him even when he sidles up to me and asks if I need a spot. He's hard to avoid, especially in the steam, but the image of him with that bald man on his knees keeps me from moving beyond an occasional glance at his washboard stomach.

My usual routine after work at the hardware store: pushups, chin-ups, sit-ups and then a swim. I'm not a barbell kind of guy, not with my skinny frame and gawkiness. I keep to myself mostly, though the old locker room with its rusty cage-like doors, worn benches and open showers is an eye opener for a raw kid like me who is trying to figure out why these blokes in their thirties and forties with fit bodies and hair on their chests are so frigging hard to resist. What's my story, anyway?

It's not the sin thing that troubles me so much. I don't cotton to religion the way Freddie does. I mean I go to confession. I give up stuff like Hershey's bars for Lent. I wore the salt and pepper uniform at St. Catherine's until I went to Boise High. I love the smell of sandalwood and taste of those wafers, and, yes, Jesus's body is rather mesmerizing in that loincloth. But I guess all the guilt stuff never stuck.

I feel more guilty holding hands with Pam or slow dancing with her. I never read the Old Testament anyway. Sure, I like Genesis and the Psalms, but all those lists and laws are just too boring to keep my interest. Give me *Men Against the Sea* any day, give me Jules Verne or even *The Yearling*. Give me *The Bear*—there's a story. When Isaac turns down his inheritance, Freddie and I jumped for joy. When he saved his dog, I knew he was my man. I would go to the mat for Coco, our boxer mix. She is my best bud next to Freddie, even though she likes Freddie a lot more.

I love the raiment, and I love midnight mass. But sin doesn't make sense to me. I can't figure out why it could be wrong to love some-body who loves you back and why it isn't a sin to hate someone for loving. So when I get off imagining guys like Kurt and even Coach at night, when I start leafing through *National Geographics* I've horded, I don't fall into some spiral of shame. I'm just surprised and amazed at what gets me hot and bothered.

Who wants to be a homo? What a life. A rock on my pinky and lavender shirts to cover my limp wrists. But what else can I do? I'll have to move to San Francisco and sell men's fashions at some department store, a yellow tape hanging from my blue blazer. Slink into dark bars after hours. Not exactly my Romeo vision of the world. Now what, I wonder after another nocturnal emission, wres-tling with a buff angel. Where the hell's this coming from?

Much of this trepidation comes not just from the way Freddie and every other nerd at school get called "queer," but also from the danger I witness on the silver screen when I watch *Rebel Without a Cause* at the drive-in. Everybody knows James Dean is beyond cool, but Plato haunts me. Talk about a crush. Nobody calls him a homo, but when he gets shot at the end, trying to defend Jim, it's pretty obvious his love for Dean has resulted in a bullet. Reminds me of Mercutio. Look, I ain't no Plato, but I sure get just as jazzed as he does looking at his friend. Maybe the Y is not the best spot for a kid like me. Maybe I should be taking a Chevy apart or building go-carts.

But here I am among the combination locks and old sweaty tiles, insecure and excited at the same time, working out in that stuffy atmosphere with the allure of its exposure, its germs and sweat-stained t-shirts, its silent sauna where racquetball players stare at wooden slats, timid in towels. Here I am with all those guys around, and not just guys my age, but real guys with jobs and muscles.

And guess who's in the pool one evening while I'm slogging through my thirty laps in plaid trunks and leaky goggles? It's Coach Williams! Working out at the Y. What could be neater than that? My friggin' football coach doing the friggin' breaststroke right next to me. I've never seen him without his button-down shirt and khakis. Never seen his bod in the flesh.

Mr. Williams is not that much older than I am. You'd never know it given his brickhouse physique, his five o'clock shadow, and the hair on his thick chest. His stomach slightly bulges, but his arms, are thick and muscular, and his round face has a stoic look that breaks into a sly smile when the mood grips him. He wears his dark hair short. Not a flat top exactly, but not much longer.

"Hi Coach," I say, lifting my hand in a wave, a bit too gleefully. He looks over and takes in my head, the only part of me not submerged.

"Why look who's here," he deadpans. "If it isn't Chin-up Tommy himself."

"That's me."

"What brings you down here to this den of iniquity?"

"Trying to get in shape, I guess." He does a take on my body, since I'm now standing in the shallows next to him.

"You're doing all right. You been working out a little, I see. You going out for the team next year?"

"Yes, sir. Probably end up warming your bench again, but I'm going to give it a shot, for sure."

He smiles at my response. "A senior, right? Going to college?" He's bobbing in the water. The air is too chilly.

"Yea. I'm applying in the fall. I want to go to Georgetown, but I'll probably end up in Berkeley or Missoula."

"You'll do well. You're a good student. I'm from Montana, actually." He pauses and looks up at the clock. He climbs out of the water, trunks and legs dripping. "Well, I'm off to shower—too cold. Have a good summer, Tom."

Why is he running off so quickly? I guess I'm feeling kind of cold too, but I'm too self-conscious to follow him. I do my final five laps, trying to beat the clock, then I climb out of the pool toward my towel, heading for the sauna. It's plenty dark inside and pretty damn hot. I find a place on the upper bench and sit with my towel underneath me, looking down at the floor, four or five bodies near me, though I'm too downtrodden by Coach's standoffishness to even look at them. They're talkin' baseball or fishing or some damn thing; I'm barely catching every third word, elbows on my knees, hands holding up my head.

What am I doing, hoping to get close to my teacher, for Pete's sake? For Peter's sake, I think, smiling cynically. I need Freddie, my anchor, but he's almost off limits about this stuff now that I know about his dad. There is no one but Peter, and Peter has a one-track mind. It isn't funny. I'm beginning to figure out it isn't part of some stupid teenage prank for me, some way to humiliate horny old men and make some spending dough. What I want, what I see in a guy like Coach Williams, has nothing to do with that idiocy, I realize, sweat now starting to bead up on my forehead. The jocks in the sauna finally leave.

My internal monologue gets interrupted by the arrival of my thought provoker. Coach is dripping again, this time from the shower. He comes in carrying his towel and sits down at the bench farthest from me. My heart is pounding furiously. Can he tell? He says nothing, doesn't even look my way, elbows on his knees. Then he rises up and flattens his back against the wooden slats. I try not to follow the ribbon of dark hair that descends from his stomach.

"We meet again," I say, laughing. "Small world." I can't help myself.

"Hey, ," he says with a sigh. I don't know what to say, so I keep glancing toward him even though his eyes are closed. He's withdrawn completely. I'm deflated, embarrassed, dripping, and drooping. I won't invade his space, I decide, getting up and reaching for the door. I mumble "see you" as I walk toward the shower, towel around my waist. The water cools me off, and I find a piece of left-over soap, lather up, scrub everywhere, trying to wash that man Marty right out of my hair. My parents have the album. They've seen *South Pacific* on Broadway during one of their junkets to cure the little town blues. They keep promising to take me, but I always end up having to feed the dog and babysit grandma.

Of course, I can't stay in that shower too long with all those sudsy butts now staring me in the face. Some of the guys are gross, which makes it easier, but some of them check me out pretty voraciously, you know, that head-to-toe treatment. I guess I'm doing the very same thing with Coach Williams. I rush to rinse off. Drying, I see in the mirror the same torso I looked at before I walked into that body shop. Oh well, it isn't that bad. I guess I just have a small frame. Maybe I'm not big boned.

At the locker, I drag my stuff out of the cage and sit on the bench, cooling off before putting my clothes on. I'm starting to cry. Can't help it. Mr. Williams is so absolutely cool. I always thought he kind of liked me, with the nickname and the pats on my back. I can't believe he doesn't care one iota about me. By some stroke of luck or tantalizing torment, he shows up a second later in the same row where I hunch over in my blue funk. He stands twisting his lock, trying to find numbers. The first try apparently doesn't work, the second either. He keeps trying to pull the lock open, creating a racket and finally shaking his head. I hear his "*Schiesse*" under his breath. He gives up and flips the Master against the metal cage, then turns and walks toward me.

"Look ," he says, "You're a good kid. You're smart and a damn fine runner. I think we both know you're not a football player, but who cares. That's not the end of the world." He leans over and puts one foot on the bench, compromising the coverage of his towel. "You know I'm not supposed to fraternize with my students outside school. I mean it's okay for me to take the team to breakfast once in a while, but I shouldn't be hanging out in saunas with one of my kids, especially one who…" He glances at his elusive lock. "You know what I mean. Just don't take it personally, okay?"

I nod. I'm just stoked he's making some contact. "I guess I thought we could just, I don't know, be friends, since we're both here," I say to him. "It's not like you're that much older than me, right?" I'm taking a chance, overly bold with my teacher, but I can't help it, "Sorry. I shouldn't have said that. I apologize, Mr. Williams."

"We *can* be friends." He spins his lock again. "As soon as I can open up this screwed-up locker and get my clothes on." He is smiling, more than his usual wry grin. I walk over and ask him for the combination. "26, 16, 7," he says. I give it a go. "Third time's the charm," I say as the lock opens, and I head back down the bench to pull on my pants. I'm leaning down to tie my laces when I catch him out of the corner of my ungovernable eyes holding his boxers up in front of his penis. It isn't hard, but it's bigger than it was in the sauna. I don't want to be crass or anything. Coach is making me crazy in ways Kurt never could. He's pulling some strings I never knew I had, strings thicker than sex, though I'm not too proud to admit that he is also a total turn on. His hasty step into those long cotton briefs paints a picture I want to frame. Sheepish, surprised even scared of my boldness, "Bye, maybe see you in the pool soon." Bounding up the stairs two by two, too jacked to wait for an answer, emerging into warm night air with pure joy.

Coach and I meet in the pool almost every day now. He's opening up a brave new world for me, one where my thing for guys doesn't have that much to do with dangling dicks and sudsy butts. Marty Williams the person—not the coach, not the history teacher, not the adult—amazes me every time we talk. I know I'm in over my head, but I can't help wanting to curl up with him, put my cheek on his chest, hug him with all my might, touch him all over his body, feel his lips on mine.

I can't tell a soul about that fantasy, much less Coach himself, who I assume sees me as a lost kid he can mentor and encourage, though part of my fantasy includes thinking he feels the same way about me. Of all my friends only Freddie might understand my crush. But Freddie has been making himself scarce lately.

My heartbeat races as I skip down the stairs of the Y, out into the evening air after a swim and talk with Coach, my head wet, my muscles tired, my mind full of stories. I bet he's never told another soul some of the things about himself he's told me. I'm like his secret confidante. Most of our talks are in the sauna after everyone else clears out, but once in a while, we find ourselves face up on the blue stretching mats upstairs next to the free weights. I usually find him doing sit-ups or push-ups and I try to keep up until we both lie on our backs after leg lifts, exhausted.

"You ever heard of the Bitterroot Valley? Ever heard of Darby? That's where I grew up on twenty acres, not more than a mile from the river," he tells me. "It's not far from Missoula, where you're applying."

"What was like to grow up in a town that tiny?" I ask, transforming myself into Arlene Francis. She's on *What's My Line?*, the game show where celebrities guess someone's occupation by endless questions. I've been trying to get Coach to reveal stuff, even if I feel like a pest sometimes.

"Pretty rough. You're lucky you've got a father like Kevin Cadigan. My dad was a hardliner. I remember he took me down to the basement and whipped me hard with his belt when I came home from high school and announced I was going to be a poet. 'No son of mine goin' to be no fairy writer,' he'd say. And down came that belt." Coach slapped his hand down hard on the floor and the sound made me skittish. "As if John Donne was light in the loafers. Only reason I ended up playing football to make Pop happy. I still got beat up when the guys found me with my notebook writing bad sonnets during recess."

I nod. "My friend Freddie Udall gets a lot of razz too, and he's not even a poet. Nobody likes me hanging out with him."

"They're just jealous. Jealousy is the worst sin."

He grows quiet and soon I have to break the tension between us. "So how did you end up here in the wonderful City of Trees?"

Coach sits now, knees to chest. He glances over at me on the floor. He knows I'm trying to pry him open, like a girl's locked diary. He rocks back and forth as I jiggle the little, squiggly key.

"I ended up in Korea. Wasn't much older than you are." He nods his head as he looks down at his bare feet on the bench. "In the Army. Now it seems unbelievable, but I thought it might let me escape, see the world, all that stuff.I lost the best friend I've ever had over there, during a night patrol at the 39th Parallel. His name was Desi and some sniper stole him from me."

On my bike rides home, I find myself out of control, racing ahead with dreams of me and Coach breaking loose from the clutches of the big little town of Boise. Yet I do worry about how possible my daydream is. We both have different orbits: I'm just a little moon whirling around the Earth and he's like Haley's comet.

The evening is all shadowy from evergreens and budding groves of maples. I'm a little agitated by Coach's reaction in the locker room, but the way he has started getting close to me the last couple of weeks is gut-punching me pretty hard. I see a huge contrast between the guy with the white shirt and tie, rolled up sleeves, and pressed chinos, shouting controlled commands at halfbacks or passing the ball to wide receivers during practice and the swarthy guy in gym shorts with dark swirls across his defined chest. I'm a sheltered nobody from Nowheresville who writes bad imitations of Yeats and chases Freddie through the foothills for kicks, and here I am sitting naked on a hot bench next to a guy who's been to hell and back. Yea, I've told him about my dad the town lawyer who's more stoic than a portrait of Abe Lincoln. I've told him about Mom, the emergency room nurse who leaves early in her spongy white shoes and vacations with her Basque family up in the mountains somewhere.

I haven't said anything to him about McKellar or Mr. Udall, of course. How can I tell my Coach I am into guys? I think he suspects—I worry he notices how I admire him. And other dudes. Especially when they're doing the butterfly in racing suits or bicep curls on the bench. I feel as if I could claim to be that scrawny kid in the Charles Atlas ads…but then I remember Coach mentioning jealousy is the worst. And I worry, maybe I'm just fascinated by his physique and it's not desire.

Tommy, Tommy, Tommy. You're fooling nobody, I tell myself on one block. *He would kill me if I said anything*, another voice sounds out after I run a stop sign. I have to keep hiding, hold my feelings in for as long as I can. Hell, just this evening, some friends of Marty's interrupted us while were lying on the mats after sit-ups, talking about our lives. I was so self-conscious I started in on some bullshit about the first practice of the season or the Giants moving to San Francisco, something acceptable for guys to discuss. Trying to be cool. I guess I wanted to protect him from the obviousness of my infatuation, which he's being nice enough to put up with.

I'm feeling different by Thursday, less ambivalent, I guess. Only one more workday at the hardware store until the weekend. It's July already. I wear shorts in the warm summer sunset, and for the first time in a couple of weeks, Coach and I are leaving the Y together. I usually head out before him to avoid "any appearance of impropriety," as my dad the lawyer says, but we got a late start and the gym is closing. It's getting dark.

"I was wondering if you want to take a walk in the park for a while before you head home?" I ask Coach while we head down the stairs outside.

"I don't know." He looks around. "I'd go in a minute, but I need to be careful about you and me."

"Can't you just drive over there and meet me at the Greek statue in the circle for a few minutes. I know a place where we can talk."

He scuffs the sidewalk with his sneakers. "I don't—"

"I just want to tell you something in private. It's important."

He sighs. He stares at my face. "All right. But you're going to have to make it quick. I'll see you in ten."

I jump on my bike and ride over to the park, pretty much empty at nine on a weeknight. Pacing beneath Pericles, I watch Marty walking toward me. He follows me into the cedar grove where we lean against separate trees. I can tell he is nervous. So am I.

"I don't want to get you into trouble." I swallow down the rush of emotions, because they will choke me. "The reason I want to be your friend...so much," I say, "... I know you're my coach and teacher, an older guy who's been around the world and seen 'bout everything... but I can't help it...I'm just feel something...."

I have to stop there, unable to confess more than I already have. I'm ready for his rejection, looking down, kicking dirt. I feel his hand on my shoulder. He holds me close to him for a long time in a hug, and then puts his hands around my face, his fingers under my wet eyes. I am trembling.

"Chin up. We've been havin' a good time this summer, having some good talks. But I'm your teacher. There are some lines here we can't cross."

From out of the corner of my eye, a light skims the grove around us from the pathway near Pericles. I put my finger to my mouth and Marty looks over his shoulder. I motion for him to head out through the thicket, and he quickly rustles away as I slip to the bottom of the tree and cross my legs. I close my eyes, hoping the torch will disappear or move on. Seconds later, a park guard walks up and flashes his light in my shut eyes.

I must mumble "Hi."

"What are you doing in here?"

"Sorry, I was just sitting here, thinking out loud. Saying my prayers," I said, with a kind of holier-than-thou attitude, adopting my altar-boy countenance. The officer points his light around the grove, suspicious. He finally shakes his head with one of those "kids-these-days" expressions. He stands looking around, his nightstick teetering on his hip, his arms folded in disbelief.

"The park closes at ten, young man. And I would not recommend leaving your bike unlocked. You've got fifteen minutes to clear out."

He turns and leaves, his light receding into the grove. I am reeling. I can't move for five minutes. Whatever the opposite of prayerful meditation is, that's my mental state. I'm scared for Marty, excited about our friendship, ticked off about the cop. I can still feel Coach's hug as I pedal home in a daze, exulted by mischief, undeterred by reticence, and spurred on by sweet transgression.

7. IDA RED

Elvina is the first person I decide to tell—about Freddie's dad, that is. I'm definitely not going to say anything to her about Coach, but the Freddie thing is eating away at me bad and I have to get some advice. Luckily, I find her at Spreckles one hot July afternoon after a few laps in the park. El is hunched over a book in a booth. She always hangs out in the same spot in the back of the place, so Mr. Spreckles won't lose business.

He has to serve her because of the new laws and such, but she's been nice enough to remove herself from the counter and start sitting in the back of the bus as long as she gets her rapturous raspberry fix and a little peace and quiet in the cool shade. She looks up with a smile when she spots me. I saunter over to say hi. She is dressed real casual today in a blue skirt and white blouse.

"Hi, Elvina. How's it goin'?"

"It's goin', honey, it's goin' just fine. What's your story? How can you run in this heat, anyway? You're one brave man."

"Do I smell bad?" I ask, sniffing my armpits.

"I don't smell a thing. You know that. Sit down, my man." Elvina raises her eyebrows and looks around as I bounce into the booth.

After settling down on the cool green seat, I look into those big white eyes. I can tell she's got my number.

"Where's Mr. Fred?" she asks. "What you comin' in here for without him?"

"I'm not married to him, you know." She gives me one of those looks that tells me to get off it and come clean "I guess we kinda had a fight. Not a fight fight," I said lifting my fists. "But a disagreement."

"'Bout what? You boys are too close to fight. Tell El what happened, now." She smiles. El wants the scoop. I spoon ice cream from my glass into my mouth in between sips of ice water, volunteering nothing. She won't be satisfied until she coaxes it out of me, which is exactly what I want to happen. El isn't the kind of person who takes no for an answer, especially from a sarcastic little whippersnapper *como yo*.

"Yea, well, it's kind of hard to explain. I'm not sure I want to get into it."

"You ain't gettin' off that easy, mister. Look, you're talking to Elvina. We've been eating sweets in here for at least four months. You going to just shuck me off?"

"You ever heard of York?" I ask her. "Or Marian Anderson?" I want to change the subject. I suck on my straw, flecks of chocolate chips clogging the passage.

"Yea, I know Marian. I heard her sing in San Francisco years ago. And I know she stayed here at the Owyhee. About the first thing they told us when we got the gig. Boise Hotel wouldn't take her. York doesn't ring bells for me, though. Who's that cat? And what's the big quiz for? I thought we are talking about Freddie. What's going on with you, boy?

"Well, we've been studying some stuff about history and different races in Coach's class. We heard about this guy York who tracked for Lewis and Clark when they came through here looking for the ocean. The first black guy in Idaho, they say."

"A slave, I bet," she tells me, placing her hand on her closed book. "Look, you going to drink that milkshake or just suck on that straw for the next two hours?" she suddenly asks, a little fed up with my evasiveness. I give up and bring the glass to my mouth, trying to avoid drips down my t-shirt. We sit in silence.

"What are you reading?" I ask her, trying another tack.

"Baldwin. *Notes of a Native Son*. My brother sent it to me. About the colored son of a preacher growing up in Harlem. A long way from this place, son," she says with a certain wistful air.

She wants me to walk her back to the Gamekeeper, only a half mile away. Her trio is planning a sound check and practice, and she wants to introduce me to the two guys she plays with. As we head over hot sidewalks to the club with my bike in tow, glares from shoppers and truck drivers unloading follow us warily. I am pretty excited. I want to hear Elvina sing. She's still giving me the silent treatment as we cross town, heat coming down like rain.

We enter through a side door of the hotel, over red and gold carpet into the dark lounge, still closed. Afternoon sun filters through the particulate air, lighting up the top hat on a drum set. We're the only ones in the low-ceilinged place, ghosted with empty swivel-stools and lounge chairs. El climbs on stage and turns on the mike, tapping it with her finger and testing 1-2-3. She asks me to sit in back and tell her how it sounds.

She starts in on Harry Belafonte's hit, "Day O, The Banana Boat Song." I sit mesmerized by her deep voice, until she points at me for the chorus, and I yell back how long the boat is. She doesn't finish, instead breaks into a version of "Maybelline," veering into an old country tune called "Ida Red," a folk song about some cheatin' heart.

She wants to know how it sounds.

"Outrageous, El. I wish Freddie were here. 'Maybelline,' is his number one."

"So why ain't he here?" she asks again.

"Like I said, we got mad about a couple of things. Then something else came along. Something kinda…I don't know, El. Not sure I wanna get into it right now. I thought the band was about to show up."

"Those two're always late. Look, something's obviously eatin' you. I'm not one to pry, especially into white folk's business, but you two are my boys and you know as sure as you were born, I'm not going to be telling nobody nothing. You been dancing around something for long enough and you can pretty damn well rest sure there ain't nothing goin' on I haven't encountered somewhere down the line." She sits down in a barrel chair and crosses her legs, strikes a match and lights a Kool, elbow on the table staring me down, her glass of water full beside her.

I finally cave in and tell her the Mr. Udall story, my head down, my heart beating, my neck and face flushed. I even have enough sweat left to feel it under my arms. I don't tell her about the JO session or about my stupid man crush on Kurt. I can't tell her a damn thing about Coach, but I give her the low-down on the fallen hat and the park scene without going into details.

"Is that the whole story?" she asks, exhaling smoke across the table as I swivel and squirm, hands in front of my mouth. "So you have to break up with Freddie because his dad goes in for a little male tail once in a while? Hmmm." El snaps her cig on the glass ashtray, then rests her chin on her palm.

"But I can't lie to Freddie. We have a pact. I can't tell him about his dad, can I? He'll have a fit."

"Son, you can *do* anything you please. The question is whether you're brave enough to face the consequences. Also sounds to me like you'd be telling Freddie as much about *you* as his dad. Am I wrong?"

"Maybe. I guess. You won't tell anyone, El, will you?"

"Got no one to tell, honey. Anyway even if there were someone, I won't be breaking my word. You know that. That's why you told me. So what are you going to do about it?"

I put my hands on my hair, staring at the table, holding the top of my skull as I confess to her I don't know what to do. I can't make up my mind, that's why Freddie and I have cooled our jets. Suddenly I hear the door open, and two guys burst into the room—one nervous and skinny with a Lucky Strike hanging out of his mouth and a fedora on his head, the other not exactly Fats Domino, but like a tackle or something, with short hair and a purple shirt. El introduces them as Claude and Jimmy, piano and drums. The skinny guy in checkered pants and a vest walks over to give El a peck on the cheek.

"How's my diva tonight? The Damekeeper. You ready to belt out some tunes or at least have a belt or two before the gig? What have we here? Little Lord Fauntleroy?"

"More string bean to me," Claude says. He holds out his hand, and I stand up to shake it. "Tom Cadigan," I say.

"Kevin's son," El puts in. "You know the lawyer that took our case."

"You got some daddy, boy. I'll say that much," Jimmy starts in. "Nobody messes with that bulldog, lemme tell you. They sure rented that place to us in a hurry once he took our case."

"That dog can hunt," Claude agrees.

I never knew El had even met my dad. First I heard of it.

"What do you think of Claude's new togs," Jimmy asks, pronouncing his name "cloud" and pinching the purple sheen of the shirt. Claude whacks his hand playfully.

"Where'd you get that number?" Elvina asks. "Can't miss it, that's for sure."

"We purchased it, Miss Thing, from one of our local haberdashers, if you must know."

"Sure you did," El says. "And I'm Marilyn Monroe."

"Penney's," Claude admits, turning away from the chat and heading up to the piano, where he starts in on "Bumble Boogie." Jimmy excuses himself and hops up on stage, laying his hands on Claude's shoulders for a second before heading toward his drums. Elvina rolls her eyes with a smile. She tells me I'll get to know these two goofballs better soon. The way she taps her butt in the ashtray tells me it's time for her to practice. "Talk to him," she says, stooping to stare me in the eye before she stands up and leaves me in the swivel chair.

Minutes later, I'm pedaling through cooling air on a ride that blows away my secret like mud falling from a fender. I move slow in low gear, sailing through shady maples feeling pretty good for a change.

8. EVERYTHING BUT THE TRUTH

So I call Freddie, ask him if he still wants to go running up at Lucky Peak next Saturday, up to the reservoir for cross-country and a dip. Dad says I can take the Willys. Have to watch the radiator though, especially in summertime. We go around eight because it's going to get too hot to run later. Fred is a crazy blazer, but I keep up best I can. He is small and light and skips over dusty trails like a jackrabbit. I'm lanky and clumsy but persistent. Once we're on the trail around the lake, Freddie waits up for me when he feels like it, Coco the boxer panting next to him. She isn't going to be left behind, especially if Freddie is in the mix.

I don't feel like getting so tired I want to puke, but I have to get my Freddie fix. I know he's moving to Nampa. I'm afraid of losing him, afraid I've already lost him by getting involved in all this guy shit. How can I tell Fred about all this stuff I wonder, bending over to lace up my high-tops? Before I can even think of an answer, Fred leaves me in the dust, taking off over the winding path as it curves around inlets of the reservoir amid yellow grass, full of hoppers this time of year. Snakes too if they bother to sunbathe. I can see his blue t-shirt as it moves through knee-tall weeds that border the rocky track.

It's too early for this, I'm thinking, making my way around, mesmerized by the cobalt lake in morning sun, glassy beside the pale gold hillside. Coke backtracks now and again to find me coming around one of the many bends as the footpath contours beside the water. Freddie waits, dreaming on a granite outcropping, picking stickers off his socks. "Okay?" is all he says, and then takes off again like a downhill racer checking in with his snowplowing companion at Sun Valley.

"I'm sweating like a pig," I comment when we finally get back to the parking lot.

"Dogs luckily don't sweat," he replies. "They pant." Coke's tongue is out, and she's sniffing hubcaps. We carry our sack of stuff over to Turner Gulch, a cove with a tiny pebble beach, silty but with some big rocks to jump off and a steep approach inaccessible except by butt or boat. We slide down the embankment as Miss Full Charge waits on shore, expecting us to tap into our endless supply of sticks. We get her in the water with a flimsy excuse for a branch and set the sack of peanut butter and banana sandwiches in the shade of a boulder. I put the Hawaiian Punch in the lake.

Freddie doesn't say much. He's probably wondering why we're on this outing, since we've grown apart this last month of summer. Still, he unlaces his shoes and pulls off his sweaty shirt, commanding his girlfriend to drop and sit if she wants to fetch again. The dog keeps us from confronting one another, plus it's only ten or eleven in the morning, the sun barely high enough to find its way into the nook where we're hiding.

"Did you bring towels?" he asks, wiping his back with his t-shirt.

"Yea, I brought one," I say, throwing his plaid trunks at him as I rummage through the canvas tote, looking for my transistor.

"What about me?" he asks. "What am I going to sit on, after I'm done serving you brunch, Mr. Cadigan?"

"The towel is for you, dickhead, not for the Coquette. Don't let her near it. I know you love her but there's a limit. It's a big towel. We can all use it." I toss the striped roll at Fred. I am throwing things at him, mad at his silent condemnation of my sexcapades, even if he doesn't know anything about them. He's telepathic, after all.

It's warm enough in the sun. I'm ready to go skinny-dipping, nascent exhibitionist that I am. I figure it's early enough. No speedboats quite yet, and I love the feel of being naked in the water with the crawdads ready to clamp a pincer on my tender genitalia. I strip and hop down the clay berm toward the cold, nut-shriveling water and then plunge in headlong. Coco waits on shore until I start swimming out farther, at which point she decides to rescue me.

"You comin?" I shout at my nerdy pal, who sits cross-legged on the towel watching the two of us. He shrugs. "You better," I shout, "or I'm going to sic my dog on you." The two of us wait for Fred, dog paddling together out in the deep blue sea, even if Turner Gulch is hardly the Costa Brava.

Coco and I head back to shore to drag in our prey.

"Your scrotum is the size of a walnut," he deadpans as I emerge from the chilly water.

"Okay, that's it. This means war. I've put up with your cast of aspersions long enough, you little bitch. It's time my bitch and I teach you a lesson." Freddie is on his feet, ready to scamper, except he has nowhere to run on this little patch of dirt with sharp rocks and a scrabble cliff. He hops along until I catch him by the shoulders.

"Tommy," he whines, "you're freezing, man." I hug him while Cokie shakes off on us. I slide my hand down his shorts as he struggles. "All right," he finally says, stripping and hiding his "privates" as he calls them with one hand. I drag him to the shore and we dive into together, swimming to the point with dog in tow. We lift her onto the flat rock and sit in the sun, knees pressed up to chests. Freddie shivers, goosebumps on his arms until the sun warms us up.

"So," he asks, "why have you been hiding from me?"

"I haven't been hiding. You've been busy with your move and your new vice-presidency. Plus you disapprove of my promiscuity."

"Yea, sure. Do you think I am going to drop you just cause you enjoy mutual masturbation with a Boise State dropout who letters in grunting? That does not mean our blood pact is now kaput. You know I'm going to stick by you no matter what. You really think I can stay mad at you? Come on. Give me a break."

I don't know what to do. Regardless of what El told me, I'm not ready to tell him his Dad is a homo or that I have professed my love to my history teacher. But I am not ready to throw our friendship away either.

"What have you been up to the past couple of weeks?" I ask cagily. Freddie pats Coco's wet stomach, saying nothing. We sit in silence as the first boat comes by with a water skier in tow. He slaloms in and out behind the inboard, raising a rooster tail before speeding across to jump the wake. The bow of the runabout seems to be heading straight for us. The distraction is welcome until it becomes ominous, the hull growing larger. At the last minute, the nose turns away and the skier zips across the wake before cutting back and spraying us with water. He's a stocky guy with big arms, wearing a long bathing suit. Coco is barking her head off.

"I know that boat," I say. "That's the Sullivans' Chris Craft." It is mahogany, with two cockpits and the engine in the middle. I think I see Skip Johnson in the back tending rope. "That was probably one of Bobby's brothers."

"Jerk," Freddie says. "Scared my baby girl." He's trying to calm Coco down, embarrassed by his nudity in a place he suddenly realizes is not paradise. "So much for our privacy," he says. "Those guys will be back no doubt. What a treat. More harassment by jocks. What I did on my summer vacation—fend off a bunch of sadistic hoods. Ain't life grand?" He shakes his head. "I'm swimming in. Let's go, Coco," he says, looking around before diving. Fred on edge. Not a great start to our picnic. When I come ashore ten minutes later, he's plopped on the beach in his trunks, staring at the lake. And it's one of those vacant looks fraught with thought, a look that puts me on the spot.

I find my suit and grab a bag of Granny Goose chips, bringing them over to the towel. Three might have been a crowd at that point. The dog and his friend on shore, me dripping, hopelessly non non-chalant in spite of my effort to get back on my friend's good side. I know something has to give. That something is me.

"I've been working out at the Y these days," I begin slowly. "I got a month's membership. Been swimming a couple of times at the old Natatorium trying to get in shape. No, really, this time I'm serious."

Freddie listens, unimpressed, taciturn. My muscles are not his main concern, at least my upper body. He wants to know what's eating me inside. Our friendship is about telling one another whatever is on our minds.

Freddie has even told me about his plans to be a philosopher, about his desire to blow up the Tabernacle in Salt Lake, about his crush on Dirk Bogarde and Gregory Peck. He doesn't call them crushes. He just thinks Peck is tall, dark, and handsome, but we both know what he means. We both joke about Peck's pecker. We don't have words for what we're up to exactly. We aren't ready to call ourselves certifiable flits in the Liberace vain. Sure, Rusty and Trent are happy to call us queers and fags every time they pass us, but we aren't ready to accept their labels. We go out with girls even though we know what we really like and are willing to admit it to one another. It's hard to explain.

"It's hard to explain," I tell him. Why doesn't Freddie have any secrets to tell me? I feel like I'm doing all the confessing. I'm trying to weasel my way out, but I know I can't. "I met Coach Williams swimming down there, and we've become pretty tight. If you say anything, I will kill you. No one can know about this. He's worried about fraternizing with his students, even though we're just friends. So please don't say anything."

"You don't need to tell me to shut up. So you're friends with Coach. Big deal."

"It's more than that, more than friends," I tell him, looking away now, picking up a jagged rock and hurling it as far as I can into the water. "Cokie, no. Stay, girl." I hate dog owners who throw sinking stones for their retrievers sadistically. "I think I'm obsessed with Coach. I mean, I totally dig him. I'm not sure it's mutual, but I go down there every day hoping to run into him, waiting for him to talk to me at the pull-up bar or looking for him on the mat doing sit-ups. He's so cool. You wouldn't believe it. He's teaching me how to weight lift and butterfly in the pool. He's got me on a workout routine and tells me all about growing up in the Bitterroot and his time in Korea. You know he studied history in Montana and writes poetry and stories on the side? He even knows e.e. cummings and loves *Rhapsody in Blue*. And wow, he's in really good shape. You should see him in the shower. And I can't believe it, but he told me he felt really close to me. He says we could do more stuff together once I graduate."

Freddie is on his stomach now, elbows propped up, hands folded on the towel. "So what stuff have you done, if you don't mind me asking? I mean the guy is our teacher. At the risk of sounding like a church father, my son, you're facing a few challenges, besides the fact that you're breaking my heart." He's only half joking, but he likes to make fun of his affection for me.

"First of all," he says, "there's this guy in our church, this Emery Bosse cat, a local parole officer for juvies, who has started whipping up rumors about a scourge of perversion spreading across our state capitol. We've been warned by our elders to beware of strange men in Buicks offering rides home or a free Pall Mall. The Pink Scare has begun in earnest. Big Brother, need I remind you, is watching. Not the kind of big brother you're hoping for. It's one thing to experiment with a bunch of classmates on the links with Marlboros and a bottle of Schnapps. It's another to get mixed up with the big boys, who supposedly know better. I mean, Jayzuzz, I sit at the dinner table with you wondering if Father can see into my soul, if he can feel my warmth for you, if he knows we've jacked off during sleepovers. If any of these shenanigans were to see the light of Latter Days, I would be crucified. And if you were known to be cavorting with your football coach, you'd be a sinner in the hands of a very angry god, even if He were Irish Catholic. Are you ready to go to reform school, ready to see Coach Williams behind bars? Have you forgotten we are living in the age of Joe McCarthy? How far exactly have you gone with...this affair?"

I'm biting my thumb, running the nail through my front teeth, listening to him do his little half sarcastic, half concerned analysis. When he stops mid thought, I am startled.

"We haven't gone anywhere. I mean, I was in his arms once, after I told him what I was feeling while we were in the park. I had kind of a breakdown. I started crying, of course. He held me and gave me a kiss. It was nothing—pure affection. It felt great, though. It felt a little like being with you but stronger and more sexual. You know what I mean. You and I, basically we're too close to fall in love with one another."

Freddie nods with resignation but maybe some approval too. He understands, I hope. He may not agree completely, but he knows we're more brothers than lovers, though incest does not seem like a bad idea to us now and again.

"I'm just saying," he resumes, "that you've got the school/teacher situation to deal with and then the age thing as well, on top of the homo issue. We aren't living in ancient Athens, man. You're living in Southern Idaho, currently under siege by Brigham Young and his gang of thought police, in case you haven't noticed. The days of horny explorers and their berdache companions have long since been made into John Wayne westerns. Hence, my worries. Your jets, I fear, may need to be cooled. Like pronto, like yesterday. Or you may be kissing Georgetown goodbye. As well as Berkeley.

"My Dad wants me with the Jesuits, but back East seems stultifying."

"Stultifying, is it? Okay, whatever. I'm just worried. These guys are nasty. I speak from experience. The Emery Bosses of the world don't make distinctions between homos and Commies and Catholics, especially liberal Catholics with fathers who work for Frank Church or other Commie pinko faggot puke. Excuse my French."

"But you don't know Coach. I mean, you're in his class and everything, but he's the real deal. And look I'm almost seventeen. I know what I'm doing. And I'm the one who has a crush on him. I mean, I'm thinking it's mutual—at least I hope so—but he's the one putting the brakes on. He's been through so much. You don't know about the life he had growing up, getting kicked out of his house by his redneck dad. Going to Korea and getting screwed by the Army. How much pressure he feels to marry Miss Winfrey. I don't know, it's just so incredible." Coco hears me getting excited, lifts up her head and stares, like I'm finally going to throw a stick or something.

"Calm down, Cokie," I say.

At this point, the predicted craft appears on the horizon again. "Oh, boy," Fred says, "looks like we've got company." He is used to harassment by the locals. He has already applied for early admission to Chicago or Northwestern or one of those philosophy schools in the Midwest. He's biding his time with the local yokels he calls "the insufferable hoi polloi."

The Chris Craft planes off as it slows in the bay, pushing its wake toward shore.

"Ahoy, mateys," Fred says. They can't hear him, thank god.

"Hey, Cadigan, what's up man?" Bobby shouts from the cockpit, his arm on the gunwale of his beautiful wood inboard, tail in the air as the boat idles.

"Not much. Who was that guy who gave us a shower?"

"My brother. Show off. I told him leave you guys alone, but he had to strut his stuff. You want to go skiing?" he asks me. "What about you, Federico Fellini, are you interested in a slalom course?"

"Yea, sure," Fred answers.

"Maybe little Freddie would like to go inner-tubing. Sitting on rubber is more his speed probably." Skip leans on the engine cover in the back of the boat.

"Shut up, Johnson," I say, "I don't see you jumping the wake. Yea, I'll go for a spin, Bobby, since you're offering." Tall Trent tosses out the slalom ski, sliding it in toward shore. He then picks up the nylon rope. I tell him to wait a sec and start swimming toward "The Sully." Bobby has killed the engine.

"Hey Cadigan," Trent yells. "I heard you made some good money down at the monkey cages in the park the other night. We were talking to McKellar." His voice reverberates off the walls of the gulch. I'm in the process of trying to get my foot in the rubber boot of the ski as I catch his comment before sinking under. After that pronouncement, I'm not sure I want to come up for air. I can't bring

myself to look back at Freddie. I just buckle the life belt and watch
the reflection of the water on the wood, my eyes like a crocodile's.

"I didn't make any money, man. I split," I finally say, trying to set
the record as straight as possible. I have the rope in my hand. "Okay
Bobby. I'm ready." He starts the engine, pulls the rope taut, and I
yell "hit it," in a pissed off, exaggeratedly deep voice that holds all
the anger I'm building up. I shove my weight against the water and
emerge somehow to my tilted position behind the boat, trying to get
Bobby to slow down. I am skipping along like a flat rock on Pond
Oreille. He finally lets up on the throttle, and I start jumping the wake
the way my Dad taught me when we rented the cabin in McCall. I
can ski as well as any of those assholes, except maybe Bobby.

If I have any notion this little ski loop might dissipate the intensity
of my conversation with Fred, I'm sorely mistaken. He looks up from
1984 while I crawl up shore to find the towel, falling on my stomach
to warm up. He isn't going to start in right away. He shows some
deference to my exhaustion, but as I soon as I catch my breath, he
has no intention of letting sleeping dogs lie.

"You want a sandwich?" he asks me. "They're getting soggy. You
better eat one before they turn to mush." He is unwrapping the tinfoil.

"In a minute," I say, turning over, looking at my amorphous
stomach, a tan mass of skin I'm unable to harden in spite of every
callisthenic known to man. Whatever. I rest on my elbows, my turn
to stare into the water's blinking sparklers, boat wakes lapping
against the shore. I know how lucky I am to have Freddie as my
main man. I can feel our belonging as we sit next to one another.

"So, yea, I ran into Kurt and those stupid dudes down in the park
a couple of weeks ago, and they asked me to hang with them for a
while," I begin my explanation, hesitant but ready. "Then these older
guys in Pontiacs and one even in a Caddy started to drive around.
They wanted to pay us money if they could suck us off or something. I wanted to ditch, but Kurt convinced me to stay, said I didn't
have to do anything. I was kind of amazed these old dudes were
wanting to get off with other guys. I mean I thought like we were

the only ones in Idaho a couple of months ago, then all of sudden these horny gin boys and suits start coming out of the woodwork. I don't think romance is their main concern, though. I figured that out pretty quick when I saw this old guy get down on his knees in front of Kurt, saw the way my idol seemed to enjoy it and started looking at me. I panicked and got out of there fast as I could. Like a prude, I guess, but I couldn't believe Kurt would sell himself like that and let me watch on top of it. It pissed me off. So Trent must have heard from him or Skip somehow. I guess I'm screwed. I don't know what I'm going to do now."

"So it wasn't Coach that was down there? I'm confused."

"No, Coach wasn't around at all. Coach and I talked another night, just by ourselves."

"Then who were those old guys?" Freddie asks point blank.

"I don't know the guy that went down on Kurt. Never seen him before. Plus it was pretty dark. It was some older guy, somebody as old as my dad. Isn't that creepy?" I stop there. I can't say anything more. I just don't feel right about telling him, so I change the subject. "No, I met Coach in the park on another night. I know it sounds like I'm living down there, but it's not what you think. I went there with Coach after the gym so we could have a moment of privacy, until this cop showed up with a flashlight. Coach got away, though."

"So these old guys are willing to pay money to have Kurt's erect member shoved down their throats? Sounds positively delightful." Fred is always capable of Lady Bracknell.

"Guess so. I mean at least they're interested in guys. That's a step in the right direction, or a genuflection maybe. But Jeez, it grosses me out. Maybe I was jealous, but I couldn't stay there, had to hightail it."

"So circle jerks are just horseplay, but sex for money is gross?" he asks rhetorically, needling me. "But, really, what kind of old dude would risk going down to the monkey cages at night just to jack off some dumb teenager? It doesn't make a whole lot of sense to me," Fred says. "Those guys must be super horny or stupid or both."

I'm eating my sandwich now, peanut butter sticking to the roof of my mouth, gluing up my plan to tell Freddie who one of those super-horny guys was. I can't unlock it. I can't burden my best friend with my secret. It's too heavy. The whole truth and nothing but the truth refrains through my brain so help me god, while Freddie twists the volume up on Muddy Waters's "Please Have Mercy." Maybe I'm doing him wrong, but I can't bring myself to hurt him with the truth. Not now. Forgive me, Freddie.

9. BUTTERFLY MAN

"Let the water buoy you," Coach says. "Keep your butt up, and pump with your hip, then pause and glide. Hip pause, hip pause." He's trying to teach me the butterfly, standing in the shallow end at the Natatorium during open swim. It's Wednesday morning and no one else is in the pool except for a few ladies in flowered bathing caps who breast-stroke down the lanes like logs in an ebb tide. Coach has agreed to give me a lesson after I saw him switching strokes with the greatest of ease. It feels more like a meltdown than a butterfly this morning. I can't seem to release my hips to let them pump and power me through the water, can't feel the oscillation I see in his body as I watch him underwater.

"Wait," he finally says. "Come over here." I walk down the lane to where he stands in his racing suit, thick forearms covered with wet black hair, motioning me to take a break and listen up. I'm trying to focus on his instructions instead of the definition of his torso as I hop toward him in the shallow end. He tells me to fill my lungs with air and just recline in the water. He holds me up gently, one hand on my thighs, one below my solar plexus. He lifts me up to let me breathe and instructs me to wave my legs and hips while he holds on to my chest.

"It's about gliding," he insists. "Let the water propel you and just pump through the element. Be patient. Don't worry about the stroke yet. Just pump three times and come up for air. Hip flex and pause." I begin to sense what he means. "Excellent," he finally says with encouragement. I spend the next hour learning how to "go with the flow" as he calls it. Coach smiles at my flapping gyrations, shakes his dark wet head and laughs at my lack of coordination. He orders me to trust my body and give up my determination to be a klutz. He calls it my inferiority complex.

We're under the hot showers now, the locker room empty weekday mid-morning in August. There are no soap dispensers so we stand beneath the warm streams, arms folded as it beats on our neck and shoulders.

"Butterflop more than butterfly," I say, shaking my head. "I think I drank a gallon of water. I hope none of those Boise matrons peed in it."

"You did fine. It's the hardest stroke to do by far. Part of it is learning to let go. At the end, you were starting to trust your lower body. For some reason, our hips get stiff. Maybe it's some cultural mindset or bodyset, especially for guys who need to be stolid. The butterfly is about moving, gliding, opening. You'll do fine. First thing, you have to stop beating yourself up about your body. I saw the way you used to look at first stringers like McKellar in the locker room last year. Let's face it, he's in great shape. But you're never going to be McKellar. He's one helluva linebacker, he's a great hustle, and a terror on the field, but he's not you. You're you. You have your own form, your own charm, your own shape. Don't fight it, move with it. Improve on it. Stop trying to be a mean linebacker."

I've heard this lecture before and am only half tuning in when I find a piece of soap in a dish across the room and grab it, suds up, and slip off my suit. I hand him the bar and ask him to wash my back. He takes the soap in his palm and looks at it for a second. He knows I'm pushing the envelope again. My swim trunks are looped around a faucet, and I'm standing there buck naked, my back to him, waiting for his touch, his rub while he holds the sliver of Ivory. He wants me to let go? Okay, I'll let go. I'm not getting a boner or anything. I just want to get my skin clean and nobody ever scrubs my back except maybe Freddie now and again.

"Okay," Coach says reluctantly, "Hold still, you little rascal." He puts one arm around my stomach and starts scrubbing my shoulders with soap. It feels great because he doesn't shy away from massaging hard, getting soap into the pores, which I need, regardless of the applicator, regardless of my lad starting to pop up, regardless of the elastic on his racing suit getting tighter. He finds zits on my butt and lets rip on those, accidentally finding my crack with the heel of his hand. The soap slips away, and he bends down to scoop it up. At that moment, I look up to see the lifeguard tromping down the locker room aisle.

"Kids swim in ten minutes, guys," he says cheerfully, his whistle around his neck. He's a guy I don't know, must be from Caldwell or something.

"Okay," I say, putting my hands to my face, rinsing the soap off my back. Coach is still squatting with the dropped soap in his hand, making motions to clean his shins. Awkward. My heart starts beating wildly. Maybe the kid has detected my semi-tumescence or maybe he saw Coach's hand on my spine or butt. My head is racing even though I know the lifeguard probably saw nothing or cares less what he saw if he did.

Coach and I are both pretty quiet after the lifeguard comes by. I have forgotten my towel, so have to borrow his. The place is empty and smells like chlorine. Coach is shaking his head while I keep smiling and shrugging my shoulders as if to say, "what can we do about it?" Big deal. Though I know it *is* a big deal. Not because the guard has happened by to discover two guys in the shower, but because I am enjoying every minute of this excitement. The secrecy, Coach's eye twinkle, the synchronicity of our body language—all of it is taking me somewhere I've never been before, dangerous though it may be. But Coach has more to lose. He's much quicker in finding his pants holes and heading to the mirror to comb his hair. I'm not sure what he's thinking, but I can tell he wants to get out of there lickety-split.

"I gotta go," he says while I'm still pulling socks over my wet feet. "Wait up."

"Nah, can't. I got to be at school. We're getting ready for the season."

"So what about Friday?" I ask. "What about my next lesson?"

"I don't know, buddy." He looks at me, a face somewhere between grimace and smile. His pout tells me he's letting himself get seduced against his better judgment, even though his own charisma is complicit. His hair combed back, wet, and perfectly styled. He holds his gym bag in his hand and puts a leg up on the bench.

"I'm happy to teach you how to swim. And yea we're good friends, but I'm getting busy. It's August and things are starting up at school, so…look, all right," he sighs, watching my crestfallen face. "I'll see you Friday for our last lesson. Be good."

He looks around the locker room and checks his collar in the mirror. I can tell from his eyes that he can't talk. Not now. Not there. I fumble for my pencil and notebook, rip off a page real quick. "Meet me at the band shell across from the cages tonight at 9." I wince at my sloppy handwriting. I slip it in his pocket as he turns and walks away, his head lowered. I don't know what he's thinking, what I'm thinking either. I have never been so forward with anyone.

My cheeks are on fire outside the Natatorium, after five minutes talking to myself in the mirror. Freddie's stare comes into my head, his admonition behind my eyes. What am I thinking? Tearing that page out of my notebook, realizing now some scribbled poem is probably on the backside of it, since my pocket-sized spiral is where I have all the first drafts of the lousy poetry I compose during down times at the hardware store.

10. HARDWARE

I've got to get over to the hardware store at noon, but I need to go home first, eat lunch, change, and then bike downtown to Mr. Brown and his cranky Ford pickup. Mr. Brown, it seems to me, needs teenage labor like a hole in his head, but Mom has prevailed upon him to enslave me for two dollars an hour this summer. She is not to be denied in certain instances, not unlike the boxer mix she has raised from puppyhood into a full-grown fulltime job. Mine is only parttime, praise Jesus, and today I thank heaven I'll be on the road again, grinding my way into third gear to avoid the cops on South Capitol.

"Gotta deliver some T Stakes out to Frank Jones's place first thing," Mr. Brown informs me. "Keep the City Council happy, that's my motto. And then you got the chicken wire out there in hell and gone—Garden City—for the Bosses, those folks playing farmers on their five acres. Best go out to Bosse's place first. Just look out for the German Shepherds. Emery's got one that will bite your head off or something lower if he gets the chance. Then there's a couple of more places, I wrote them down." He hands me his scribbled notes torn from a spiral notepad.

"And stay within the speed limit, please, young man. I don't want Ralph Evans lumbering in here with his nightstick again. You crazy kids better stay out of the trouble you've been gettin' into down there in the park by the way. That's what I hear, anyway. Heard it's been a fun little summer for some of you fellas down there by the cages. There's talk, young man, talk. I just hope you haven't gotten mixed up with any of those hoods. Juvies. Wouldn't want see a Zubiri boy caught up in that kind of stuff. No siree, Bob."

It takes me a good half hour to find the Bosse spread. When I drive up, his kids are playing in the yard, so I roll down the window and ask about the dog.

"Don't worry about Rufus," the girl assures me even though she is considerably smaller than her pet. I'm unlatching the tailgate when I feel a snout bump me on the leg, attached to a hound with ears up and tail unemotionally quiet between his legs. His black and brown coat as handsome as I've seen, still my better instincts check any inclination to give him a big wet sloppy kiss.

"Hello, Rufus," I say gingerly. "It's a pleasure to meet you. Don't suppose you're in the habit of sitting and shaking for strangers." It's hard to be charming when you're about to be torn apart. "Oh, hi, Mr. Bosse," I say, looking up at the tall man with wire-rimmed glasses who has creeped up on me from the other side. "Here's your chicken wire," I continue. "Where'd you like me to put it?" I look around at the dirty white clapboard house, spare car parts hanging out like bad sculpture in rusty fields. Bosse has a long head. I've seen him before at school, talking to the principal whenever he brings some expelled kid back into the fold. He looks at me rather sternly.

"Hello, son," he says. I feel like I'm in one of those Gary Cooper movies. Shane Cadigan. 'Hi paw.' "Don't I know you from somewhere?" Bosse continues. "You're Kevin Cadigan's boy, aren't you?"

"Yes, sir."

"Thought so." Dad is none too popular out here in the hinterlands. He's made some waves with a few trials, saving Indians from jail and white lawmen. His reputation as "one of them librels" follows me around, not that I'm a reactionary or anything. I admire my paw. I'm not about to join the John Birch Society quite yet, in spite of mounting pressure from the Young Republicans on campus. I actually like the United Nations, though I'm pretty sure Officer Bosse is not interested in my brand of politics.

"Just leave the wire in the driveway, Tom." He calls me by my first name, which sounds oddly ominous. How does he know me? I heave the roll out of the car on to the gravel and move it out of the way of the truck. Mr. Bosse has his hands on his hips. He's already told his kids to "git" back in the yard. Rufus seems about as threatening as Fred Mertz at that point. Mr. Bosse folds his arms as I climb in the cab.

"Alrighty, then," I say in my chipper, delivery boy best. I find the receipt on the seat of the truck and hand it to him. "Well, I'll be off then, Mr. Bosse. Bye now." I search for reverse under the wary eyes of family and animals, jamming the stick into place and jerking backwards down the driveway as the touchy clutch finally engages. I'm happy to get the hell out of that Fun House, I can tell you that much. Wouldn't want to sit around Bosse's table for supper eatin' squirrel stew and grits.

The Jones's colonial, once I find it, features a parabolic driveway and some grand juniper hedges. I see a detached garage and as it turns out, a servant's entrance, where I am directed by a uniformed maid as I drive up. I twist the knob on the radio, the Chordettes crooning "Mr. Sandman," and I hear the story of my lonesome nights, hoping that Coach shared my lonely heart like Pagliacci. Would Mr. Mart Williams please come to the bandstand? I know the other teachers call him Mart, though I'm not quite there yet. Life is real cool.

As I drive around back, I don't see Mr. Jones. I'm hoping his son, the famous Frankie Junior, star wide receiver and tennis champion might be around. I read about him in the papers, knew him in school before he graduated, though just to say hi. Scores off the charts and handsome too, he was a junior when I started at Boise. Kid has it all, not the least of which is that he managed to fly this coop.

I'm walking toward the truck bed to unload the heavy green and white stakes when an old, wizened and beanied gardener unhinges a wooden gate and emerges in his green overalls. Basque dude, I can tell. My mom's folk. His hands are weathered and worn and his shoulders are stooped, but he's still as sturdy as a Spanish chestnut tree.

"Hey, look who's here," he says to me. I'm not sure who he is at first, our Basque picnics having casts of thousands, only organized once or twice a year. "If it isn't Gloria's boy. All grown up. Look at you, taller than a cypress. I can't believe it. Driving a truck, too. Aren't we the cat's meow."

"Oh hi, Mr. Urquidi," I remember now. The dance leader at the picnics. The guy with the red and white costume. How could I forget? He is shaking me by the arms, looking me over, getting a load of my skin and bones. He can't believe how tall I am. The Basques don't grow like Cadigans, I guess. He starts to talk about my cheese consumption, about the way Gloria is not feeding me enough flank steak—one of those gastronomical tangents grownups like to go off on when they see sagging jeans.

"So where do you want Mr. Jones's stakes, Mirenny?" We all call him by his first name even though he is an *anciano*—a venerable old owl with eyes in the back of his head. He helps me with the stakes.

"You such a handsome boy. And so light in the hair. How can you be Basque? Tell me that. What's the world?" He shakes his head, beaming at the miracle that is me, a half-breed American, never to be a sheepherder in the Sierra, never to live in dark stone rooms in Alvara, never to keep the sheep from wolves.

"You wouldn't happen to know if Frankie is around, would you?" I ask on a lark.

"Frankie, Jr.? The golden boy? Yea, he's playing tennis in the back with that funny friend of his. I say nothing. You decide about that man from the *teatro*. *Mariposa*." He spits out the Spanish, shaking his head in disapproval. "Just follow the path down there." He nods. "Watch the roses. I was just trimming. Go, make an interruption. He needs that."

Mr. U points down the edged gravel path, past the formal flower garden with its low hedges, the long path surrounded by more juniper hedges and in the center of the privet-rimmed roses. At the end of the walkway, I hear the thwamp of rackets against a ball and feel awkward suddenly, the delivery boy sneaking up on the well-heeled

Joneses. How could I be so impertinent as to disturb their set, these two gentlemen with their Maxply rackets and Fred Perry shoes, alligators stitched on their proud pectorals. I start turning red again, feel my heart pound as I unlatch another gate and enter into the lanai beside a green hard court, where Frankie is rallying with an older man. Well, I mean in his thirties, maybe forty. Doesn't take me long to recognize our part-time drama teacher, Mr. Dir the local celebrity. Singer, songwriter, actor, entertainer extraordinaire. A fun guy who knows how to put on a damn good show, but also the kind of dandy the salt of the earth like Mirenny finds intolerable. Melvin Dir is slated to launch a play in the fall, and Freddie and I are thinking of trying out for it. I had no idea Frankie and Mel, as we call him behind his back, were chums.

They both look up as I enter, Frankie halting his forehand in midstroke at my appearance, the ball flying into the chain link. "Well, hello there," Frankie says with what appears to be a little James Mason in his voice. He has no idea who I am, and seems quite taken aback by my appearance on his estate. Mel comes to my rescue as he approaches the net.

"You remember Tommy Cadigan don't you, Frank? He ran cross country the year you graduated, I believe."

"Oh yea, now I do," Frankie recovers his Boise-ness. "How you doin'? What brings you out here?" There is no one in sight. I can see the flat pool through another hedge, a sweating pitcher of lemonade and towels on the table under a striped awning. It's an idyllic, deserted little paradise in the suburbs of Boise. Could have been Connecticut, whatever that looks like. I'm thinking Katharine Hepburn and Cary Grant. The players dress white, and Mel is perspiring quite a bit under his polo.

"Sorry to break in," I say, starting to realize I might be intruding on more than a 40-love game. "I was delivering some T-stakes from Brown's, and Mirenny told me to come down and say hello."

"He would," Frankie says. "He owns the place. I love him, but this garden has become his life. He's quite a little despot when it comes to his territory." Frankie picks up a towel off the chair, wipes the sweat from his brow. "Mel...Mr. Dir here...was just giving me a terrible thrashing, so your timing is impeccable." Frank goes on, his diction only half ironic. "Have a glass of lemonade before you get back in the truck. Brown can wait, the old busy body. I remember working for him myself one summer before we went up to Sandpoint. We usually spend most of July up at the lake." The heir putting on airs. Mel can see me raising my eyebrows at his ex-student's haughtiness. He undoubtedly knows I'm trying to get my bearings around the two of them at two in the afternoon playing tennis in eighty-degree heat at the Jones estate. Where's the party?

The ice in my glass soothes, and the tart lemonade gives me a rush. I relax and check the place out. The Joneses' home is astonishing, with clipped shrubs and the net perfectly strung. Even the tennis balls are still white. This is the life, I decide. This will all be mine after my first three or four bestsellers. Mr. Dir is looking a little sheepish, a towel around his neck now.

"Frankie and I are just getting caught up," he explains. "My star student, and performer. You remember the *As You Like It* we did, don't you? Two or three years ago? Could it be that long? It was quite a smash. Frankie was a stunning Orlando, of course. We had an absolute ball that year, didn't we, Frank? And the girl who played Rosalind—Gracie Udall, was it?—turned into a quite convincing Ganymede. Of course she wasn't a boy, as the bard would have had it, but Gracie was quite a *tom*boy if you recall. It's a mixed up world in that play. That's what we love about it. I think you'd just started at Boise, but it was a fabulous production. You know Frankie has been away for a year."

"So Gracie Udall acted in that Shakespeare play?" I ask.

"Yep," Frankie nods, falling back to his Boiseness. "She's in my ward." He looks at me. "That's right, you used to hang out with her little brother. Now I remember. The one with the black glasses."

"Fred."

"Yes, Fred Udall. I just saw him last weekend. What an odd little duck. Brainy, yea, brainy and aloof. I wonder how long he'll stay in the stake. Yea, so you're Freddie's friend? It's all coming back to me." He begins to relax and get more alert at the same time.

"Yea. So what's it like back East, in the Army?"

"Great," Frank says, holding his glass between his thighs rather rigidly. "Couldn't be better. It's tough. They give us freshmen a hard time, I can tell you that, but the classes are pretty amazing." He sips his drink and glances at Mel, who sits with his legs crossed.

"Do they have initiations and hazing like you hear about?"

"Well, It's all top secret, of course. But let's just say there are no holes barred." He looks over to Mr. Dir with a sly grin. "One kid woke up naked in a canoe on the Hudson. Another, well, I don't want to go into the details, but he came to in the wrong bed. Or the right one, as the case may be."

Frankie chuckles again, eyeing Mel. There is a Morse code or something going on between these guys. I can't figure it out. Mel invites me stay for a quick dip in the pool, tells me I don't need a suit. They always swim nude because no one is around anyway. Frankie's foot is moving pretty fast. Mr. Dir has pulled out a non-filter and is puffing away when I rise and say goodbye.

"Toodeloo," Mr. Dir says. "We'll see you in September. You simply must try out for *Tea and Sympathy*." Gravel crunches underfoot as I hurry back to my time clock, Mirenny lifting his pruning shears and shaking his head as I wave goodbye.

I remember the two soaker hoses still in in the truck bed. Mr. Brown is going to shit bricks. I look at the address of the next delivery and then at the receipt. My heart skips a beat as I recognize the U word and realize I'm off to Freddie's old place for the first time since things went bump in the night. I'm scared to death of running into the man with the dropped hat. Hopefully, Mr. Udall will still be at work, but the chance of me facing him or him me unnerves me as I find my way back to the North End.

Hell, maybe Fred will be there with his face buried in *Thus Spoke Zarathustra* or one of his other unreadable books, lying on the porch swing with Welch's grape juice and his Fig Newtons if that snack is not beyond his sugar quotient. 'We wouldn't want a hyperactive child now, would we?' I say, channeling Mrs. Udall. 'That much green Jell-O might send you to perdition, young man.' Poor Freddie. The sooner he heads to Africa, the better. It's going to be hot in those black slacks, though.

I get there, and I'm standing in the driveway, the order wrong. It's almost five and rush hour is about to bring home the father I can't face. "Gee whiz, Mrs. Udall, the invoice says two soaker hoses."

"Well, Tommy, I know I told Mr. Brown to send over four of them. That's why I wanted them delivered. I just don't know what to do. Tomorrow I'm going over to Nampa first thing in the morning to set them up. I wonder if you wouldn't mind too terribly dropping them off later this evening or tomorrow morning early. I'm going to call that Wally Brown right now. Just unload the two you have and wait right here."

Off the lovely Mrs. Udall goes through the side door to the kitchen, ignoring my protest that I'm off at five thirty, and don't work mornings and Brown's store closes at six and doesn't open until nine. She isn't about to hear excuses. I'm looking around for Fred, but he isn't on the porch. Suddenly, Gracie appears in a pair of pedal pushers and a sweatshirt, rushing out the front door and down the steps with a catcher's mitt under her arm.

"Can't talk, got to go to softball practice," she yells in a rather rambunctious voice. Great to see you. Freddie's upstairs." Ganymede, wow. Try Ma Perkins. I haven't seen her in a while. Gracie, I thought, had gone off to Salt Lake for school, but she must be home for a summer visit. I want to go up to Freddie's room and jump on top of him but have to restrain myself. Mrs. U comes back, tells me Mr. Brown will get the hoses to her.

"By the way," she says, "he would like you to return to the store right away." She turns on a dime and leaves me in the driveway.

Driving back, I think about what it must be like to have all those kids and a successful husband who works for the Idaho National Bank, to be building a new home in Nampa and be active in a Mormon ward. They're thriving in ways my father never would because he refuses to give up his criminal defense practice, refuses to represent a corporation or two so we can remodel the kitchen. His principles are keeping me in baggy ski pants and bamboo poles. I'm an embarrassment on the slopes, looking like a relic hung up on the wall of some lodge while all the jetsetters schuss down with their Head skis, looking out for Sonja Henie or Papa Hemingway.

What must it be like to be Mrs. Udall when her husband Edward is sucking off teenagers on the sly? But how can I cast stones when Pam and I foxtrot at the prom and send gushy notes to one another? Surely there is a huge difference between fake dating and faking a Mormon marriage, isn't there? Surely Mr. Udall has more at stake given his position in LDS. The whole thing boggles my mind. I just want to forget all the consequences, forget those folded arms of Emery Bosse, forget everything but Coach.

Brown orders me to run the extra hoses back out in spite of the end of my shift. I call home before I leave and race out in the truck, swearing to drive by and toss the green snakes in the driveway. Besides, I have to get home. My life's in orbit. I could care less about Mr. U, who also likes guys apparently, but why not love them if you like them that much, I'm thinking when I pull into that driveway and leave the engine running.

"What are you doing, back door man?" Fred comes out of the house and jumps up to the side of the cab. "Trying to slip away, you little sneak? No way."

"Look, Fred, I'm on the clock. This is a late delivery, and I don't have time to dawdle. We're going tomorrow to see El, right?"

"Well, I'm pleased you have penciled me into your busy calendar, Mr. Cadigan. I'm so happy you've blocked off a few hours to entertain your deranged childhood friend." He folds his hands in prayer and jumps off the truck, backing away with a Siamese bow.

"Freddeee," I say. "Stop it. I'd love to come in, but Brown will can me. He told me to come back with the truck right away. Jayzuzz, Fred." I run over to him and grab him around the waist, tackling him. We tumble onto the ground, and he somehow gets on top of me and pins me down on the cool grass in the front yard. "Please, don't kill me, Sheriff. I didn't mean to hurt nobody," I cry. He has his hands on my wrists but his glasses are falling down his nose as I buck madly. Just as he reaches up to push them in, I flip him.

"Son," Mr. Udall says from the front porch, "your mother wants you in here for dinner." He's in white shirtsleeves, his thin tie knot loosened at the collar, the low notes of his forceful command carrying an exaggerated perturbedness. I stare at him in fright as Fred gets to his feet. I stay on my knees, frozen at the sight of the six-foot elder, his Vitalis hair slicked back, wingtips shined. He stares me down. I'm the first to blink.

"Stop the rough housing," he says with a grimace. "You boys are too big for that kind of stuff, anyway." He turns and leaves, unfazed, stone-faced, undaunted. Fred asks me what's the matter, and I make something up about my knee or elbow, getting up, brushing off, telling him I'll see him tomorrow, my heart thumping wildly. I drive down the road grinding gears again, about to explode. I don't know who to turn to. Whom? Whatever. Who wrote the book of love?

11. EXIT BEAR

It isn't dark by nine that night. It's getting there, though. The band shell in the park hanging over me like a shadow of some dinosaur, pigeons gurgling and hooting. I'm still in my white T and jeans sitting there peeling off the rubber label from my worn-out sneakers, thinking about Freddie and his dad and his sister.

Mom just shook her head as I hopped on my old bike and told her I'd be back in by eleven. Dad didn't care, in his office getting ready for some stupid trial, his head stuck in *Idaho Reports* or *The Nation*. I ate my fish sticks and cold asparagus, then took off with a Fudgesicle in my hand. Mom cuts me some slack though. She knows summertime in Idaho, and she isn't going to get in the way of her teenage kid as long as he doesn't screw up big time, and she assumes I guess that isn't going to happen.

Coach Williams is late, but he may not even show up given the risk of getting caught. But, come on, who goes down to this part of the river at night? Nobody. Freddie knows the place I plan to take Coach, but he's the only one. It's a little hollow amidst the trees that line the Boise River beside the park.

But what if he does show up? What am I going to tell him? That I want to be his friend forever? How can I dream of such a thing with my history teacher, my coach, my man, years older than me? My heels are banging pretty hard off the side of the bandstand, and I'm thinking how absurd and calculating I've become with my coy notes and persistent flirtation. What a creep I've turned into.

Coach is wearing a short-sleeve madras shirt, khakis, and white tennis shoes. He walks down the lane with one hand in his pocket, his shuffle unmistakable as he looks around, holding a book in his other hand. It's nine thirty by the time he saunters under the overhanging trees as the river in sunset sheens behind him. His stance is wide, his small mouth and big cheeks barely visible as he approaches the bandstand unaware of my presence until he spots my feet drumming.

"Hi, Tom," he says, almost as cool and baritoned as Mr. Udall. Startled by his formality, I look into his eyes, scared for a second. Do I really know this guy?

"I brought you this." Coach hands me a book. "It's about William Drummond, a fur trader out here in the Rockies during the eighteen hundreds. Kind of interesting, especially if you read between the lines. Thought you might like it."

"Thanks, Coach," I say softly, taking the book and looking at the cover, the picture of a Daniel Boone-ish type with a rifle. "You scared me there for a minute. Weren't sure you'd make it. It's boss that you showed up. I really appreciate it. And this book. I'll give it back when..."

"It's yours. I found it yesterday and set it aside for you. I want you to keep it. Whatever happens," he says, both hands in his pockets now. A long silence lingers between us. "Let's go for a drive," he finally says. "Tell you what. Just head over to the library, and I'll come by and you can hop in. You know the Black Studebaker."

"Yea, I know your car. What about my bike?"

"Stash it."

"Got to be back by eleven."

"No problem. I'll see you in a sec." He turns and walks off, business-like and unemotional. His tone carries a strange edge, distinctly more military than that of the sweet man who is teaching me to butterfly. And what about my grotto, what about my forest of Arden, my midsummer night's dream? I'm anxious, unsure what to do; I can't very well bail at this point. I'm the one that asked to see him, but his odd demeanor makes me uneasy. I'm not ready for a date in the Studebaker, a Coke and fries at the Howdy Pardner with the girls on skates in short shorts. Do I want to cruise the strip with Coach Williams?

He tells me to relax when I get in the car. He smiles and puts a hand on my knee, "I know a place where we can be alone." I expect him to pull out a fifth of Jack and hand me the bottle, but instead he just pushes in the lighter and lights a Camel, asks me if I want a smoke. I decline. He knows I don't smoke.

We head north out of town up Sunset Lane, windows rolled down, a warm breeze sweeping through the car and some dumb oldie called "Make Yourself Comfortable" playing vaguely in the background. It was Sarah Vaughn, my Dad's favorite singer. Maybe Coach is more like guys my Dad's age. Maybe he isn't as cool as I thought, acting like some old fart for crying out loud. I sit moving my knees in and out as the roadster accelerates around turns, weaving up into the hills north of town. I know the route. I've driven up here with Pam on dates, and we made out on the overlook. Was Coach taking me there?

And why for the love of god is he suddenly driving like a fiend, his tires screaming around turns as our shoulders bump together. His maniacal grin is scaring the bejesus out of me as he asks me to find the rum under the seat of the car. We're going fifty in a thirty mile an hour zone and barely missing the guardrails. Is he drunk? Poking me in the ribs, he sings along with Fats Domino's "Ain't That a Shame," the volume on high, bobbing up and down like he's hopped up on dope or something, telling me I'm the one to blame. I white knuckle the seat, wondering what's gotten into this mild-mannered guy, when all of a sudden a siren cries out behind us, red lights flashing as the black and white cop slows Coach to a stop.

Marty pulls over and jumps out of the car, slips his wallet out of his back pocket while the big-hipped cop lumbers over, ticket book in his hand. I sit there wishing I had a baseball cap or could sneak into the trunk. What if the cop knows me or my dad? Luckily, I don't recognize him through the rearview window. I can hear snippets of the conversation. Marty is apologizing, admitting he's showing off for his young friend, whom he's trying to teach to drive mountain roads. He's being foolish, he admits.

"Bad example," the cop says, and then he takes another look at the man he is citing and realizes he's the football coach. They start shooting the shit about the upcoming season when the cop peers in the window to look at me. I nod my head and smile nervously.

"Steady, big fella," Coach says to me, getting in the car once the fuzz pulls out in front of us and makes a U-turn. "Everything's under control. We got a warning is all. I weaseled my way out. 'Yes, officer. No, officer. I apologize, officer.' The usual bull."

"Did he know me?" I'm worried, staring at Mr. Hyde, who has his pedal to the metal again, but is looking out the rearview mirror as he squeezes my thigh.

"I don't know. Did he?" Coach snarls. "And what difference does it make if he did? Who gives a flying f? This is our night. No poli is going to get in our way."

"But I got to be back at eleven."

"Poor Tommy Cadigan," Coach snivels, "has to get back to Mommy before he turns into a pumpkin. Come on, man, grow up. We'll be lucky if we're home by eleven tomorrow. I mean we haven't even cracked the bottle yet, my boy. And the hot springs are still a ways away." He grins wildly at me and turns the radio up again, but the tunes are starting to crackle as we head out of town.

I've never been up to Haven Hot Springs but have heard about it. Lots of bad-ass bikers up there and a long hike in to the place, too. What is Coach thinking? He grabs my hand and brings it to his crotch, the Ron Rico bottle sloshing between us. He's smoking another Camel, gyrating under my limp hand. I feel like I'm in a nightmare. This guy I idolize is suddenly morphing into Kurt or some weird combination of Freddie's Dad and those raunchy juvies at the monkey cages.

"Coach," I manage to say.

"Call me Mart. No need to stand on ceremony anymore. Not if we are going to the hot springs" His grin reminds me of the Joker from my Batman comic books.

"But that place is miles from here."

"That's the idea: get the hell out of Dodge. You'll finally get your chance to get into my pants,. He presses my hand down on his zipper. He laughs.

"Yea, but, Coach, I wasn't expect—"

"Don't give me that line. You've been creaming your briefs over me for the last two years. So now you're finally going to get what you want." He snickers at me with a stupid "hardy, har" so totally out of character I'm taken even more aback than I already am. I'm cringing, holding back my signature tears. I have no idea where we are or what time it is. I only know I'm totally turned off by this sex-craved freak next to me in the cockpit. He suddenly veers left onto a dirt road and races over potholes at a crazy speed, fir trees passing in a whir, all kinds of critters with red eyes scattering as the Studebaker leaves a trail of dust. We come to a meadow with a stream running through it, the sky full of stars. I escape the car as soon as it stops.

Coach follows me with his bottle of rum, tells me not to worry we'll just soak, and we head up a path to the pools, a mile hike through the forest to a grotto. It must not be the Haven, because it's too small, too deserted. Coach doesn't seem so drunk now as we skedaddle up the rocky path, me jumping every time he comes close.

"Fifteen men on a dead man's chest. Yo ho, ho, and a bottle of rum. Drink and the devil had done the rest…ten fathoms deep on the road to hell, ho, ho, ho and a bottle of rum." I can't believe this is happening. Coach belting out drinking songs? Goosing me on the path? None of it makes any sense. Does he really think I'm enjoying his aggression? Damned if the place isn't empty when we get there, with four or five pools, some full of pine needles and soot, the last two clearer, hotter, surrounded by rocks. Coach doesn't take long to strip.

I hear him laugh as I slip my underwear down my legs.

We slide into the hot water in the grotto, spooky and quiet, tree trunks towering over us like sentries. I am shivering cold even in the hot water, plenty scared, hoping Coach will calm down. I don't know what he's going to do to me if he doesn't come around. He kneels in the water in front of me and then rises up, grabbing my ribs and guiding my trunk toward him as he positions himself under me.

I can feel him getting hard beneath me. I'm half struggling, but he has me in a bear hug and is pressing his cock into my butt. His head is turned to the side as I try to look at him, to get him to kiss me or something, but he won't meet my eyes. He has one hand on his penis, directing it under me. I squirm and struggle to move out of his grasp, but he's too damn strong. I'm half in love with him so I wonder what I should do, his boner pressing against my butt cheeks, him thrusting now, trying to get inside me.

"Wait, please, wait. Please, stop for a second." I push hard against his shoulders with my arms, and he abruptly turns and looks me in the eyes.

He glares at me but backs off, squatting in the middle of the pool, his arms like swan wings waving through the water.

Relieved to have him off me, I push myself back as far as possible into the side of the pool, only about five or six feet around anyway and not more than waist deep. The water is plenty hot in one spot but cooler where I lean against a submerged ledge. I'm shaking, and I start to cry. Sometimes I can't stop crying. It's some—not a disease exactly—but some kind of psycho-physio thing that my parents have looked into, my so-called emotional incontinence. I'm borderline PBA, almost diagnosed with pseudobulbar affect. One doctor in Seattle thinks I am pre-epileptic and wants to put me on medication, but I manage to hide it as much as I can. Freddie knows about my crying spells, how even pop songs can trigger them. I just have to deal with it. Part of it is my emotional make up. Part of it, I have to admit, is probably psychosomatic.

Anyway, I'm crying pretty bad, and I think Coach knows. He's seen me before on the bench when some guy calls me Caddy after

I miss a tackle or something. I'm not sobbing so hard I can't talk, though. Just blubbering a little, stuttering, starting and stopping. Coach kneels in the middle of the pool with his arms out, witnessing my breakdown. He's not about to come to my rescue. Not this time, not like the time in the park near Pericles.

"I guess... I don't know. I want to. With you. But I was hoping we could just maybe talk and make out or something. I've never done anything...like sex before—"

"Oh, that's not what I hear. You went down to the monkey cages. Made some money while you were down there.. You aren't the naïve little prude you pretend to be.."

"Who told you that? They're lying."

"I'm done being wrapped around your pinky. You and your swimming lessons and your heart-to-heart talks." Coach moves around in the water now, pushes himself back to the other side of the pool. He stands up and puts his hands on his hips, his upper body in front me under the dim moonlight, backdropped by a web of pine branches. I know I want that body, but only if it comes with Coach, with the Coach I know or the Coach I dream about. The Coach I thought I knew, not the one who has gone ape on me. I look down at the water then up into his face.

"I was with McKellar. He talked me into staying, then these older guys came and one of them got on his knees and started going at it with Kurt, and I took off. "

I'm half way out when Coach comes up behind and grabs me by the waist to pull me back in. I want to kick and scream, but he holds me close to him, puts one hand over my mouth and whispers in my ear to calm down. My legs are strong, and I'm at least as tall as he is if not half as big and built. I'm pushing up from the silty bottom, writhing in the water when I see the black hulk sniffing around our pile of clothes, pawing the bottle of rum, a black ball bigger than a go-cart or a small sofa, smelly as hell and ugly as sin. Coach is holding me as we watch the curious animal turn his nose toward us for a few seconds then scamper off.

"There goes Winnie." Coach is trying to appear unfazed and cute, but I feel the tension in his arms, still around mine.

"Was that a bear? Jeezus."

"Couldn't get the top off the rum bottle, I guess," Coach says. "When he started checking us out, I got nervous. Gone now, I hope." He stands up and peers into the dark. "Well, that's enough excitement for one night."

"Very funny." I leave his clutches, turn around to face him, sniffling, my eyes still blurring. "You got it wrong. I'm here because you care about me. And I'm totally cranked when I'm around you."

I stop and sigh, drawing my butt up on a rock beside the pond and sitting there, head down, staring at my stupid wiener, wondering how my dick got me into this mess. Or my heart. I can't say anything. There's nothing to say. I thought I loved Coach, thought I loved everything about him. But I'm not ready to go all the way with him. I'm not ready to go all the way with anybody. I don't even know what all the way really is with a guy, though Coach was planning on giving me a crash course. He keeps treading water in the middle of the pool, while I sit head down on the lip.

"I never did anything for money." I glance into the dark, hoping yet fearing some sight of the bear. "And yea I've fooled around with guys here and there. We did some jerking off, I'm not going to deny that. I mean come on, I'm a kid. You're not going to tell me you didn't screw around once in a while. But I'm not out there doing it to make money. I would never do that in a million years. You have to…"

"I wouldn't make claims you can't keep," Coach says. "You never know what you may have to do if you end up trying to stay alive as a homo in this world," he tells me bluntly. "But I believe you, kid. I should have confronted you head on, but I just panicked when I heard about it this afternoon. Especially after this morning, learning the butterfly. This morning was pretty precious. They don't come around like that very often. Not for me anyway, and then to find out you were pulling my chain. I just got mad and wanted to get even. It was kind of crazy."

Coach looks sheepish, maybe a little ashamed. He has shown me another side of his personality altogether. I guess he knows that, but even though I'm shaken up and still reeling, I'm unwilling to be deterred.

"At this point in my life I'm not looking for a summer job getting blow jobs, Coach. If Kurt and those guys want to do it, that's their thing. I mean, it's just not for me is all I'm saying. I'm not in this for money. I don't even know very much about most of the sex stuff. I just want to be close to you. Until tonight. Until this whole weird thing started in the car. Now, I don't know. I think I just want to go home."

"Look, Tommy, you can't just screw up and then go running back to Mommy. We're both in too deep. Rumor has it you and some other guys have been making some extra cash off a bunch of bankers in the park. Maybe it's not true, but it's out there. And let's face it, people have seen us together. We've done stuff together. I've taken risks, and I'd take them again if I knew I could trust you. Yes, I'll take you home in a second. Don't worry. I shouldn't have let things get this far out of hand.

"I know what's happening with you. I was a queer kid, too. I grew up in a town a lot smaller than this, and I was running around in high school trying to get laid one way or another. Not for dough, either. But I hung out at the rest stop outside Darby, down by the bridge in Hamilton. I went looking and did it with some pretty raunchy truckers at some pretty dingy bars. But I don't want to be double-crossed, even by a sixteen-year-old. Especially when he makes me believe he's got a heart. You know I'm still in my twenties, Tommy. I've been in only one relationship that's meant anything to me my whole life, and he died in front of my eyes, so if somebody else is going to come along and try to make me think he loves me or wants to be close, I'm not going to let him take me for a ride. He ain't going to screw with me. I don't care if you're one of my students or if you are years younger, you aren't going to mess with my head, Tommy. If you want to screw around, if you want to do it with some sugar daddy that's one thing, but you're not going to try to steal my heart and get away with it. Not after

Desi. He can't be replaced by any cracker teenager who wants to mess with my mind."

"Ask Freddie, he knows. I mean I know I'm not supposed to say anything, but he's my closest friend, and he knows the way I feel about you. I would never lie to you. I just want you to be the gentle guy you were this morning. I'm crazy about you, I admit it, but I can't do it this way. I'm not ready. I just need to hold you for a while. I'm not ready."

I'm about to burst out in tears again, mired in that messed-up muddied pool, being a dumb-ass kid, so embarrassed. Coach sits on the rock ledge across from my breakdown. I figure he's probably wondering what in the name of heaven he's gotten himself into, but before I know it, he wades across, takes me in his arms, and gives the top of my wet head a kiss. I throw my arms around him and let it all out.

"I don't even know how I got to be this way, Coach. I mean, Jesus, what if everyone finds out I'm a homo? What will they do to me? Where am I supposed to go? Am I going to jail or something? Do I have to run away to LA or hide out in San Francisco? What am I going to do? I mean, you have to know what it's like. It's so great to be with somebody real like you, someone who loves guys, who wants more than wankers in the stacks or some smelly bathroom or something. Shit, I can't live like that. I want to love somebody. I don't want to suck anonymous dick in the bus station for the rest of my life. Maybe I'm being a stupid prude, an uppity snob. You're the first person that has made it real for me. I mean Freddie understands, but it's different. We are best buds. With you, I feel like the flame is going plenty strong. Please don't give up on me. You can't. I mean even if we can't go any further, please don't hate me. Please at least let me know you trust me, let me know you believe me when I tell you how I feel. I realize your friend in Korea is still with you and everything. I would never tread on his memory. And I'm sorry, sorry I ever went near the monkey cages. But please don't treat me like you did tonight."

Our conversation is not over. Coach admits he has flipped out, says he's sorry, holds me close and looks me in the eye. We hug again, but nothing happens down there, nothing major that is. I can't afford to get horny right now, given all my protests, so I have to back off. He continues explaining, telling me he wanted to teach me a lesson, that I'm the first person he has let under his skin since Korea.

His dead friend Desi still wakes him up at night, and not just because he'd been picked off by sniper. They'd also taken leave together at the Great Barrier Reef right before it happened. They'd bunked together for a long, long time before the hot night in the hotel with the fan and trade winds and beer and a long day's sun. Though both of them had done it with guys before, neither of them had ever fallen in love, whatever that means, Coach says. "Desi." He names him, sitting there in the pool with me. "Good old Desi. Yep."

And we hang out there for a minute under the dark, quarter-moon sky before we finally get out to go back home. Coach says, "Sorry kid. Didn't mean to scare you. I lost it for a moment. Some of the stuff that happened to me in the Army started coming back. Believe me, I know how you feel. I'm feeling it really bad too, feeling how close you're getting, how right it seems in my heart, but how dangerous in my head. You know, Tommy, we got to be real careful in this neighborhood. You know that, right?"

His honesty triggers something inside me. I tell him about Freddie's father. He doesn't say much about it. We're suddenly within the city limits on the way to my house. It's late, and we are both worn out. I'm hoping Coach will tell me what the hell to do, but he just sits with his window rolled down and his elbow on the door. I tell him Freddie doesn't know yet. He looks over at me and finally says, "Judge not. You're right to keep your mouth shut, but with your buddy, I can't say. That's your call, Tommy. Nothing's easy when it comes to this stuff between guys." He just lifts his shoulder and turns up the radio. Laconic sucker, back to the Coach I know and love.

He drops me off a block from home and I race back. There will be hell to pay, but damned if I'm willing to pay it after a night like that.

12. BLACK-BALLED

"Yea, she played Rosalind," Freddie tells me. It's Thursday, and we're riding our bikes downtown, rainwater stripes up our butts and backs. It was Thursday when I went to bed and it's Thursday when I wake up to a note from my mother telling me to clean my room, empty wastebaskets, sweep out the garage, and call her when I'm done.

When I phone, she wants to know where the dickens I was last night. "Out driving around," I tell her. With whom, she asks. Just friends, I answer meekly. The upshot of it all is my grounding for the weekend. I am destined to spend Saturday and Sunday doing crossword puzzles and skimming tedious novels like *Silas Marner* or *Ethan Frome*, required summer reading about stolid lonely men facing ethical dilemmas. Dimmesdales.

It's raining, so I skip out of some of the work, eat three or four bowls of Cheerios with tons of milk and bananas and sugar, sneak another root beer popsicle, and call Freddie. He is ready to meet El at the Gamekeeper. Three hours and many chores later, we meet half way, I fetch my wet bike from the park, and we head downtown. It has let up a bit, just sprinkling, so we put our hoods up over our sweatshirts. We almost have to shout.

"So your sis and Frankie Jr. were pretty tight?" I ask.

"Nah. He told you that? Gracie can't stand Frank Jones. So full of himself. She never sees him nowadays, except at church. So Mr. Dir wants us to try out for the new play?"

"Yea, think so." I pedal fast to avoid traffic, almost too much exhaust to talk. Fins are pulling out from parking spaces, wet shoppers running amok, unaccustomed to steady rain in early August. We finally reach the big turn-of-the-century Owyhee Hotel at the corner of 5th and Main and take our bikes around the back to the alley. We're soaked. We knock on the green metal door, but there's no answer. Turns out it's open, so we just head in, hiding our bikes behind a dumpster. Inside is dark, the place smelling of spilled booze and unemptied ashtrays.

"She said she'd be here." We plop down in club chairs and put our wet feet up, pretending we're in the movies. It's a dark and seedy afternoon.

"I have a leetle surprise for you in de basement," Fred says. He's rubbing his hands and snorting Peter Lorre. He lifts his eyebrows. "I theenk you will be very pleeesed," he chortles.

We settle in for a wait. Maybe we're early. Fred wants to know what happened.

"When?" I ask.

He squints at me. "You look so worn out, Thomas. I'm just so worried about you." He's jumpy, Freddie is. What's eatin' him? I wonder. Forget me. What about *you*? I want to say, but it won't work. Not with the steady stare of Cotton Mather. Jayzuzz. So I just spill the beans. Tell him about the Studebaker and that smelly bear hide, tell him almost everything about what went on in the hot springs, tell him about the cop stopping us, the Long John Silver song.

I even tell him about the book Coach gave me, which is soaked and wrinkled since I left it with my bike. I'd slipped it into the inner pocket of my slicker while we rode to the hotel. I draw it out and hand it to Freddie. Hard bound, thank god, but still wet as hell. The jacket is embossed with a drawing of a guy that resembles Kit Carson except his beaver hat, which looks more like a Louis XIV bouffant. *William Drummond and the Fur Trade.*

"This book is sopped," Freddie says. "Looks like you got some explaining to do. So, when did he give it to you?"

"Before I got into his hot rod." Freddie shakes his head, smiling. I can tell by the way he's shaking his head he wants to start lecturing me again. He's looking at me like *I* was Mr. Hyde, not Coach, just staring at me with a mixture of jealousy, admonition, and fear.

"Are you mad at me?"

"You love him?" There are no out-loud answers to either of our questions, though some deep place says yes to both. Freddie's anger has to do with consequences, I presume. My love has to do with some state beyond infatuation, some place on the other side of idolization. We sit in the silence of the dark nightclub. We're in front of a round cocktail table in fake leather chairs that swivel off balance. A shaft of cloudy daylight turns the lounge into a chapel.

Freddie picks up the book out of habit, his way of blocking out what I know he sees are all the faults he finds with his family, his religion, his eyes, his body, his school, and now maybe his friend. We often wonder how long we can survive if we really pursue these homo-romantic impulses. What are we thinking, he often asks me when we lie in bed at night during sleepovers in separate single beds as we talk long into darkness about how doomed we are to think we might make life work with our "predilection," as he calls it. Freddie's books are his medicine, his place of survival.

And in this book, Fred finds a small piece of lined paper wedged in between the fly leaf and title page. It's damp but still almost legible. On one side a scribbled note, on the other a poem Freddie reads aloud:

> *I watch the clock. It watches me.*
> *Ahead in my head my break*
> *waits for you in the pool*
> *blue suit down a blue lane*
> *iris in bloom, in a vase, in the swim,*
> *my butterfly, my chin surf,*
> *my breath-away, my*

"It's smeared after that. I can't make it out. Is it 'life' or 'heart'? No, you wouldn't dip that far into sentimental soup, I hope." He shrugs. I want to stop his commentary, as I see him read Coach's signature on the next page. I know it by heart now. "To Tommy," he'd written, "For you, I'll risk everything. MW." I don't want Freddie's irreverence to ruin Coach's gift—or my poem.

The lights snap on in the nick of time and in walks the trio, making a ruckus, arguing about something. Freddie and I stay hidden in the dark corner, listening to the three of them. El is on Claude's case, telling him he'd better shape up or he's going to get run out on a rail.

"You think I give a rat's ass?" Claude says. "What do I want with this cow town anyway?" He's keeping his voice down a bit as he speaks, looking around. El tells him to mind his manners if he wants the gig to last, says something I can't hear about the police, something like, "we ain't in North Beach no more." By that time, Jimmy is testing the snare and staring at us in the corner.

"Well, well, well. What have we here? If it ain't Prince Charming, with a sidekick this time."

"That's Freddie," El points out, noticing us with some surprise. "I hope you gentlemen were not eavesdropping. Claude and I were having a little discussion about his behavior on West Main Street."

"None of your damn business," Claude says to El, nodding to us in the corner, sitting down to the piano. Claude starts moving all over the keyboard in anger—"What'd I Say" and "Rocket 88" and 'Johnny B Goode"—all the rock and roll songs jazzed and sped up as he warms up, ignoring all of us as he lets off steam by pounding the ivories. Reminds me of Freddie and his books. Cloud, as Jimmy calls him, wears a light blue flannel shirt over his t-shirt today. He sits back straight at his bench, round-faced, brow-knitted, tortured by his tunes.

"Claude misses San Francisco," Elvina tells us as she takes off her raincoat and rests her umbrella at the edge of the stage. "He misses Tommy's Joint. That's right, there's a joint named after you. Except Tommy over there in San Fran, that Tommy's a girl. She's a butch, but she runs the place over there. Yea, he misses the clubs—misses the 440."

Claude starts playing, then El begins to sing "Misty."

"You guys heard my friend Johnny Mathis, right?" He hasn't recorded that one yet, she says, but he sings it at the clubs in North Beach." El is on stage, testing the microphone, plugging in amps, unstringing wires.

Claude switches to "Stormy Weather," starting to sing about some man he is no longer together with, about the rain in his brain, his husky voice sounding breathy through a live mike near the keyboard. El watches her temperamental pianist bellow into the keys.

A voice rings out from the back, picking up the song as it starts in on the blues. Looking up, we spot Mel Dir in his camel hair coat and slicked back pompadour, his pressed slacks and tasseled loafers, trying to look like Efrem Zimbalist Jr. He does, in fact, have the suave. He croons in a soft baritone, and they're taking turns now, singing about rocking chairs and loneliness, until suddenly Freddie stands up and jumps in right as the song brings the Lord and prayer into the picture. And so the trio goes on until Claude stops playing.

"How's our famous band?" Mel Dir asks, walking up to the stage and kissing the top of Claude's head as if it were a shrine. "Miss Elvina." Mel bows to the bandleader with mock chivalry. I had no idea Mel Dir knows them. I should have figured as much. He is in show biz, after all, and there isn't much show biz in spudland.

El doesn't seem too pleased with Dir's distraction of her piano man. She merely nods and starts tapping the mike again. Mel is a little slick, a little glib, but it *is* the theatre after all, dahling. He isn't as flamboyant as Liberace, at any rate. Elvina wants to know how her voice sounds in the back. I tell her to turn it up. She then calls us to help with some wires and mike stands. We're honored to play band boys for the afternoon.

She starts to talk to us about Johnny Mathis again. He went to San Francisco State to study English just like she did. Everyone was interested in the writing scene in the city.

"Johnny was torn between sports and music," she says, "but he was a shy kid, with a beautiful trim lanky body and a manner that got him into trouble. Kids made fun of his voice from the very beginning, even in choir at high school," she recalls. "His voice was so beautiful and he was so beautiful that the frat boys and the football team ganged up on him. They black-balled him in college, wouldn't go to his concerts. It was hell for him, but when he came down to our 440 Club in North Beach, he found his niche. The Bohemians hung out down there. Then the talent scouts scooped him up. And now he's at the Copacabana five nights a week," she nods. "Now those black ballers got their comeuppance."

"Those phonies," Dir says. "I know they're listening to his records right now. I knew Johnny, too. And Orlovsky and that crowd. I knew them all when I lived out there. Johnny, he's the sweetest man in the world. And he will put all those bigots to shame, I will tell you," he looks at Claude. Freddie and I are all ears. We can't believe they know these famous singers and writers, can't believe they lived the scene in San Francisco.

"So you met Ginsberg?" Freddie asks Dir. "Tell us what he was like. Such a revolutionary writer. I just wonder what kind of person he is."

"Kind of ugly, actually," Mel says. "Kind of unkempt. New Yorky. But smart and funny and a little shy. And most of all willing to lay it on the line. Willing to call America out on its military industry, its racism, its hypocrisy. On its lobotomies and shock therapies and castration of homosexuals."

Jimmy's drumroll interrupted us. "The H word," he announces from his stool with a cymbal slap. "The love that dare not sing its name."

"Especially in bossy Boise," Claude said. "Where the boys are boss, but the bosses are..."

"Bitches," Dir says. We're jaw-dropped as we hear Jimmy punctuating the talk with his pedal and brushes.

"Okay, gentlemen," El interrupts. "Enough is enough. These young men came down to hear us play. And to what do we owe the pleasure of your company, Mr. Dir?"

Mel moves sheepishly away from the piano. He has come to see Claude about a private party he's setting up at the Joneses, he says. But what luck, he interrupts himself, to run into the young

Mr. Udall, who has such a "charming voice." Dir puts his hand on Freddie's shoulder.

"I'm so glad we ran into to one another, young man. You will try out for *Tea and Sympathy* this fall, won't you? And in the meantime I'd love to tell you more about my wild times. What are you up tomorrow afternoon? Lunch maybe?"

Freddie appears surprised yet intrigued. Claude has stopped playing and lit up a smoke, elbows propped up on the piano. Inside my head, I'm trying to tell Freddie to avoid Dir's grasp. El is watching her watch. A pregnant pause hangs on the scuffed black stage, and Freddie is on the spot.

"Of course, Tommy Cadigan is welcome to come along if he's not too busy playing hide the football in the park with some of our local linebackers." I look up realizing that half the town may have gotten wind of my time beside the monkey cages. Who's spreading this manure, and why is Mel Dir kicking it around? I want to kick his ass, and I actually take a couple of steps toward him, but he's the high school drama teacher and I know my place.

"I'd be happy to talk to you," Fred says, adopting his officious tone. "But I can't say I'm as interested in their sex lives as I am in their politics."

"Mel," Elvina insists. "I'm going to have to ask you to skedaddle, if you don't mind. Scoot. Now. Or else Claude is going to bounce you out of here like a big beach ball." Mel looks up, annoyed.

"'Lawdy, Lawdy, Miss Claudie,'" Mel says., "Okay, I'm out of here. I'll see you, Fred Udall, tomorrow in the restaurant out front. Right here. At one. Don't be late. I have all the dish on the Beats. Snyder, Whalen. All the skinny on the cool grey city of love." Mel waltzes across the dance floor toward the double doors that lead to the lobby while Claude plays "Somewhere Over the Rainbow." Freddie sits on the stage cross-legged in a trance, while I head to the bathroom. He's in heaven that afternoon listening to the band, and I'm on cloud nine knowing he's there.

We learn a lot Thursday. A different world has opened up to us. We have found out there is a place for people like us, even if it is an underworld in a dark bar after hours with police ready to pounce at the slightest provocation. Even if we are unspeakable, even if we are outlaws, we can go places where we'll find others like us.

Before we leave, El sits us down in a corner and tells us that everything that went down that afternoon must be kept within those four walls. She says we are young, we have to find our way in the world, and we shouldn't go listening to grownups who want to tell us what to do. She is advising us to listen to our hearts instead of Dir or even her.

"You can't always hear what your soul is saying," she says. "And yes, you gotta be careful. The police are everywhere and not just in uniforms. But you must find a way to hear your heartbeat and follow it, follow its rhythm. Ain't that right Jimmy?" she asks, looking over at his checkered cap. And off he goes on one of his solos, a really slow one on the congas.

13. HOOKED

Coach and I are driving through the Palouse in the Stude again, this time in the morning slant light of a golden Rockies summer, just the two of us, going north up to Lolo where the Mormons are gathering. The Udalls are staying at the lodge, and I've been invited to join Fred to spend a few days with his family. Coach has agreed to drop me off on his way to see his clan in Darby. I want to go with him to Montana, but such dreams surpass even my wheel of fortune. I guess I have to be content with our little day trip, which in itself is a minor miracle.

"So Captain Drummond Stewart probably tromped around this neck of the woods with his friend Antoine Clement, you think?" I ask Coach in the car, letting him know I had read part of the biography he'd given me. "Do you think they were more than friends—in 1830? Was that even possible?"

"Stranger things have happened," Coach says, rolling his window up to talk more comfortably. "The book goes out of its way to avoid even considering it, but that says something in itself. History, as you've heard me say a million times, has its own history. Historians are creatures of their times and they gather facts based on what is believable to them. We know Stewart never married, and we know he fathered an illegitimate child at an early age. The book talks about the rash of sodomy arrests, pillories, and trials in England during the 1830s when it writes of Lord Byron's wildness and Stewart's worship of him. The writer mentions life sentences and forced immigration to Australia.

"Maybe we should head to the Great Barrier Reef before it's too late," Coach half jokes. "Stewart probably had to get the hell out of Dodge himself, but in this case, Dodge was not hicksville. It was London, the big city. He was coming over to Dodge, actually, which makes it so damn ironic. Came out here to the Rockies, now one of the most conservative places in the country, to get laid by guys and fall in love with one. Incredible.

"Must have been before Brigham Young showed up," I laugh, trying to sound smart.

"Yeah, the Mormons didn't land in Salt Lake until the 1840s, I think. Too bad we don't have H.G.'s time machine. It would be fabulous to go back and find out what really happened at Fremont Lake when Stewart went back there with his British bachelor buddies and put on tent parties."

"But nowadays if you want to be queer in the not so wild west," I say, "you have to go back to Europe or San Francisco and become a bohemian dodging bar raids. Or so says Nellie Mel."

"Don't throw stones. Dir is a damn good actor, director, and singer. And he has the courage to make a go of it in Boise. More power to him is what I say."

"I just don't want him pawing Freddie."

"I think Fred Udall can take care of himself."

"Maybe you're right, Captain." I smile at him. Yeah, I'm being protective. But that's how I am. "But what if *we* get caught?"

Coach stops for gas at the first town between Boise and McCall, pulling up to a chipped white pump at the Flying A. A tall, mean-looking guy in dirty overalls emerges from the dark garage, wiping his hands on a blackened rag. I jump out of the car and run over to the Coke machine, just as I hear the gas man say, "Nice lookin' boy you got there." I slow down to stay within earshot. I want to hear Coach's answer and only stop listening when I slip the dime into the slot and shove down the metal lever. I buy one for Coach too.

"Well, he isn't exactly my boy. I'm giving him a ride up to church camp."

"Not your boy, huh? Whose kid is he then if you don't mind me askin'?"

"Excuse me?" Coach says sharply, an indirect command to back off.

"Loads a camps up there. What camp might you be takin' the boy to?"

"It's up at the Lochsa Lodge." He isn't going to give the grease monkey any more information. Overalls saunters over to the front to lift the hood and check the dipstick.

"Cousin had one of these old Studebakers. What year's this anyway?"

"51."

"Oil's good. They can run hot, I'll tell you that much. Where'd you get her?"

"In Montana. Jeez, we gotta get a move on." Coach checks his watch, closes the hood, and motions for me to get in. He gives Jed three dollars and we pull out rather precipitously, as Freddie would say.

"What a chump," I say as we settle back on the blacktop. "Why doesn't he MYOB. He's like one of those rocking chair guys outside the saloon in *Gunsmoke*."

"What time did you tell Freddie you'd be there?" It isn't even noon. We have poles in the back and plenty of time to fish for a couple of hours on the way up, but the driving turns out to be slow going around the lake because of construction. After a while, we stop talking. The only channel is Stuart Hamblen and his Cowboy Church of the Air.

Doesn't take long for Coach to twist the knob down. He finally tells me he hasn't forgotten my question but needed to sit on it for a while. First of all, he doubts we'll get caught since no one has seen us and nobody knows we are doing anything. Secondly, if we were to get spotted in the act, we will just have to deny any accusations because the law we'd be charged with is an unjust law, and civil disobedience requires us not to play their game. "Lewd and lasciv-ious conduct, like what we've been up to here and there, is a lesser offense than a crime against nature, like the one I was stupidly going to perform the other night in some blind revenge. I definitely would spend plenty of time in jail if convicted, especially because you are a minor. I could be sentenced to life if they catch us in flagrante delicto. I've told you from the start, this thing is no laughing matter. It's not like going steady with Pam Wells. *You* have done nothing by the way. Everything that has happened physically has been instigated by me. Remember that."

"That's bull, Coach. You know darn well I started this whole thing. I'm the one that followed you into the sauna every day. I'm the one who got you to come to the park. I've read *Romeo and Juliet.* I'm the one who climbed those orchard walls. I know what we're getting into, but no matter how hopelessly romantic it sounds, my love for you is 'proof against their enmity,' as Romeo says."

"Tell that to a jury from Boise. From anywhere, actually." He looks out the window and then back at the road, shaking his head. "I don't know what I'm getting myself into," he says. "This is so incredibly reckless. You're a minor for Chrissake, and I'm your GD coach and teacher. I'm supposed to be the adult here. What do I think I'm doing? You don't know the consequences. You're a sheltered kid who's just excited by finding out about guys who like guys. I can't take advantage of that. I don't want to ruin your life."

He's gripping the steering wheel so hard I can see his knuckles whitening. I know he's thought before about everything he's telling me, but articulating it must be making it real.

We're driving up the Lochsa now, having covered long stretches of wide water that run under the bridge where the Selway flows in. I ask Coach to stop, tell him I have to pee. I'm losing my cool a little after his excited outburst and increased speed around turns, vaguely reminiscent of his earlier mania. "I gotta go," I tell him, which is true on a couple of levels. He tells me to shut up and cross my legs, announcing our fishing spot is just around a couple of corners anyway. "Not far at all," he says. Is he calming down?

We pull off on a short dirt road that dips down beside the river. I don't see any other cars. When he stops, I put my palms on his cheeks, turning his head toward me. "I know what we're getting into. It would be nice to say I'm too immature to understand what this is all about. Maybe I am just a stupid kid, but I know the way I feel about you. And it's real. Why does everyone want to turn me into an infant? Look, I've known since I was thirteen that I could not keep my eyes off men. I was paging through *National Geographics* before I was ten.

"So give me a break. I'm the one that should be protecting you. If we're caught, they will excuse me for fooling around because they'll think I'm a helpless kid, experimenting for kicks like punks will do. But you're an adult, and we all know that adults, like those suits at the monkey cages, are rational and intelligent and know better." I stop, disturbed by a dose of sarcasm in the midst of my sincerity.

"I don't know," I continue, releasing him and looking out at the river, glimmering in the midday sun, rushing through boulders. "Maybe we are out of our heads. Maybe you're right. Maybe we're driving off a cliff. Maybe I should just repress it all, go to my room and beat off to memories of divers at the Olympics or stupid Kurt McKellar. That's even a bigger bunch of BS, though. Hide for the rest of my life? Get married and drive out to rest stops? Talk about hypocrisy. All I know is I love you, and I want to be with you. If that's a crime, so be it. Drummond and Antoine made it happen, why can't we?"

"You're a brave hunter, Tommy," Coach says after a long pause, smoothing his hand through my hair, his eyes wet. He takes my head in his hands and holds my scalp to his nose and lips, saying nothing. I can smell his sweat mixed with Ivory soap, me near his chest, my eyes closed.

"Let's soak our heads on it," he finally says, breaking the trance. "And take that promised piss." We jump out of the hot car, still partially in shade. The light is intense, reflecting blindly on the water, heat held in big grains of golden sand. I jump right in, wearing my cutoffs. Coach goes to the trunk and fishes out his suit. Before long, we're wading upstream and diving shallow into the current as it takes us down, until we swim hard toward the bank and emerge falling down on the sand.

When Coach opens his eyes, he has a smile on his face. The ends of his mouth are up, and I'm grinning to see the whites of his eyes. There isn't much to say. We know the place we're in right now is good. We know this moment is a gift from the river god. I drink in the smell of Coppertone as Coach kneels over me and spreads the white lotion the way he washed my back in the shower, and he rubs it in good up on the shoulders where I'm feeling the remnants of fear we left in the car.

"Since we're in this thing together," he finally says, "you better know a little more about my story in the war." He keeps talking with his eyes closed while I turn over and rest on my back watching a huge white cloud like an iceberg sail across heaven.

"Well, the first thing you have to know is Desi was not really one of the guys. He had his ukulele he bought in Hawaii and his Shakespeare book, and he sat in the corner all the time practicing and reading. Don't get me wrong, he was a really gentle guy, not very big but wiry, kind of weird and shy. Everyone gave him a hard time, some even called him queer now and again and he'd get pissed. Desi made it a point to volunteer for every dangerous mission he could think of in order to prove he was a man or whatever, even though I kept telling him to forget those lunkheads. But they got under his skin. The night he got killed, he was out proving himself at Bloody Ridge with me tagging along because I was worried about him. Sure enough he gets picked off by a sniper while we're on watch. After he gets shot, I'm shaking him so hard, I just kept trying to wake him up, like he was drunk or asleep or something even though he was bleeding all over. I kept yelling at him, telling him we had to get out of there until they pulled me off him and took me back to the barracks. Then I just sat there in kind of a trance.

"I guess my battalion sergeant knew something was going on, because I wasn't saying anything and wasn't interested in eating for a couple of days. I followed orders, but I was pretty much a zombie. The priest nursed me until he got it out of me. I told him Desi was the first person I loved who ever loved me back, he was the first person who meant it when he held me in his arms. And Father Cruickshank just looked at me but didn't flinch too much or anything. He'd probably heard all kinds of stuff, I can tell you that. He consoled me, said he understood I was very close to Private Clairveaux and we make intimate friendships in the army and learn to love our brothers as ourselves. I kept telling him this wasn't brotherly love, this was the real thing, the whole shebang, but he just ignored me and absolved me of my sins.

"That was just the beginning of the big eraser. They sent me back to headquarters in Seoul for a week and this other chaplain kept coming into my room once a day and asked me if I was feeling better. And I kept telling him, 'Look man, I've lost the first person I have ever slept with and loved, the first person I have shared everything with, the first person I ever made real love to.' I was twenty, but I was proud of what I had with Des. I wasn't going to let them deny it. I knew the consequences but didn't give a shit. They kept giving me medicine, saying I would soon come to my senses. I needed time to rest, they kept saying.

"It was Kafkaesque. I swear. An absolute nightmare. No one would listen to me, no one would even acknowledge what I was going through. They just treated me like I was insane. They took me to Honolulu and put me in a psych ward—kept asking me questions and giving me tests."

Coach stops and rolls over on to his side and looks at me. I'm on my back. We're warming up, but I can't go in the water until I hear him out.

"Are you sure you want to hear about this? Should we just go in again and forget it?" Coach asks me.

"I want to know what happened," I say, still looking up at the sky.

"All right. They decided they were going to try aversion therapy, where they hook these electrodes up to you and show you all these muscle guys and every time you get turned on, they deliver a little shock to your balls. Then they show you Jayne Mansfield or some other bombshell and don't shock you. So Dr. Hall would come in wearing his white coat and start talking to me about a sure-fire way of getting over my problem. I was scared and pissed. But I couldn't get out of there. It was a psych ward and guards were everywhere.

"And then a week later this new priest came in, some old Jesuit guy from Detroit. I just broke down in front of him, begged him to get me out of that place. He heard me out and then told me to calm down. Said he knew what was up, and that he felt the same way I did. He'd lived with it his whole life. He had a plan to get me out of there. It would take some time he told me. I had to get physically sick first, so they would lay off the shock and then I had to tell the doctors that I was confessing to Father Bede and needed a week of prayer.

"So I started to get less rabid, less radical. I grew cagey. I barfed a lot. I got a Bible, started quoting Matthew. I was an altar boy, after all. I started acting like I had slowly come out of a trance. When they asked me about Des, I just said I thought it was better not to talk about it for now. I told the docs it was in the past, told them I wanted to go home to Montana for a while, wanted to sort things out. It was tricky, but I finally got discharged honorably and sent home."

I hear Coach out, lying there, looking up at the intense blue sky accented by frigates of clouds, frightened by his story. I'm getting in deep and my feet are getting plenty cold. When I look over, I see Coach watching me with his head propped on his elbow. I can't mask the fear in my eyes, but I know I have to hold his hand, however briefly, know I have to roll over on my side and look him in the eye.

"So when I met you," he continues, smoothing out the sand with the side of his hand, eyes glued to the ground. "I didn't know how to handle it. In so many ways you remind me of him.

"I'm your teacher; you're under my trust. I have an ethical duty toward you, and there are boundaries I'm not supposed to cross. But you've brought it all back to me, all the hurt—but all the joy too, the realization I can love another guy and it can be real in spite of all the doctors and priests and cops. So I decided if it's true you do really love me with open eyes and an honest heart, we may have to give it a go. So, to be honest, I don't know what I'm doing, but I know I don't want to give you up. Crazy as that is.

"C'mon," he says, suddenly changing the subject, "let's jump back in to get rid of my telltale bulge, then we can cast our nets for an hour or so to see if we can fill up our baskets." He stands up, and I chase him down to the water and leap on his back, trying to wrestle the thick man down. I'm taller than he is, and he lets me tackle him as we both head into the backwater of the big pool.

We both know how to fly fish. My dad has taken me up to the Madison near Yellowstone a couple of times, and once we drove to Oregon and took boats down the Rogue. Coach grew up fishing. We have to walk up river a half mile to find some water, but we finally spot some holes and shady bank water, and of course I spend what seems like hours trying to tie my tippet, trying to get the line through the eye of the caddis. Coach ties on a big hopper and is way out in front of me, already casting to the side of a falls, wading in his old tennis shoes, all those flies stuck to his fishing vest. What a stud, I think, watching his round dark head, his mouth turned down, watching the easy loop of his cast, his concentration and patience.

I picture him on the sidelines during games, in his nondescript slacks with grass stains, his blue nylon warm-up jacket. His dark hair is cut short, and he's shuffling and pacing, hands in his pockets. Quiet, stoic, almost shy, yet assured, letting his players make their decisions. No pep talks, no prayers, no yelling. Just a look in a huddle and a soft-spoken suggestion. That's Coach. He's not interested in championships or trophies. He'd rather get us to play hard and do our best. And we stay focused and believe in ourselves because he shows us how.

It doesn't take long before his rod bends like a crooked staff as he holds it up. It's wobbling. He's letting the fish get tired. It's a fighter it turns out, a rainbow. We joke about size. How long is it? It's a big fish, well over a foot. Coach has caught the big one, but we've got to go soon after he lands it. We find our way to the road and walk down to our spot. It's getting late, and we head back to a Studebaker that refuses to turn over.

14. CHERRY HILL

Two hours later we're in a tow truck headed to a gas station in Myrtle Beach, north of Lewiston. Coach and I spent time under the hood but we couldn't figure it out. She wasn't overheated. We thought it might be the battery or alternator, but the charge seemed just fine. Coach finally thumbed his way into town to get help, and the three of us with Studebaker hitched up are now headed in the wrong direction.

The driver might be twenty, wearing torn jeans, work boots, a dirty old tee. He's puffing Luckies from a pack on the dash, the three of us bouncing down the road, knocking arms in a truck filled with muddy receipts, a crowded ashtray, and a box of hose clamps on the floor.

"It's a bitch," he says. "You ain't gettin' to Lolo today. You guys might have to spend the night down here in Myrtle Beach, population minus five. Maybe you can shack up at the Cherry Hill. He's got cabins. Can't see Mike working on it until later today. You could crash on my floor if it comes to that, but I got a tiny place outside Lewiston, even further south. Where you guys comin' from?" he asks.

"Boise," I say.

"Ah, the booming metropolis. Our capitol. My big sister's down there. Married a Mormon dude. Strict as hell. He comes up here and stares at my empties. Fuck 'em, fuck 'em all is what I say. I don't want to offend you boys. You aren't eee-van-gelicals, are ya?"

"No way."

"Good, those folks chap my ass. Look, if I want to smoke a pack a day and drink a six a Coors, what's it to them? If I want to screw up my life, that's my goddamn business. I ain't hurtin' nobody, for shit's sake. I sure ain't knocking up five gals at once like those poly whatever they are over there in Hamilton. I don't need no angels. I get a steak down at Lucky's and then do some two-step dancing on Saturday. That's all the heaven I need. That's what I tell my sis. Keep that Bible-thumper away from me or I'll have a crack at him." This monologue is interspersed with clouds of smoke, chortles, and smiling nods our way as we head toward the nearest mechanic.

We decide to rent one of the old clapboard cabins at the Cherry Hill Resort. Nobody asks any questions once they find out Coach is taking me to church camp. He makes a big deal of my Mormon destination around the nosey Myrtle Beachers, and he plays the father figure at the diner, ordering me to not to play with my fry pile. My mom is gonna call the lodge in Lolo to let Freddie's folks know I'll be up there tomorrow. She has instructed me to behave myself and not harass Coach Williams with my sass.

"Mind your manners and act like a gentleman. Make sure to treat him to breakfast. You can afford that, Tommy, with what I gave you. Okay, my sweetest, you be a good boy."

Our little cabin at the Cherry Hill resort overlooks the Clearwater River. After we take turns showering, we climb into our underwear and under our separate covers with the TV off because there is nothing to watch. It's after ten, dark outside, the two of us shacked up in a knotty pine cabin that smells of smoke and Lysol, the beds saggy. But the sheets are clean, and the Bible sits on the table between us. I pick it up and find Leviticus and show Chapter 18 to my cabin mate. He flips to the New Testament and reads the Letter to the Romans.

"We're an abomination," I say.

"Yea," he replies, "I don't reckon there's much way round that, ma boy." There is some Walter Brennan in there. "But so are Jonathan and David apparently, whose souls are knit together."

"Why is it a sin to love?" I ask, mixing naiveté with genuine wonder.

"It's not, but it *is* a sin to make love to another man if you are a man. And a sin to get a divorce, a sin to hang up your laundry on

Friday night or lust after someone in your heart even if you don't do anything about it. There're lots of sins, which doesn't excuse what we're up to. The question is how do we reconcile our love for one another with the teachings of the church? How can God condemn our hugs? Who are we harming?"

"But do we even have a right to ask that question? How can we doubt the gospel?" I'm a good altar boy. I've learned my catechism.

"We are sinners," he repeats, lying on his bed, looking up at the ceiling. "But we are also two souls who long for one another. I can only speak for myself. I don't really know how to square my love of men with my faith. I don't pretend to know what God thinks of the love I have for you, even after all the praying I've done. But I do know where my heart is when we're together. I know there's something sacred about us, as wrong as it seems by conventional standards—even to me at weak moments."

He bows his head, so full of anguish during his halting sermon, so full of his willingness to respect the church that now damns us for following our hearts, so bravely or foolishly willing to tempt fate. He reaches over and turns the light off on the bedside table between us and we lie still, both pretending to sleep. At least I am wide awake, waiting for a half hour before I make my move and climb under the covers beside him.

"Tommy, I don't know," he says with some misgiving, but then he allows me to put my arm around him as he holds his head in his hands, almost praying. Not for forgiveness but for a blessing, a blessing of the beauty and holiness of the love we are about to make.

The rest is not just history. The rest is two guys in a single bed trying not to roll off on to a smelly carpet. Two guys awkwardly learning how to exchange tongues and touch lips, two men turning red and closing their eyes and kissing. We feel chests and nipples, pulling off our shorts and pulling the covers up because it's getting cool. We're naked now, pressed together with hard ons. I'm on top of him rubbing, and I can feel his whole body in waves of pressure against my chest and stomach against my cock. I can't hold on much longer, but I don't want to come too soon.

I want him to come too, I want him to come with me as I kiss him, with him on top of me now but not in me because we don't want to do that yet. We can't fuck yet. We just want to hold each other, touch each other, touch one another's cocks. We want to jack each other off, but I'm at the breaking point while he's on top of me, and I'm holding on to his thick muscular back while he's kissing me.

I can't help it any more. I just cave in and say screw it and come all over him and my stomach, and he stops rubbing and holds me tight for a minute. My breath calms down, and I don't know who or where I am for a second. When I open my eyes, I see him looking at me and stroking me. And then after a few minutes, I kiss him and he kneels across me. I press against his stomach and he starts rocking and moving up and down. He finally falls backward and comes up in the air, like a geyser, his eyes closed in pleasure before he lands beside me, sighing. When he opens his eyes, he sees my tears and reaches over to gather me into his arms.

15. THE THEATRE

Of course, Freddie gets the starring role of fey prep-school folksinger Tom Lee in *Tea and Sympathy*. No surprise there, not with Mel Dir directing. I tried out too, not willing to let Freddie alone with touchy feely Dir, and I got cast as Al, roommate and only friend of Sister Boy Tom. Al's a jock who longs to be captain of the baseball team even at the price of giving up his femmy roommate who reads love poetry and sings sappy folk songs.

The coincidence with my own private Idaho story is unnerving, leading me to ask what Dir knows and when he found it out, but the play is racy and current enough that even without my liaison with Mr. Williams, one might have expected mischievous Mel to push the dramatic envelope by choosing this script. And it might quickly come to a halt once the PTA becomes aware of its sexual content. Dir plans to downplay some of the intimate scenes to make the work high-school friendly.

Unlike the movie, Anderson's play has no qualms about naming the bookish Tom Lee a queer boy. How much Mr. Dir is going to cut from the script is still up in the air, but the scene we find ourselves rehearsing this late afternoon comes at the climax of the play.

Tom attempts to head off to Ellie's love shack to prove his manhood, but housemother Laura, played by Miss Winfrey, waylays him and asks Tom in for a spot of tea and a little more than sympathy if she were honest.

I sit in the old auditorium with the attached wooden seats, one leg over an arm rest, hanging a couple of seats away from the piano teacher, Mr. Garrison, who is miscast as Laura Reynolds's husband, the coach and housemaster. Garrison is a good enough guy, but he is a bit too precious to play the doddering, whistle-blowing coach projecting his own queerness on to the confused Tommy Lee. So Mr. Garrison is trying to butch himself up since he is playing the macho husband who prefers the butt-patting sidelines to a candlelight evening with his lovely wife. Garrison and I are hanging out ten rows up, trying to memorize our lines, no longer tickled pink by Mr. Dir's witty directions. So we sit, nervously tapping our feet against the seat backs, watching Mrs. Winfrey and Freddie during their climactic little encounter, following along in the script.

> *Tom*: Why are you so nice to me?
> *Laura.* Why—I—
> *Tom.* You're not this way to the rest of the fellows.
> *Laura.* No, I know I'm not. Do you mind my
> being nice to you?
> *Tom.* I just wondered why.
> *Laura.* I guess, Tom—I guess it's because I like you.
> *Tom.* No one else seems to. Why do you?
> *Laura.* I don't know—I—
> *Tom.* Is it *because* no one else likes me? Is it just pity?
> *Laura.* No, Tom, no, of course not—It's well—it's because
> you've been nice to me—very considerate....
> *Tom.* Mr. Reynolds knows you like me.
> *Laura.* I suppose so. I haven't kept it a secret.
> *Tom.* Is that why he hates me so?
> *Laura.* I don't think he hates you.
> *Tom.* Yes, he hates me. Why lie? I think everyone here
> hates me but you. But they won't.
> *Laura.* Of course they won't.
> *Tom.* He hates me because he made a flop with me.
> I know all about it. My father put me in this house two
> years ago, and when he left me he said to your

husband 'Make a man out of him.' He's failed, and he's mad,
and then you came along, and were nice to me—out of pity.
Laura: No, Tom, not pity. I'm too selfish a woman to
like you just out of pity....
Tom. There's so much I don't understand...
Laura. Tom, don't go out. Won't you let me teach
you how to dance?
Tom. Oh God—God.
Laura. Tom—Tom—

"Okay, okay," Dir interrupts. "Let's stop for a second, shall we?
Now my dears need I remind you that this scene is really in some
ways the very climax, so to speak, of the drama, so we must reach
the right pitch. Laura must be taken totally aback by Tom's sudden
passion at the end of this scene, even if in our version it will be just
a hug, not a kiss. Laura is finally getting what she wants, which, as
Wilde tells us, is the only thing more traumatic than not getting it. So
when Tommy embraces her, she is aghast, exposed, shocked. That's
why you pull away, Lois. You realize you have crossed a big red line.
You are now in the arms of one of your husband's students," Dir
pauses, looking out into space. "Got it, Lo?"

"Mel, I am not sure this script is going to fly. The principal will
never go for it," she warns. "What happened to the Cox adaptation
of Melville's *Billy Budd* I gave you? Wouldn't that play have been
more appropriate for a secondary school audience? I mean we all
know you love controversy, and I'm willing to work with you on
this script, but has Mrs. Orcello approved this play?"

"It's on her desk, Lo. And I have not heard word boo. I looked at
the *Billy Budd* adaptation, love, but just couldn't find any life in it.
The prose is just too stiff, too wooden, if you catch my drift." Miss
Winfrey shakes her head and digs her nose back into her Samuel
French quarto. We aren't off book yet. It's only the third week in
September. Dir shuffles over to Freddie and puts his greasy paw on
his shoulder.

"Now, Fred," he says, "We have covered this ground before, I believe. This is a crucial scene and you need, if I may be so bold, to get your head out of your ass...ignments in algebra and become emotionally involved with Tommy. You have your blue suit on, you've taken a couple of swigs of Jack, you are on the way to the Joynt to pick up Ellie and head up to her garret. You're hellbent on losing your virginity or your life. Give me sex or give me death."

Dir laughs at his wit, being his own greatest fan. "Okay, okay, Lois." He glances over at his colleague sheepishly, looking out at Garrison as well. "I'll reign myself in. But Fred, my dear, look, when you tell Laura, the woman you are secretly crushed on, that soon they won't hate you anymore, you are announcing your intentions to score—"

"But wait," Freddie interrupts, turning away from his precious director, walking away in his crumpled cuffed corduroys and the Buster Brown shoes his mother makes him wear. "I can't figure this thing out," he sighs in exasperation. "Is my Tommy character actually a fairy? I know he is accused of being one. He is rumored to swim naked with Mr. Harris at the beach and loves to arrange flowers and sings French Art songs. But you are telling me he also has the hots for his den mother? I don't get it. Maybe this hug is just a kind of a romantic stab in the dark, but then at the end it is suggested they apparently went all the way. It just doesn't add up."

"Life doesn't always make sense, Mr. Udall. Tom Lee is seventeen. He's confused. And the play is not about whether someone has homosexual tendencies or not. Who cares? If Kinsey is right, one out of ten of us have such leanings. No, my dears, the play is about prejudice and conformity, conformity to gender roles. It's about being normal—or else."

Something suddenly makes me yell out. "But isn't it really about homosexuality? I mean if Tom Lee looks like a duck and swims like a duck and quacks like one, well, why isn't he a duck? Why turn him into this let's-sleep-with-Mommy kind of guy? If he's queer, he's queer."

"Now hold on a minute, Tom," Miss Winfrey raises her voice firmly from the stage. "You know we have talked about this in class.

The play is dramatizing prejudice. It's questioning the boundaries of what it means to be a man and, in Laura's case, what it means to be a good wife."

"I'm the one with the homosexual tendencies," Mr. Garrison suddenly blurts out. He's talking about his character, but it oddly sounds more personal.

"How am I supposed to hug my English teacher?" Freddie asks out of the blue, blurting it out as he stands leaning on the stage frame.

"Okay, okay." Mel says with exasperation. "Enough, please. The point is, Tommy, there are a lot of ducks in the pond and the off ducks are often hard to spot. The play is about pre-judgment as Miss Winfrey reminds us"

"So what if Tom Lee is doing more than swimming bare with Mr. Harris, then what? Then would all this bashing be somehow legit?" I ask from my seat in the audience, getting too heated for my own good. I don't care at that point if I'm a teenager with homework and TV shows to watch, don't give a damn if I'm supposed to be talking on the phone with Pam or playing ball with the guys. I know my outburst is out of line to say the least, but I can't help it.

Dir stands there wide-eyed looking at Miss Winfrey, who turns and shakes her head at Mr. Garrison in his seat with the crease down his slacks and his polished loafers.

"That's what kills me about this play," I continue, starting to raise my voice. "What if Tommy Lee were a fag like Allen Ginsberg or Walt Whitman? Then what? Then there's no drama at all, then no one cares if he commits hari kari with the kitchen knife. That's why I hate this stupid play. It doesn't make sense!" I yell, jumping up in a fit and shouting "Jayzuzz" into the balcony, then stomping out of the theatre.

I run to the fence and grab the mesh, shaking it uncontrollably. I know I'm creating a scene, I know the shaking clangs across the practice field, a noise soon drowned out by the football team marching from practice toward the locker room. They're on the other side of the chain link, but I can see Trent and Runt and Skip and the rest of the guys I've grown up with on the team I was cut from. Or I cut myself from. It doesn't matter. I am off. Coach said no way, and not only that, he now avoids me on campus entirely. But now when he sees me shaking the fence with all my might, he turns and looks at me with knitted brows, asking me with his look if I'm all right. I nod yes and slide down the links on my back, sitting on the cold walkway.

Freddie is watching me from behind. I need a smoke, pull out an old pack of Winstons I've stolen from my Dad's dresser. I light one, watching Fred watching me. He saunters over and slides down next to me, even though he's not pleased I'm smoking. We sit silently beside one another, our knees up against our chests, me staring at the ground, flicking the filter nervously with my thumb. So self-conscious, so serious, so angry. And on top of that, like some sappy top forty song, so much in love.

"Sorry," I say. Freddie—what would I do without him?

"It's just a play," he reminds me, drumming his fist on my knee.

"Is it?"

"I know it's hitting home. Maybe that's why Mel picked it."

"Mel, is it? So we're on a first name basis with that flamer, are we?"

"Well, you should talk. Yea, we've kind of become friends. We've been getting together before rehearsal and stuff, talking about San Francisco and the Beats. He's a wealth of information. City Lights and North Beach. Everything is so cool there. You wouldn't believe it. I wish we could just take off and go live in Berkeley or next to Coit Tower or something. Just get a place near the bay. I could go to Cal and study with philosophers or mystics in Big Sur. It sounds ideal. Get out of this place. We need to get out of here, with all these rumors flying about sex rings."

"What are you talking about?" I ask, looking up from my blue funk.

"Mel told me today Bosse and some other guys have hired a private investigator from Washington DC, some Army guy who used to work for the government hunting down homosexuals in the military. I hear they've set him up in an old house on 16th Street, and he's calling in people for questioning, talking to a bunch of juvies and kids about selling themselves for money to local bigwigs, muckety-mucks in the city. I think his name is Schmidt or maybe Schlitz."

"You have to be kidding," I say, my anger turning to anxiety.

"Mel mentioned it in passing. He thinks it'll blow over. Once they start looking into what's going on in Boise, there will be too much at stake to bring it out in the open. Plus, Mel thinks Bosse is a kook, a John Bircher hoping to bring the McCarthy hearings to the Rockies. We'll see about that. Emery Bosse scares me."

"Who have they started questioning? Kurt?"

"I'm not privy to any more information, Mr. Cadigan. Look, just be careful. I doubt anything will come of it. Mel says it's just some holier-than-thou guy trying to start a witch-hunt. He doesn't think anyone is going to pay attention to him. So I wouldn't worry too much."

Easy for Freddie to say. Me not worry about his dad getting caught? About me getting caught? About Coach? I light another cigarette. Freddie stands up, letting me know we have to get back into rehearsal. His bomb drop about Bosse has changed my mood from rage to worry, but I have to hide that swing. I've seen our parole officer's German Shepherd, a poodle compared to his master.

What if I am hauled in for interrogation by Emery and his G men, put under oath to tell the whole truth, then what? Jayzuss. This whole thing is suddenly getting weird and Freddie, who watches me take a huge burning drag off the Winston, grabs the butt out of my fingers, drops it to the ground, and squishes it with his Busters, telling me we have to get back, telling me not to worry about Bosse, telling me we have nothing to hide.

He'd be a helluva lot more concerned if he knew who was unzipping down there at the monkey cages, but I still can't bring myself to tell him. Now I know I have to talk to El again. She's the only one besides my elusive coach who knows. The thought of Mr. Udall getting caught gives me the heebies, but I have to try to suppress my jitters.

"What if they interview McKellar?" I ask. "Or what if they pull you in?" We are walking back to the dark theatre.

"Come on, Tom," Freddie says. "Let's not turn our little wanking sessions into federal offenses. We're not in an episode of *Dragnet*. It's *Tea and Sympathy*, remember?" He's following me through the lobby, trying to peel my low tops, successful just as I swing open the doors to the stage. Our dearest Mr. Dir is waiting with a Pall Mall in his mouth and script in hand, lining out certain sections of the text.

"And what's this Mel malarkey, Fredster?" I whisper to my friend as we walk down the aisle. "You're not letting him under your temple undergarments, are you?"

"*Ferme la bouche*, Cadigan." Fred stops me, shoving my arm and heading stage center.

Freddie gets into part, and they run through the scene again. This time he passes masterfully as the misunderstood non-homosexual, impetuously grabbing Miss Winfrey in his arms in the climax of the scene. She is taller by six inches, so Mel has Laura lean on the back of the couch. I have to say Miss Winfrey is also rising to the occasion as a result of Freddie ripping up the stage. She has never been assaulted quite so convincingly by one of her students.

When Tom Lee attempts to kiss her after the initial embrace, Laura Reynolds gets cold feet and asks him to back off. Tommy takes her recalcitrance personally and rushes out the door to his ill-fated tryst with easy Ellie, the loveless hookup who convinces Tom he needs to kill himself because he can't get it up with a woman. Luckily, he is disarmed by bystanders, and Laura sacrifices herself to the successful loss of Tom's virginity by becoming the woman of his dreams. That climax, needless to say, takes place off stage.

At the end of the scene, I watch Freddie rush out the door with melodramatic conviction, slamming it so hard he knocks the set down. Miss Winfrey is so overwhelmed, she's hardly able to run after him as required by the script. It's all Freddie. After the crashing door, Mel cheers.

"Bravo, bravo, Federico! And Lo, what a wonderful reaction— stunned on the back of the couch, almost unable to run after him. I love the change in stage direction. Let's keep it. Yes, let's stick with this staging. Wow, don't you agree, you two out there?" Dir looks out at Mr. Garrison and me.

"Mr. Cadigan, do you still find this play worthless after seeing a performance like that? Maybe this is as far as Anderson could go and still have his play not banned in Boston, I don't know. I only know this is good drama," he says, calling a halt to the rehearsal.

I still have my doubts. I still see the play as a cure-the-queer story. It reminds me of what Coach went through in Hawaii. Its message seems to be that even the queerest of boys can be normal. Anderson's script may be playing with gender roles, but it's all hitting too close to home. I'm not ready to stir from my seat even after Freddie picks up his books and comes bounding up the aisle, triumphant. There's something hypocritical about this story of the slandered lover boy, his life ruined by a false accusation of a kind of love I'm cherishing at this very moment. I am naked in the dunes with the fired teacher Mr. Harris and loving every minute of it.

And damn it, what's wrong with that? Why should I do everything in my power to avoid it, to get Pam into bed and become a happy tight end at the prom? Why should my fate be the most abominable known to man or woman? And who the hell is this guy Freddie mentioned at break, this Schlesinger guy from Washington anyway?

16. CLAUDETTE AT LE BOIS

Back to the lima-bean green soda fountain, Mr. Spreckles in his white paper sailor hat and that big mixer where he makes the coffee shakes, poured thick and lumpy into funnel-shaped glasses. He always gives us a long-stemmed spoon to boot. This concoction is usually my manna from heaven after facing down broccoli spears beside pork chops and applesauce at the dinner table.

I've arrived today in search of my confidante, but El's booth is empty. I swivel at the counter, making small talk with Mr. S, fending off questions about the football team. I'm no longer on the roster, I inform him, and the Braves are one and three because their second-string defensive end has opted for a minor part in Mr. Dir's upcoming production. Spreckles nods silently, his baggy eyes glancing upward with disapproval at the mention of Dir. Mel is notorious.

The quarterback is out with a hamstring injury, I explain. The team is being forced to rely on short passes, and there are turnovers and missed field goals with our new kicker. I try to make excuses for Coach, but the old timers at the counter are not buying them. They want victories, trophies, headlines. They expect it after four winning seasons with Marty Williams. I finally return to my straw, then politely inquire about the whereabouts of Miss Elvina. Spreckles hasn't seen her in three days, this time a shoulder shrug instead of an eye roll.

"I'm not sure she'll be back, to tell you the truth," he mumbles, passing his wet rag over the counter.

I'm about to head over to the Gamekeeper when El out of the blue shows up in her dark brown polo coat and big black handbag. Is she happy to see me? At first, I can't tell. I try to be cool, looking up from the straw in my mouth and raising my eyes as she slides into the booth with a big sigh, pulling her coat off once settled. I gather my glass and canister and remove myself to the bouncy booth where she has found her spot. Spreckles nods and begins to open the raspberry sherbet bin, mindless in the comfort of routine, a ritual too familiar to need formal orders.

"I'm glad you showed up," I say to her as I slip into the booth.

"How are youse Tommy?" She sounds tired.

"Are you okay? You look a little strung out."

"It's been a tough week. Claude took off, and we can't find anyone who will sit in on piano. There's a GI down in Mountain Home, but that's a helluva drive, and he can only make it when he has leave. Dir can fill in but he's not very good. This guy Garrison came down once, but we can't make it without a steady piano man."

"So what happened to Claude?"

"Don't know for sure. Jimmy does, but he's being cagey. I can guess well enough. You know we been arguing 'bout stuff, about Claude hanging out at Le Bois and outside Bing's Dance Hall after hours with Dir and those guys, getting drunk and rowdy and, behaving in what we might call an indiscreet manner. Honey, have you ever heard of drag before?"

I look at her, wanting to appear worldly, thinking vaguely of souped-up Chevys on the strip, hot rods and laying rubber, engines with big metal exhaust pipes and deafening rumbles. She reads my silence like an open book.

"Look, babe, Claude is a drag queen. He is Claudette Hautbert when the opportunity arises, which it does not in the City of Boise— at least not in public. So a two-hundred-and-ten-pound woman hanging out in Bing's parking lot at midnight is not kosher in Idaho, especially when that broad is a Negro man. Anyway," she continues, "word got around after one of his tricks, some hood in his twenties named Halverson, stooled on him in front of a private dick holed up in a house around here, investigating male hookers for some reason—some vice squad goon. I don't know. No doubt Dir got wind of it and told Claude to scram before the poli come looking for him up in Riverside.

"That's my version, anyway. Jimmy has the details. I'm not sure what to do now. We might have to leave too. They may come after Jimmy, who is, mind you, no drag queen but is not exactly—" She stops midsentence as an open-eared Mr. Spreckles shows up with Raspberry Rapture in hand.

"Elvina," he says, "glad to see you back. I hear you might be leaving the Owyhee soon. Rumor has it."

She smiles. "Rumor has a lot of things, Mr. Spreckles. Wow, this freeze looks perfect. Just what the doctor ordered. I can't thank you enough for fixing it the way I like."

"Much obliged." He walks off with a wry grin.

"What's that all about?" I whisper, leaning over.

She puts her straw to her lips, telling me to cool my jets, without saying anything of course. I lean back in my bouncy cushion and pick up my tin to see if anything is left, my spoon clanging impolitely against the sides.

"Would you like another?"

"No, thank you. Sorry. So now that Mr. S has gone into the kitchen…"

"Tom, look. This is not your battle. Claude is a good man and a first-rate musician. We've been together for over ten years. But his high jinx have begun to become the talk of the town, at least among the merchants. Hence the polite prompt from Mr. Spreckles. He's one surprised guy to see me show my black face in in his place, not that he cares about color. So I'm getting the cold shoulder. People aren't coming to the shows. We're being quietly run out of town. The boss is meeting with me tonight. He wants me to stay, of course, because we've been packing them in up till now. We'll see." She sits

back and stares at her frozen dessert as if unable to find the energy
to pick up her spoon.

"Who is this Halverson guy and what was he doing in that house?
El, what am I going to do? I'm hearing all this stuff about some
investigator in a house on 16th Street, and I'm starting to go ape
with worry. I haven't said a word to Freddie about anything. I can't
do it. I even saw his dad at church camp. I spent two days with his
family out there. We said nothing. Talk about elephant in the living
room. But if Schleeburger or whatever his name gets hold of it, I'm
screwed. Or Mr. U is screwed or we both are."

"What are you worried about, son? You didn't do anything," El
insists. "You ran away, you bumped into a suit by mistake. He's the
man got something to worry about. Not you, hon." She is keeping
her eye on the counter, being even more vigilant than usual.

"It's not that simple, El, not that simple," I'm foot tapping uncontrollably and turning raspberry, my hands in my pockets, my mouth
dry. She pushes her glass of water over to me and tells me to relax.
I can walk her back to the club in a few minutes, she says. Help
her work on some cowboy songs she's practicing. "Don't Fence Me
In" for one, though she knows Cole Porter has stolen it and made
it famous. Ernie Ford's "Sixteen Tons," and a sappy Jim Reeves hit
called "I Guess I'm Crazy." She starts singing about her foolish heart
as we stroll down the street.

Then she stops singing and walking, leans against the wall of the
Shoetorium we're passing and tells me to come clean, cut the coy
act, spill the damn beans.

"You can't be that shaken up by Freddie's father and his wandering
willy for crying out loud," she guesses.

I squirm. I have promised Coach to keep my mouth shut, but I'm
worried about him, and we haven't had a chance to talk in weeks.
He's avoiding me like the plague, busy with football, super cautious
about our being seen together. We've passed a few notes, like high
school sweethearts. At first he wrote about how he was trying to
figure out where and when we could meet and how much he missed

me, but a couple of weeks later, he wrote that "things" were too busy and too "tricky." We'd have to wait, maybe until Thanksgiving.

I write him back the sappiest replies, telling him I am starving for his arms. Every night before bed, I imagine his warm body next to mine, fall asleep hanging on to a pillow or a brown boxer I pretend is him. It's torture, though, being so close, passing him in the crowded corridor at school with just a smile and a nod.

"What if I told you there was more going on than that one time at the cages?" I start in. "More than just running away from those guys that night? What if I told you I can't say anything about it because I've sworn not to, but I have to tell somebody because I'm in a huge bind? I can't say anything more, but it's totally different. I'm in love with a guy who's older than me, a guy in his 20s. I can't allow him to get caught by these people. I have to protect him no matter what. If anything happens to him, I'm going to kill myself. It's my fault. I followed him around, I found him. I've fallen for him and I don't know what to do. Who can I go to with this stuff? My Dad? Jesus, he'll kill me."

I'm trying to stay calm. We're in public, after all. I have my sweat-shirt sleeve up to my eyes at this point and am searching wildly around to see who is watching. El tells me to follow her. She knows I'm making a scene. Public displays of emotion don't happen in broad daylight in downtown Boise while a white teenager accompanies a black jazz singer to her workplace. So we head through the alley once more into the dim nightclub with its swiveling club chairs. She sits me down and brings a Coke over.

"And now Pam tells me she wants to drop me," I add. "She says I won't pay any attention to her. She's going to the prom with some-one else. She won't continue 'this charade,' she calls it. Which is fine. I don't care about the stupid prom anyway, and I can't blame her or anything, but El, everybody is asking me what's up. Freddie told me about this investigator and now you tell me about Claude. Like who's next?" At least I'm not crying anymore. Just sitting there panicked, feeling trapped, glad to be inside that stultifying bar in broad daylight. This dark club is the only place I can be safe since sunny Boise feels like a prison these days.

"Okay," El says, sitting down and lighting up one of her Kools, offering me one. I hate Menthols but take one anyway. "Look, Tommy, I pretty much figured out something else was afoot. I mean you've been coming out over the past months in some very sweet ways. You're looser, you're moving with a kind of panache, you're taking more risks with your words and emotions. El can tell. Tommy's in love. It's written all over your sweatshirt." She smiles deeply and chuckles to herself. "So, that's good. Love is good, love is a flock of birds breaking out across the sky. I love love. I sing about it every night, and I know how crazy and exhilarating it can be.

"But you aren't legal, boy. You can't just drag the strip with your thirty-year-old man in his Mustang, hon. It cannot happen in this here pop stand. Like I told Claude, Claudette can hang outside Bing's or do whatever she want to do, but she's going to have to face the consequences. What we do is up to us, what what we do does to others is not something we can control. People hate Negros, Tommy. People hate homosexuals. That might be changing in some parts of the world, but it's changing very slow and that change is not going to come here anytime too soon." I see the smoke streaming out of her nostrils as she stabs out her cig, leans back, and crosses her legs to look at me.

"You love him?"

"Yes, ma'am."

"I ain't prying, but I'll tell you what. You got yourself in a pretty tight bind here. You got your best friend's dad, who you've found out is bumping uglies with boys in the park, even though he hangs out with the Mormons that started this whole commotion. Yea, they're behind Bosse and his hit man. Jimmy told me that much. Then you got your 'friend' falling in love with a seventeen-year-old senior in high school who is applying to college and has a pretty damn bright future ahead of him as the next poet laureate, and then you got your dad, a lawyer who has scraped out a reputation as one of the only level-headed public defenders this side of the Mississippi. Forgot about him, did you? Well, don't, son. Don't forget who you are, Tommy Cadigan. Don't forget what your father means to a lot of the folk around of this town, including me. So your plate is full, boy. Your plate is heaping."

I lift my hands as I slouch across from her, spreading out my fingers over my head. I stare at her. "So what's my Dad got to do with all of this? He doesn't know anything."

"He will, Tommy. He will. If this thing ever gets out, he's going to be in the thick of it, whether you are or not. There's going to be some fireworks down the road in that courthouse. You can count on that. But anyway, look, I love you, Thomas. You are a good kid. You're in deep, but you got to reach back and grab hold of what you know to be right. As your paw said to us when we wanted to rent the place, I'm going to do justice. Didn't say nothin' about no law. I guess that's good advice. What that might look like, I can't say. Maybe this thing will blow over. Nobody's been arrested yet. But they got some folk running scared. Mel will tell you that. Hang tight, my man. And when the time comes, do justice."

El has thrown a wrench in the works—my father. Ethics. I haven't been thinking about him. I can't. He and Mom have their own life. I love them, but I'm not about to share my sex life with either of them, even if my sex life is about to go public, at which point, hell, I'll have no choice. Jesus H. Christ. I'm starting to swear, starting to smoke. I'm a hellbent homo, but it isn't funny. It's wild, but it isn't funny funny. It is crazy funny. But lives are at stake, I'm realizing. I can't just blow Boise up and not give a damn. She stands and heads over to the stage, takes out some music, starts singing "Just One of Those Things," starts sounding off about gossamer wings and fabulous nights.

"This love's not going to cool down," I tell her when she stops her warm up. "This one's going to keep burning. I got news for you."

"Who knows about you and your man, anyway?"

"Nobody. Well, Freddie knows I idolize the guy. Freddie knows how I feel about him, but he doesn't know what happened this summer."

"What are you going to do if you have to stick your hand on a Bible, boy?"

"I don't know." Knees to chest now, swiveling, hands around the caps. "I don't know what I'm going to do. I can't put him in jail. I won't incriminate him."

"Can you lie under oath?" she asks. She's going hard on me, with those wing-tipped glasses and her polished nails. She's getting my goat on purpose. I know she's testing me, know she wants to let me know what I'm in for. Wants to get me ready. "You're a Cadigan, young man, don't forget that. Your father means something around here."

We hear a knock on the alley door, both of us looking up in surprise. El points and I get up and head out the front door into the hotel lobby. I skirt down to the bathroom, which is thankfully vacant. In the mirror, pale cheeks and red splotches tell my story. I smell my pits, clamming from tension, pull out my sweatshirt from my body, airing myself out, trying to take a pee, wash my hands. After five minutes, I figure I can't stay in there forever. Anyway, this bellhop suddenly barges in, and I just bolt. I find El in the lobby chatting with the concierge. She nods toward me to head back into the club. Freddie is sitting in my chair.

"Fred," I say.

"Hello, Thomas," my other half replies, pushing his glasses in. He's wearing his uniform, black pants, white shirt, and those ridiculous brown oxfords. I can tell he is on a mission. "I come with a message from Mr. Dir. He has called a practice this evening at six thirty. It's kind of an emergency. I've been deputized to track you down, even though I told him I was not my brother's keeper and you've made yourself scarce these days."

"How'd you find me?"

"Well, I didn't ask our football coach, if that's what you're thinking. I'm not unaware of your recent estrangement from Mr. Right. And since you're never home these days, deductive reasoning led me to your milkshake haunt, and after a few discreet inquiries, I smelled my way down here."

"That bad, huh?" I ask, sniffing my pits. "Or that easy?" Freddie is looking over my shoulder at El who stands at the bar. She tells us she needs to get ready for her meeting. It's getting on six. But she wants to say a couple of things to us now she has us captive.

"I've never seen two kids closer than you boys. I can tell from the way you move around each other. Like clockwork, like choreography almost. It's rhythm, pure rhythm." It's a gift, she says, to find a friend. "Hold on to it for all you're worth. No matter what comes, don't break up this duet." The other thing she wants to tell us before we go on our merry way to practice, the other thing is trickier, she admits. It has to do with what Freddie is studying, what he's interested in. It has to do with the truth—how to know when to tell it, how to tell it, and whom to tell it to. She doesn't know the answer, but life is a long series of truth tests and our job as kids is to pass those tests.

Freddie and I look at one another, not knowing what to make of her mysterious philosophy but grateful to hear it. Before we can ask her any questions, she sits down to the piano and plays Gershwin's "Someone to Watch over Me." We wave goodbye to her as she continues playing, watching us find the back door. Freddie walks his bike with me back to Spreckles where mine is locked up. We ain't sayin' nothin'. He can hear my sniffles, though. He knows.

17. THE "F" WORD

"Mr. Garrison is no longer with us," Mel Dir announces. "We are looking for an understudy for the part of Mr. Reynolds to replace Mr. Garrsion, and I have approached Marty Williams, who would be a natural choice since he is already friends with his colleague, Miss Winfrey. He has said he will consider it. He's supposed to drop by later this evening."

"What happened to Mr. Garrison?" I ask, worried but excited about Coach coming on set, if only to have him in my field of vision for a few hours.

"He has taken a leave of absence," Dir says. "He had to leave school suddenly due to an emergency in his family back East. That's all I know, I am afraid. I might also add that the play is being reviewed by the principal's office. I have received a list of preliminary emendations to the text, which I will pass on to you. We will have to delete all references to the "q" word, of course, and we have also been instructed to rule out the word "fairy." It looks like Spenser's epic and Tinker Bell have been banned in Boise. Other than these bowdlerizations, however, we have the green light for our production unless we hear otherwise from the PTA in the next couple of weeks."

"Why not just cut the queer stuff completely," I say. "Then we can have a nice little love story between Mrs. Reynolds and her devoted folksinger."

"That's pretty much what we're left with anyway," Fred adds, coming for once to my rescue.

"Boys, please," Mel says. "Can we confine the literary criticism to Miss Winfrey's English class? Your job is to perform a drama that has suddenly become even more powerful by the administration's concerns over its content. This censorship makes *T and S* that much more exciting, in case you haven't noticed. Okay Tommy and Lois, center stage please. Remember in this scene Al has received orders from his father to "change roommates next year or else." Al has come down to inform Mr. Reynolds of his switch. Okay, let's start where we left off.

> *Al.* My father's called me three times. How he ever found out about Harris and Tom swimming naked I don't know. But he did…and he wants me to change for next year…
>
> *Laura.* Al, you've lived with Tom. You know him better than anyone else knows him. If you do this, it's as good as finishing him so far as this school is concerned—and maybe farther.
>
> *Al.* Well, he does act sort of queer, Mrs. Reynolds. He—

"Wait a minute," I say, going off book. "The 'q' word, Mr. D. What now?"

"Odd," Mel says quickly. "For now 'odd' will do. Okay, let's start again," Mr. Dir commands.

> *Al.* Well, he does act sort of odd, Mrs. Reynolds. He—
>
> *Laura.* You never said this before. You never paid any attention before. What do you mean…odd?"
>
> *Al.* Well, like the fellows say, he sort of walks lightly, if you know what I mean. Sometimes the way he moves—the things he talks about—long-hair music all the time.
>
> *Laura.* All right. He wants to be a singer. So he talks about it.
>
> *Al.* He's never had a girl up for any of the dances.

Laura. Al, there are good explanations for all these things you're saying. They're silly—and prejudiced—and arguments all dug up to suit a point of view…Al, look at me, what if I were to start the rumor tomorrow that you were—well, odd as you put it?

Al. No one would believe it.

Laura. Why not?

Al. Well, because—

Laura. Because you're big and brawny and an athlete. What they call a top guy and a hard hitter.

Al. Well, yes.

Laura. You've got some things to learn, Al. I've been around a little, and I've met men, just like you—same set up—who weren't men, some of them married and with children.

Dir stops us. "Okay, good. Lo, nicely done. You oughta be in pictures. And nice pause on 'odd' Tommy. Love the hesitation even in using the 'o' word, love it. But you're going to have to buff up a bit for the part. Right now you aren't exactly looking like Ted Williams. So you need to start pumping some iron. The point is, Cadigan, Al has a choice between Tom Lee or the baseball team. And peer pressure has pushed him toward the easy way out, regardless of whether some of the ball players might themselves be boys in the band.

"Which leads us to our next little snippet. Wait, I think I see a ghost in the dark shadows out there in the theatre. Avaunt, 'never shake thy gory locks at me.' If it isn't Marty Williams. Hail fellow, well met. Are you ready to play the part of Reynolds in our tragedia?"

Coach comes out of the darkness and is on stage now smiling while I stand as close to him as I've been in weeks.

"Well, Mel," he says. "I'm a very busy man, as you know, but if you're in a serious bind, I might be able to fit you in. Especially since Lois has twisted my arm."

Mel gives him a play book and a pat on the lower back, or is it the upper butt, at which point Miss Winfrey and Mr. Williams, read from one of the other climaxes of the play, the collapse of their marriage in the wake of their disagreement over the Tommy Lee problem. Laura has just announced she is leaving her husband Bill:

> *Bill.* Laura, we'll discuss this, if we must, later on.
> *Laura.* Bill! There'll be no later on. I'm leaving you.
> *Bill.* Over this thing?
> *Laura.* Yes, this *thing*, and all the other *things* in our marriage.
> *Bill.* For God's sake, Laura, what are you talking about?
> *Laura.* I'm talking about love and honor and manliness, and tenderness, and persecution. I'm talking about a lot. You haven't understood any of it...
> *Bill.* And you're doing this—all because of this—this fairy?

"Fairy!" I erupt stupidly from the sidelines. "There it is again! Fairy, fairy, fairy, very fairy!" Everyone stops and stares at me like I'm crazy, which admittedly is not far from the truth at that point. Crazy and jealous of Lois and Marty on stage together, working so well as the angry couple, without me. I can't stand to watch it.

"Hairy fairy," Fred mumbles. "Scary hairy fairy with gory locks." He's trying to make up for my ridiculous outburst with a little dumb rhyming of his own, trying to protect me from the consequences of my outburst. Dir stares us down with a sigh. Miss Winfrey is also looking at her watch, which is too small to read anyway, while Coach stands up there with a puzzled grin.

"Sorry, Marty," Mel says. "We have been told by the powers that be we cannot use the 'f' word in the production, and these juvenile delinquents are acting out around that dictate. Children, please. Mart, take that line from the top. We are using the word 'odd.'"

> *Bill.* And you are doing this—all because of this—odd...ball?
> *Laura.* This boy, Bill—this boy is more of a man than you are.
> *Bill.* Sure—Ask Ellie.

Laura. Because it was distasteful for him. Because for
him there has to be love. He's more of a man than you are.
Bill. Yes, sure.
Laura. Manliness is not all swagger and swearing and
mountain climbing. Manliness is also tenderness, gentleness,
consideration. You men think you can decide on who is a
man, when only a woman can really know.
Bill. Ellie's a woman. Ask Ellie.
Laura. You've resented me—almost from the day you married
me. You never wanted to marry really. Did they kid you into
it? Does a would-be headmaster have to be married?
Or what was it, Bill? You would have been far happier going
off on your jaunts with the boys, having them to your rooms
for feeds and bull-sessions…Did it ever occur to you that you
persecute in Tom, that boy up there, you persecute in him
the thing you fear in yourself?
 Bill. I hope you will be gone when I come back from dinner.
Laura. I will be—Oh, Bill, I'm sorry. I shouldn't have said
that—it was cruel. This was the weakness you cried out for
me to save you from, wasn't it—And I have tried.

"Nice read through, Coach," Dir remarks. "Remember, once she
insinuates your own homosexuality, you are enraged. She has hit a
nerve by mentioning your jaunts with the boys, and the truth is one
of the most dangerous words in our vocabulary. Everyone wants
it, but no one wants to hear it when it arrives. Hence, your bolt for
the door. We will work on blocking later, but I wanted to give you a
taste for the part, Mart. I thought you would be perfect for it." He
raises his eyebrows as he looks in my direction. Freddie glances at
me. What does Dir know? Even Coach seems to have a hard time
sloughing off that last remark. "What are you insinuating, Mellie?"
I expect him to say, but Coach is not as foolhardy as I am. At least
in some ways.

18. BANANA OUT

Fred has to hightail it home once rehearsal is over. Slowly walking toward my bicycle in the dark, I glance over my shoulder every other second to see if Coach might come out of the big double doors. I tuck my cuffs into my white socks, fiddling with the combo on the lock, lingering hopelessly around the rack for as long as possible without seeming like I'm planning to steal a bike.

Coach finally emerges with Miss Winfrey, and they stand talking outside the auditorium. I ride off into the sunset but stop at the edge of the field and look back to see if Coach might be walking to the parking lot by himself. I spot the dark figure, his short steps, his mixture of meander and deliberateness. I can't restrain myself, so I ride back toward him, thinking of an excuse. I left a notebook in the auditorium, I have to go to the bathroom. Any fiction to see him alone for a few minutes.

"Hi," I say, braking and stepping off my pedals, approaching the man I sleep with every night even though he's not in my bed.

He glances around furtively. "How's it going?"

"Can we talk?"

He smiles at me, his hand on his old briefcase, full of essays on Appomattox or the Dred Scott decision, no doubt. He's glancing over my head toward the parking lot, then he tells me to lock up my bike and meet him at the gym door in a couple of minutes, to make sure no one sees me.

Coach has an office down the corridor from the lockers and showers, a glassed-in cubicle across from a new stainless-steel whirlpool.

He doesn't turn any lights on when I come in, so the building stays dark and shadowed. We walk down to his office, trying not to bang into rattily lockers. He turns on a desk lamp and sits down in his swivel chair.

"Well," he looks at me. "What would you like to talk about, Mr. Cadigan?" he says, half joking, spinning a sharpened yellow pencil on his industrial desk. Under the lamplight, I feel like I'm being interrogated in front of Eliot Ness. Maybe Freddie was wrong. Maybe my life is an episode of *Ellery Queen*. But I don't have time to play cops and robbers tonight.

"I miss you. It just seems so insane…I know it's dangerous. Why is Garrison gone by the way?" I ask, paranoid about all these disappearances.

"Don't know," he says. "His wife's still here. No one can figure it out." I tell him about the house on 16th Street and the guy from Washington the biggies have hired to ferret out sex-ring perverts. I tell him about Claude's disappearance. Coach starts drumming his fingers on his chair. "*Schiesse*," he says quietly. He wants to know who the hell Claude is. I give him the low down on Claudette Hot Bear. He knows the group. Has Coach been to Bing's too?"

"What are we going to do?" I ask him, scared and aroused at the same time, but not scared of being excited, scared of the consequences. There's a difference. "If we get caught, we're totally screwed."

"I'm aware of that, Tommy. We're getting into some deep *caca*. But Garrison? Well, actually he is the kind of guy who would hit the panic button if he were up to anything. I don't know. God, I can't believe this. Everywhere we go, they come after us." He puts his elbows on the desk, cupping the top of his head with his palms. We sit in silence for what seems like minutes while he digs his fingers into his skull. Is he about to have another one of his fits? I stand and walk around to the back to his chair, putting my hand on his slumped shoulders, massaging them, finally letting my hands fall between his arms and resting my head on top of his hands.

His chair starts rolling under our weight but he holds it still with his feet, finally taking hold of my wrists and bringing them to his cheeks. He swivels around and sits me on his lap. Our mouths meet in a kiss that shuts up the world with its endless do's and don'ts's, locked in an embrace, unable and unwilling to articulate the rules we're breaking, risks we're taking, probabilities of detection, discipline, and punishment.

I can feel Marty getting hard underneath me, and I shift my weight in response, getting him in between my legs and trying to ignore the pressure on my own belt. Maybe our touch begins as a moment of pure caress and tenderness, pure silent hug and comfort, but neither of us can ignore the call of our cocks for long. To be blunt, we have to unzip and get the red things out, even if we don't take our pants off, even if we're on school grounds after hours in the football coach's office. I can't keep feeling him through the cotton of his stupid trousers. I have to pull it out. And he, reluctantly at first and finally with my help, does the same to me as we kiss and stroke and thrust and head toward climax. I try desperately to hold off long enough that Coach can go with me, grabbing his wrist for a second because the touch was too much, my face buried in the smell of his shoulder I am feeling the veins on his neck when we hear the snap of lights in the locker room down the hall.

"Fuck," Coach says, the first time I've heard him use the other "f" word. He reaches for his zipper and crams himself into his pants. He grabs me and puts me under his desk, pretzled and stuffed into the three-sided hole. How can I fit in there? How can I not fit in there? Coach slides his seat sideways, takes off his coat and drapes it over the back and side of his chair, pressing it against me. Coach tilts back and puts his feet up as the yellow bucket wheels into the corridor toward coach's office, which is glassed in from midway up. Thank god, there's some vanity protection.

"Hi Sam," Coach says as the paunchy janitor comes in.

"Working late, are ya?" Sammy replies, finding the trash can beside the desk. He's been with the school since the beginning of time, white-haired now and pretty much in control of the entire campus.

"Yea, I'm burning the midnight oil, a bit Sammy," Marty says. "Trying to get some plays in order." Coach puts his legs down, his knees rammed against my cheeks.

"Thought I heard some noises when I came in," Sam says, perching one cheek on the desk. "Don't worry none, Coach. Nothing's going to happen to you."

I freeze.

"Last coach went winless two seasons in a row before he got canned," Sammy says. "You've still got a few games left. My advice is simple. Straight up the middle. Your guards aren't fast enough to pull. Just get them to make a hole, dammit, and then let Trent run right up through it. Or send that greenhorn QB up. Just run the ball, boy. Get some Elmer's. Turnovers, Marty, turnovers. Dang it. Hold on to the damn football for Pete's sake. And then do something with that kicker, for the love of god. That's my two cents. If you send 'em up the middle, you'll squeeze out a win over Pocatella. You mark my words. Course it's your call, coach. Don't let me tell you what to do." Big belly laugh. Coach is making laughing noises, too.

"You don't want me to sweep in here I take it. Clear out your empties from those big drawers?"

"Nah, not tonight Sammy. I got to get to work and then get home. Thanks, though." Sam rolls the cart down the hall and out the door to the pool. We wait another few minutes, then Coach pulls me out and kisses me on the cheek. We're both jumpy, but he keeps his head, gets the lights off and sees me out once the coast is clear. We can't really say much, but we hug before he opens the door to make sure the janitor has buggered off. A hug and a quick kiss. More than a peck, the tips of our tongues meet. I can still remember the sensation.

19. THE BIRTHDAY BOY

I meet Dad in the kitchen one Sunday around nine about three weeks later. Thanks to Pope Pius and the Vatican Council, we can still eat our hotdogs and eggs and make it to Communion at eleven o'clock Mass, the fast only one hour now. Dad wears his plaid bathrobe over blue cotton pajamas. He's a big, lumbering man, six two and pushing two hundred ten. He shuffles around in his size twelve slippers looking for the cast iron frying pan that is about to produce his specialty, hopefully without burning down the house.

I'm in charge of toast after a glass or two of Minute Maid orange juice. He's percolating Hills Brothers coffee on the back burner. We're getting away with murder while Mom takes her beauty sleep on Sundays, pretty much destroying any semblance of order in the kitchen. I slip in the Wonder Bread and find cold butter and boysenberry jam in the icebox. Dad breaks eggs into hot-dog grease, leaving dripping shells on the counter, shaking the pepper like a martini mixer.

I manage to singe the toast only slightly and pile slabs of butter on the stack. We head to the kitchen table and open up *The Statesman*. I usually go straight to *Blondie* and *Peanuts*, but the headline on the front page catches my eye: "Three Boise Men Admit Sex Charges." My dad seems impressed I'm actually reading the news.

The article tells of an investigation "into immoral acts involving teenage boys." My heart drops into my stomach, and a shiver runs down my neck and arms. The second paragraph says the probe is being undertaken at the behest of local probation officer Emery Bosse, who claims the authorities have barely scratched the surface, with evidence against other adults and as many as a hundred boys. Bosse has hired Howard Schleiner, an ex-CIA investigator who has rooted homosexuals out of Washington D.C., to come to Boise and nip this "lewd and lascivious conduct" in the bud. Three arrests have already been made.

"What are you reading about so voraciously, Tom? Have you suddenly become a political bug?"

"This thing about sex charges." I wish I had perused the article on the addition of "In God We Trust" to our currency instead. I shove the front page over to my father the barrister, who is adding yet more pepper to his Oscar Mayer scramble.

"Why a parole officer instead of the prosecutor's office? And who is this Howard Schleiner character, hired by this mysterious client?" Dad's peering at the paper through his half-moon reading glasses, his nose slightly elevated.

"My birthday's coming up," I say, desperately trying to change the subject. "I was thinking of going to the movies with Fred and Pam and whoever on Friday. *Rebel Without a Cause.*"

"If your mom agrees. She does love a birthday party so you better make it home in time for cake and candles."

"I gotta shower," I say, rising from the table and heading to the sink with my dishes. Dad has not stopped reading since his inquiry. His eggs get cold. I bound up the stairs two by two with my heart pounding. I'll be in deep if Mr. Udall is arrested, in even deeper if that Howard guy comes knocking at 615 16th Street, asking Mrs. Cadigan when her son will be home. This is one sin I have no intention of confessing. It will remain my secret for now. I don't want it muddied by the likes of God and country and Boise. My dad is another story. I can't face him yet. I can't burden him with the complications of my love at this point. Can I?

And really, I hadn't done anything with that man in the Cadillac. Sure, I watched Kurt get hard, but that was it. Guilt by association? Is voyeurism a crime? I'm in a fix, but no one can fix it but me. All because I am turned on by McKellar. Can I get arrested for dreaming of his biceps? I suddenly realize it's going to be one rough shower, one rough Mass, one rough Sunday. What about the confession I forgot to go to yesterday, and the last ten Saturdays? And what if I continue to avoid Communion? There's already been quite a few raised eyebrows around that omission. Mom especially. Not much misses her purview, in church anyway.

I'm trying not to think about Coach as the hot water beats against my scalp. Our love has nothing to do with Bosse and his posse. They know nothing about us and never will. Anyway, no one is going to find out, I assure myself, covered with soap and getting totally hard thinking about Coach, remembering his taste, realizing I have to get out of that shower, face the sermon, and keep my head down.

20. HOMOITIS

My destination a one-story clapboard on the corner of 16th and State Streets, its white paint dirty, trim an off-colored grey, an unassuming bungalow unfenced and unlandscaped except for a few junipers against the front. An empty porch gathers dust to the right of three wooden stairs leading to a storm door and bell. A light glows from behind drawn shades. It's snowing, but I have ridden my bike anyway. It isn't sticking. I arrive after school one day during the week after my November birthday.

Emery Bosse comes to the door after I ring the bell. I can't explain why I've agreed to talk to him and Schleiner. Bosse found me at school and told me he'd talked to Skip Johnson and Kurt McKellar, and they'd mentioned me as someone who could help them with their investigation. I should have gone to my dad and spilled the beans at that point, but I have Coach to think about, and then there's Edward Udall. I can throw out a million stupid reasons why I've decided to cooperate, like not wanting to seem obstructive, like wanting to give these creeps a piece of my mind, like wanting to protect Freddie, and like being scared shitless and not wanting to admit it to myself or anyone else.

After the editorial in the paper about "crushing the monster," Boise High is pretty much on high alert over the scandal. The "cancerous growth" having taken root in the city, it has spread at a rate even faster among the one hundred boys at our school. We're all looking at one another in the hallways, wondering which of us has blown or been blown by the shoe repairman, the guy who works at the men's section of Mode's, or the loading dock worker.

We're all poor victims of these criminal deviates as well as a whole host of other more respectable deplorables who promise to emerge once the surface is scratched. The *Statesman* wants this sordid and sinister mess to be "cleaned and disinfected." We're all potential juvies now, slamming our algebra books into our lockers and checking one another out. Skip has warned me Bosse is a bounty hunter and I'd better cooperate. He tells me Schleiner is a decent, straight guy.

Hence my appearance at that front door in my dirty blue parka, fat snowflakes floating down like fallout from some H bomb. The door has opened on to a hallway carpeted in a tufted wall-to-wall beige that cannot hide its wear and tear. Bosse lets me in without saying much, but right beside him stands an attractive guy, forty-something with a V-neck sweater and a handsome face. His light blond hair is parted perfectly, a few lines on his forehead, and his smile warm and startling white. He would make an excellent doubles partner, it seems to me. A tour leader through Bavaria, perhaps. I can see myself sailing with him off Hyannis port, wherever that is. He seems like he probably lives on Cape Cod or Annapolis in his off time. He wears Topsiders and creased slacks and a pale pink shirt under his black sweater. Sporty devil.

"Thanks for coming, Tommy," he says, extending his firm grip. "I'm Howard Schleiner. Sorry this place is so dingy, but we wanted a spot that was in the center of town. We're not here to arrest anyone, so don't worry. No handcuffs. We're just trying to find out what might be going on, and your name has come up a couple of times. This is not about blaming anybody or putting you on the spot. Emery and I are here to give kids a chance to talk about what is going on without feeling like they're in trouble or anything like that. Come on into the living room, Tommy. Can I get you a Coke or anything?"

"Sure, a Coke would be nice," I say. He asks me if I want ice and I say sure again. I love to suck on cubes. Freddie tells me it means I'm sexually repressed. Where does he read that stuff? The cloth couch is long and green with two cushions. Schleiner asks me to have a seat as he pulls up his wicker barrel chair toward the long low coffee table between us.

A couple of standing lamps keep the living room bathed in soft light. On the table some magazines—*Sports Illustrated* and a couple of muscle mags whose covers have pictures of men with tanned oiled bodies and skimpy bathing suits. Curious selection, I'm thinking, as Emery brings the Coke in on a tray with a cup of coffee for Mr. Schleiner, alias call-me-Howie. He's doing everything in his power to put me at ease, even motioning for Ichabod Crane to get lost in the kitchen. He does have a yellow pad and pencil on his lap, however.

"Taking notes?" I ask.

"Well, I have been hired to present a report once my fact-finding is done. I don't need to write anything down verbatim, and hell, if you are put off by it, we can just talk, Tommy," he says, throwing the pad on the coffee table and stretching out his pink arms. He relaxes in his chair and takes a deep breath.

"Long day," he says. "How's school?"

"Boring. I'm a senior, ready to get out."

"Yea, I remember senioritis. I had a bad case too, back in Maryland. Are you out for football this season? I'm going to the game this weekend."

"Not this year. I decided not to." My new friend is already moving into troubled waters.

"That's weird, a guy in shape like you. I hear almost anybody who tries out can at least sit on the bench. You have a run in with that famous coach over there? What's his name?

"Mr. Williams."

"Yea. I know you played junior year and almost all you guys try out. I mean, look at you. Tall, lanky, probably a good runner, I would say. What gives?" Howie is looking me over now, staring at my untucked flannel shirt. They've hung up my jacket in the hallway closet, and Emery slips in a bowl of pretzels and disappears again behind the swinging door to the kitchen. Yea, so Howie is getting off on my long thin body, making me feel like a sexy track star.

Maybe he wants a blowjob. Maybe not. My foot is tapping. I suddenly want out of that stuffy sitting room. It smells like my grandmother's apartment, like thirty years of beef stew and Campbell's tomato soup, like a lifetime of tuna fish sandwiches. We are silent for a few seconds while Schleiner smiles at my diminutive crotch puffed up by the fold of my cords. He can't tell what's in that cotton package. Neither can I after a cold shower. I'm trying to be Mr. Sarcastic, Mr. Tough Kid, Mr. Aloof. He can see through that guise with the ease of Sigmund Freud or Father O'Neill.

"Well, Tommy, let's get started. This is damn messy business we got going on here, let's face it. We got guys my age and older, lots of them married with children, trying to solicit sex from a bunch of young teens who are just out to have some kicks, who don't know any better. We've got these despicable cretins hanging out in the library and the Y and the skating rink and who knows where, the Riverside Ball Room and Bing's dance hall, we got them preying on these young men, offering them money for sex.

"I don't need to dance around this problem with a senior like you. You know the score, even if you decided not to play football this year for some unknown reason. Ha, ha. Can't figure that one out." Still harping on my football coach.

"Mr. Schleiner, I can't catch. I'm uncoordinated. I run track, play tennis. I'm not lettering in anything. I appreciate your compliments, but I don't even have a mitt."

"That's funny, Tommy, funny. No mitt." Schleiner chuckles, shifting in his bamboo-backed chair. He crosses his legs like a politician in an interview and hunches over a bit. He has the most translucent blue eyes and his brows are still blond. He seems Swedish. I can see him on one of those Sun Valley resort posters, one of those low angle shots with a snowflake sweater. Maybe sunglasses. Staring off at the snow-capped peaks. Handsome dude, have to give him that.

"Well, let's cut to the chase, Tom. We've talked to your friends Kurt and Skip Johnson. We've actually received written statements from them, which we've got here somewhere." He pulls out a manila folder from the bottom shelf of the coffee table. "If you want to read them later, you're welcome to. So we kind of know what was going on down there at the monkey cages this summer. And of course, Emery and I have talked to a number of local police officers and folks at the Y and the park service. We've even contacted some local storekeepers and teachers. So we're not completely in the dark here, if you catch my drift." He pauses. He wants to see me squirm. He's going in for the kill, I can tell. I brace myself. Have you ever swallowed an ice cube whole by mistake? Felt it go cold down your throat?

"First thing I tell all you boys is that nothing is going to happen to you for talking to us. We're here to get these sick men off the streets. We just want to protect Boise from these chicken hawks, as we call them in the service. Yea, I did some time in the Army and helped get some of these men out of our military. And now some folks from church and community groups here in Boise have brought me on board to help out with your problem."

He reaches down and takes a swallow from his coffee, then stands up and pulls his sweater off, revealing his body. Howie's in damn good shape, and he's relaxing now, mentioning how hot it's getting in the room, kicking off his Topsiders and putting a foot on the table edge. He doesn't want to put any pressure on me.

"So you were down there this summer, am I right?" he finally asks me.

"You mean the park?"

"Yes, I mean the park, Tom. In July."

"Yea, I was down there and ran into Kurt." I know a little bit about testifying. My Dad has let me know about just answering the question.

"Do you want to tell us what happened?"

"I was riding my bike through the park and found Kurt and some other dudes down by the cages."

"We know that, Tommy. What we want to know is who you got involved with down there. Do you know the dirty old men that offered you money for sex? If we don't find out, they'll be out there trying to prey on more kids. We want you to help us nab them and get them off the streets. So a couple of guys drove up?"

"Yea, two cars came by."

"Did you recognize them?"

"The cars?"

"Yes."

"What make were they?"

"A Pontiac and a Caddy."

"Did you have sex with the men in those cars?"

"No," I say.

"What were you doing down there if you weren't having sex with them?"

"I was hanging out with Kurt, and he convinced me to stick around, but when the bald guy started doing it with Kurt, I bolted.

"He was bald?"

"Yea, mostly," I say. "I saw the top of his head."

"And why did you decide to leave?"

"Because I was flipping out."

"If you were so agitated, why did you stick around in the first place?" He is trying to push me into a corner.

"Because Kurt talked me into it." Yea, sure, Howie, seems to reply with his body language, leaning back. Sure, it's all Kurt's doing.

"That's not what he said. McKellar's story is a bit different, if you want to read it. Kurt says you idolize him, as he puts it. Kurt says you got pissed because the old guy was doing him, and the two of you were not together. He claims you got angry and ran away. Kurt claims you banged into the other guy when you were running away. Kurt saw that. So, Tom, level with me. Tell me if you recognized those old guys that night."

"I didn't recognize the other guy when I knocked into him." It's the truth, technically. I only figured out it was Mr. Udall later, riding home. I'm not going to tell them about Udall, even if I have to lie. I'm not under oath. Are they tape-recording me? I look around. "I just ran away, jumped on my bike and got out of there."

"Are you jealous of Kurt?" Howie asks me. "Be honest, Tommy, nothing's going to happen to you. We're just figuring things out here. You're a big boy. Just turned seventeen, I understand. It's not you we're after. If you have a problem, best to come clean and get some help now."

"Everybody looks up to McKellar," I say defensively.

"Even your teachers?"

"I don't know. I doubt it." What is he getting at? Was he talking about Garrison?

"I wouldn't be so sure of that," he says. "Look, I don't want to pull teeth all afternoon. I got to get back to my hotel, too. If you don't want to tell me the truth, that's fine. We will find out one way or the other. We just wanted to give you the chance. But if you're going to sit here and waste our time…"

"What truth are you talking about? I told you what happened that night."

"We think there's more going on than a chance meeting this summer. We think you might have been down at the park this summer other times."

"I run and ride around in the park all the time."

"Late at night?"

"When it's hot, sure."

"And do you have sex there?"

"No. Look, Mr. Schleiner. I want to help. But I don't know what you want me to say." I'm sweating at this point and plenty red down my neck. Howie notices. He sees me madly tapping my foot. He sees my unfinished Coke sweating on the coffee table. He sees me avoiding eye contact and then peering into his ice-blue eyes, looking at his five ten Army body, looking at his arms filling out the sleeves of his pale pink shirt, at the blond hairs of his wrist.

He sighs and picks up his yellow pad and starts to write rather fiercely in big letters. He looks up and smiles warmly, shaking his head. "You're a tough nut. I respect that. When I was overseas, we had guys that were pretty cagey, too. But part of my job is to figure out what's what. I have reason to believe you might not be telling me all you know about these desperate homosexuals, some of whom are ravishing boys, even in your school. And the sad thing is that these vultures are ruining the lives of some of their victims. These poor kids will never be able to live completely happy lives again. They will be drummed out of college and the armed services and all kinds of jobs. I feel sorry for these boys, some of them much younger than you. Their lives will be ruined by these sickos."

He stops and throws down his pad and pencil on the coffee table. The pencil jumps on to the carpet and I lean down to pick it up, shaking as I hand it to him. He notices. I watch his eyes as I rise from my crouch, can see him eyeing the white skin of my back as I bring the pencil to his outstretched hand. I could almost swear he would happily take me into the bedroom, but what do I know?

We stand up, my pants sticking to my thighs. I shake them with my legs and walk toward the door while Schleiner goes to the closet to get my coat. Lon Chaney appears again in the foyer, staring at me like a bloodhound. He has left the German shepherd at home, apparently. I had expected him to be chained up on the porch. The two men thank me profusely for coming in, tell me that they will "see me around." They would be talking to others "in the community." Schleiner's cordiality is so chilling, the snow feels warm. He grabs my arm while he shakes my clammy hand, tells me not to worry, that everything will be all right. I almost slip on the slushy wooden stairs getting out of there, get damn wet riding home even if it's only a mile. It's starting to come down, big wet heavy flakes, almost like white rain. Some of it sticks on the cut lawns outside the neat bungalows along 16th.

21. PROMISE KEEPERS

"You're next," I tell Freddie the next weekend while we're hanging out at my house, me replaying my interrogation. We're upstairs in my room, on our respective single beds with those uncomfortable maple headboards. The slanted roof outside my window holds at least eight inches of snow and the heater fan is churning as fast as its little engine can from down in the basement. On my desk a bunch of shirts belong in the hamper, dirty jeans on top of some *World Book* volumes, on the sill St. Christopher shoulders a rather precocious Jesus who carries some weird ball. My room is not a complete mess.

Coco lounges with Freddie on the baby blue cotton bedspread, in seventh heaven. Her boyfriend is back. It's November 10, the day before Veteran's Day. Outside, it's minus five with the wind chill. We're reading, or trying to read anyway.

"The paper said Cooper got life for lewd and lascivious conduct," Fred announces. "Must have been multiple counts. He pled guilty. So you still think all this stuff is exciting and fun? Schleiner called Mr. Dir in there the day before you went, you know."

"I wonder what he fessed up to," I say, thinking back to Howie's statement about interviewing teachers, worried about what Freddie might have told Dir about Coach and me, or what Dir may have figured out on his own. "Did you say anything to Dir?"

"Dir's not stupid. He has his radar. Your crush on Mr. Williams has been pretty obvious from the moment he came on the set, maybe even before. Mel knows we're both odd kids, both off horses, but he doesn't know what we've done or not done. I mean you got a kiss from Coach in a cedar grove last summer. Big deal. Is that lewd and lascivious conduct? Even if it was made with the intent of arousal, how could they prove it? And the monkey cage thing—I don't know. He knows stuff was going on down in the park. He knows Kurt. But do you really think Mel would mouth off to Hans Schleiner?"

"His name is Howard, Fred, not Hans. Jayzuzz. The war is over. This thing is getting out of control. I don't know what to do. Screw these stupid stories. I can't read 'Barn Burning' right now. I can't do anything." I throw down *Great American Short Stories*, sit on the edge of the bed, start to rock nervously back and forth. Freddie and Coco monitor me. She starts snapping that tail in a mad wag then stops when she sees me holding my head. Freddie rolls over on his side and props his elbow up. What can I say to my best friend, my blood brother from whom I vowed never to keep a secret? Tell him about his horny father? The Cherry Hill? "I'm going to have to talk to my dad," I finally say out loud, glaring at the worn oval carpet covered with dog hairs. "I can't do this anymore. I can't."

Yes, I start crying. Who wouldn't? With the prosecutors and investigators and letters to the editors. Mothers running around school asking what has happened to their boys, staring at me like a poor victim turned pervert. I can't walk into the Smoke Shop to look at a *Sports Illustrated* without some wing-lensed matron in an overcoat and scarf shaking her head, like I'd just bought her nephew another Sugar Daddy and jerked him off during the intermission of *Davy Crockett.*

Our town is going crazy, and school is twice as bad. Play practice got canceled, and Freddie spends his free time in the library reading *Lord of the Flies* and biographies of Abe Lincoln. He doesn't dare show himself too often in the hallways. And me, everybody knows I am one of the Masturbators. Son of the kooky Democrat lawyer in ruffled suits who owns that run-down old Craftsman almost downtown, his son riding around on some rusty bike without supervision. Freddie and I are both personae non-grata.

Freddie is staring at my head. He's looking into my brain cells, deciphering the waves or swells or whatever they are. Coco has her head on his thigh. She's a slut, like me. I'm so fed up with my hard-ons. Every morning I wake up on my stomach with that thing pressing against my poor mattress. If she were alive that Simmons mattress girl in the ads would be big with child. If she were a guy, well, we'd be having the time of our lives.

"Are you my blood brother?" Freddie asks me out of the blue.

"What if there are things I can't tell you?" I know he's calling me on our pact. "What if I've been sworn to secrecy by someone else? What if stuff I know could hurt you, hurt a bunch of people? What if *you* did stuff with Mr. Melvin you can't tell *me* about?"

"It's a test. It's easy to make a promise, hard to keep one. Maybe some promises are not worth keeping, maybe some promises can't withstand all the challenges they face. Not every rule needs rigid adherence."

"You sound like some textbook. Look, I'm in trouble, Freddie. I'm beyond philosophy. Plus how do I know you didn't tell Dir Coach was kissing me in the park? How do I know you and Mellie weren't feeling each other up during your chats at the Owyhee? Huh? Are you keeping *your* promise?"

"Dir made some vague overtures, of course, but I rebuffed them. He's not my type. I don't do Leslie Howard or Cary Grant, especially if they are pudgy. He told me he knew you and Coach were close. He knows you guys were hanging at the Y this summer. He's a terrific gossip as you've probably figured out. A smart and funny one. I might even call him a courageous one if gossips can ever be courageous. He's not going to put up with this Pretty How Town, *My Friend Flicka* malarkey. He knows the Boise underbelly and is not afraid to embrace it.

"I neither confirmed nor denied any of his speculations about you, counselor. So there's the scoop on our director, who may be driving across Nevada as we speak. All hell is breaking loose, and we're sitting in your bedroom trying to be witty. I can barely get from Trig to Chemistry without being stoned to death just because I'm an egghead. So, you want to tell me why you're upset, or do you want to call the whole thing off?" Freddie looks down at me from his cross-legged perch on his bed.

"I was just trying to figure out," I finally say, "what would motivate a father with a family and a good job to drive down to the monkey cages in the middle of a summer night to have sex. I mean, I'm as horny as the next dude..."

"Hornier."

"Okay, hornier than thou. Sex—exactly what's gotten me into this morass," I sigh. "Anyway, I guess I can sympathize with the need to make it with another member of the male sex. Maybe it's even kind of neat to think these bigwigs are willing to go down to our level, but the risk and the consequences...." I'm shaking my head in disbelief. I don't even know I've tipped my hand in the middle of this train wreck of out-loud thought. I'm sitting on the floor, back propped up on the mattress, mixing metaphors. The dog is getting in our way. The floor her playground, and she thinks I'm ready to bite her. "Coco," I say, mildly annoyed by her tongue.

"What are you trying to tell me?" Freddie asks. "I thought you knew nothing about those guys in the park."

"Shit, man. You're the best friend I've ever had. You mean everything to me—even more than Coach, as dumb as that comparison is. Look, okay I'll tell you. That night I didn't show up in Lolo because Coach's car broke down? How do you think we spent it? What do you think happened at the Cherry Hill Resort in Myrtle Beach for crying out loud? Do you think Coach and I just said our prayers and fell asleep like two tired cowboys? Do you think I could leave it alone? That's what I'm talking about," I say, raising my leg and kicking the side of the bed Freddie is on, sliding down on my back and fending off the nervous dog. My hands are in the air now.

"I just can't keep it my pants, like you've said. But it's more than that with Coach. I don't know, Freddie. Now you know what I promised Coach not to tell anybody. You're not pissed because I did it with someone else besides you, are you?"

"We've been through that," Fred says. "You know my feelings. I'm not going to deny them. But I know we're kids too. I know I have to get out there and try to fend off the Mel Dirs of the world, and probably the Melody Dirs and the dear little freshman in college who are going to have a crush on the cross-country boy with black glasses. We might come back to one another, but I know we both need to hit the road for a while, go our separate ways.

"If you want to know the truth, I already figured out you were in pretty deep with Mr. Williams, if not physically then definitely in your heart. You can run but you cannot hide from the Lord. Or from Fred's spectacles for that matter. But I wasn't asking you about the Cherry Hill, appropriate as that name might be for a virgin."

"Look, Fred, we didn't go that far. I'm a black sheep admittedly, but we just slept together."

"Spare me the gory details, *mon ami*—and the sheep jokes. I am more interested in your musings about these married men who are about to be indicted according to the paper, more curious about those guys who have already been arrested. Mel tells me you know more than you're telling about the monkey cages. I didn't even tell him you were down there."

"He's a shit disturber is what he is."

"Like my little sister," Fred says. "Last night she started getting on Gracie's case about her softball sweatshirts. Started razzing her about getting married—to her girlfriends no less. Mom and Dad can't shut her up. She's worse than I ever was."

"Doesn't your Dad reign her in What about your little brother Duncan?"

"Duncan is the good boy. Duncan plays baseball. Duncan likes duck hunting. Duncan this and Duncan that. He thinks I'm a freak even though he's two years younger. He avoids me like the plague now that he's at the high school. Dad worships the ground he walks on. Duncan is the golden boy. He leaves disciplining my little sis to Mom."

My heart is starting to boil as I roll on my side and stand up, walking over to the window to watch sleet slant across the old lattice with a dusty window clamped over it. "Freddie, look, I'll tell you what I know, but before I do you have to realize I'm not going to ever swear to it under oath or admit it to any cop or judge or jury or investigator. I have already stretched the bands of our trust. Look, okay..." I'm pacing now, my head down. I can't look at him.

"...one of the guys I bumped into down at the cages that night was your dad."

PART TWO

To the tune of "Sweet Little Sixteen"
by Chuck Berry

1. LEWD AND LASCIVIOUS

"Now, Mr. McKellar, did you have occasion to spend time at the YMCA during the summer of 1955?"

"Yes," Kurt answers. He is wearing grey polyester slacks and a white shirt with a diamond pattern, his t-shirt visible at his open collar. The ex-linebacker is on the stand, called as a witness in the *State of Idaho v. Martin Williams*.

"Could you tell the court what you observed between the defendant and the young high-school student Tom Cadigan at that location?"

"Objection, your honor," Marty's lawyer, Ruth Libby, interrupts. "The characterization of Mr. Cadigan is prejudicial. He was almost seventeen last summer. Hardly the child the prosecutor seeks to characterize him as, I must point out."

"Counsel," the judge says, "let me remind you and the jury that for purposes of Section 18.580A of the Idaho Criminal Code, lewd and lascivious conduct applies to a minor child who is sixteen or seventeen. I am not going to argue semantics at this juncture. Suffice it to say the prosecutor has sufficiently established the victim in this case was sixteen at the time in question. Proceed, Mr. Hathorne."

"With all due respect, your honor," Ruth persists, "it is our contention Mr. Cadigan was neither an innocent youth nor a victim in this case." I sit on my hands in the gallery on a wooden fold down chair, listening to these people talk about me in a courtroom, powerless to interject, frustrated and angered by the government's decision to prosecute my love for Coach as a crime.

"We note your objection, Miss Libby. You may continue, counsel." I can tell Judge Danforth, a flat-topped burly man with drunk-red cheeks and a set of hairy knuckles, is becoming perturbed by Ruth's attempt to impede the progress.

"Mr. McKellar, tell the jury what you saw at the Y last summer," the judge says to the witness, trying to cut to the chase. Kurt sits up, alert in the witness box, relishing attention but nervous.

"Yea, well, sir, not too much, I guess. Coach was down there sometimes in the evening. And Tommy would show up, and I guess they were lying down on the mats and talking or doing pushups or sit-ups or whatever. Coach would give Tommy a spot on the bench press. It seemed like Coach was partnering up with Tommy, helping him get big. Tommy's kind of scrawny, and he was always trying to get some definition. Thing was, though, every time I asked Tommy if he wanted help, he refused, but when Coach arrived, he was all over him. Kind of strange. They were pretty tight."

"Did you see them in the locker room?"

"Yea. Well not at first, but later in August. I saw them in the sauna talking and then they were soaping up together in the shower. Yea, sometimes laughing and talking. Having a pretty good time. Coach is a cool, pretty no-nonsense guy. But I guess with Tommy, he kind of took him under his wing. Tommy was always trying to get good at stuff, trying to lift more weight. But it's not in the cards. He doesn't have the body for it. I guess that's why he liked me—at first anyway. Yea, until he started hangin' with Coach. Then I was like a leper or something."

"Did you see them have any physical contact?"

"Yea, well, you know…" Kurt hesitates, glancing at the gallery, then Ruth, and then at the judge. "Like holding Tommy's waist during pull-ups or his legs down for sit-ups, maybe keeping his arms steady for barbells. Just the usual spots was all. I guess I saw them checking each other out a lot in the showers and stuff, I don't know. I can't really talk about it here. Not with ladies in the room."

"Mr. McKellar," the prosecutor, Blaine Hathorne, continues, "I know this is hard for you. These matters are difficult to talk about.

We all understand that. But the law requires us to ask these questions if we are to show the elements of lewd and lascivious conduct, and we have no other choice than to bring out some very unpleasant things. We are trying to determine whether Coach Williams solicited Tommy Cadigan to engage in a sexual act, even if there was no act itself."

"Objection, argumentative. Your honor, counsel is giving his version of the law to the witness. He's not even asking a question."

"Sustained. Mr. Hathorne, you must ask questions that gather evidence of the solicitation, not tell us what solicitation is. We have already established that the defendant is guilty if he either *committed* acts upon the body of the alleged victim, or if he *solicited* the commission of such acts through verbal or physical action. Your job, counsel, is to show how the defendant enticed the victim into some form of sexual arousal even if they had no physical contact. I am assuming you are not trying to establish Mr. McKellar witnessed any such contact. That is a separate and more egregious offense which the prosecution, I take it, will broach with other witnesses."

"Yes, your honor."

"Very well, enough said on that front. Let's try to get on with it, here. Mr. McKellar. Could you tell the court if you saw or heard anything that might suggest Mr. Williams was asking for something sexual from Tom Cadigan?"

"Well, Judge, like I said, it's pretty hard to talk about this stuff in public, but you know how some guys act in the shower, like the way they suds up and stuff. And Coach, I'd never seen him shower before, but you know, with Tommy in there, he would go at it pretty good, if you know what I mean."

"Go at it?"

"Yea, like clean himself all over in a way that was pretty obvious."

"You mean he was exhibiting himself?" Hathorne asks.

"Objection, calls for a conclusion from the witness."

"Overruled," the judge snaps. "Exhibition may have a number of definitions, not necessarily legal."

"I don't know what you mean by that anyway," Kurt says. "Coach never did anything to Tommy that I saw. They just had all this eye contact and soaping up and well, Tommy, I just kind of noticed, maybe he was, you know, kind of...getting bigger down there. I mean like, you know, Tommy was on the team for a while and I saw him a lot, like in the showers and such. He wasn't like really that well-endowed. He was okay, you know, average, but it was just like, well, sometimes with Coach there he just..."

"Did Mr. William's actions arouse Tommy Cadigan?" Hathorne asks.

"Objection, your honor. The question is leading. It calls for a conclusion and speculation."

"Sustained, Miss Libby."

"I just noticed," Kurt says, "Tommy kept looking at Coach in the shower and he was getting bigger so he had to hide it or whatever. I don't know. Tommy's a weird kid. He's not a wimp or nothing. No way. It's just with Coach around, I guess he just got kind of excited or something."

"Thank you, Kurt. I have nothing further, your honor."

Ruth asks for a recess before cross-examination.

2. DRAGNET

Where do I begin? How humiliating to listen to that jerk talk about Coach and me at the Y, while I sit there, silent in the gallery of Courtroom 1B on West Jefferson in the middle of town. I've been blind with rage for most of 1956, wondering how the hell it has all come to this—how my love for Coach is being exposed in a wood-paneled courtroom with the gallery and jury full of disgust and excitement, lapping up evidence of my average-sized dick swelling at the sight of my love taking a shower.

Yes, my love, dammit. You think I am too young to use that word? Too horny? Too immature? Too perverted? For me still, it is love. Even at this moment sitting in the gallery, trying to figure out how I got from the floor of my bedroom talking to Freddie to waking up six months later in a courthouse where Coach slumps at a wooden table next to my Dad's law school buddy, Ruth Libby.

Ruth is from Coeur d'Alene up on the Panhandle, one of a handful of women lawyers in our great state of good old boys. She has agreed to take the case because my dad can't. Coach, damn fool that he is, has decided to plead not guilty against everyone's advice, insisting on his innocence under some measure of justice that has nothing to do with the Idaho criminal code.

Lewd and lascivious conduct. Encouraging me to play with myself in the shower. Enticing me, according to Kurt. Ruth will get him after the break. Ruth will kill him, I tell myself as I slump behind the bar in the third row. She's talking to my father while Marty remains nonplussed but unswerving, unable to turn and look at me.

He's dressed in his narrow olive necktie and charcoal gray suit, his black cap-toed shoes poised beneath the grainy maple table. He leans forward in a rib-backed wooden chair.

All eyes are on the sodomite, Coach Williams, our ever-popular football leader who has led the Braves to two state championships in four years. The devil may assume a pleasing shape, scripture tells us, abuse the weak and vulnerable youth and lure them unsuspecting into steamy perversions of lechery. Abomination. Having allegedly destroyed my life, Coach is poised to ravish other Boise boys, turning them into hopeless and homeless homos for the rest of their sad days.

The same eyes that watch the despicable corruptor of youth are also watching me, the seventeen-year-old victim of the sick pedophile, a poor contaminated boy whose only hope now is counseling, the military, and marriage. There is no cure other than God's grace. All eyes are on me, victim of that infamous crime against nature. That charge, the more egregious of the two, will never stick. How can it? We have never screwed one another, as much as we may have wanted to.

When I went to school on Veteran's Day last November four months ago, I was more worried about Freddie, who had left me without a word after my revelation of his Dad's visit to the monkey cages. I guess I was caught off guard when everybody started buzzing about Coach's arrest a day later. It happened so fast. At assembly, the principal told us that our town was currently going through "a difficult time," and that boys in any grade should speak directly to Mr. Bosse about "odd behavior" by adults they might have encountered.

He tried to calm us down, telling us the routine at Boise High would remain the same. Pam, who was mad at me anyway, and her friends stood in the hallway, their French books clasped against their chests. They gathered in tight circles outside the multipurpose room, saying "hi" to me in the most nasty of tones as I shuffled by. Every time I glanced back at them, I could see my classmates glaring above their whispers.

My friendship with the arrested history teacher was no secret then or now. Everyone is being very "nice," but obviously giving me a wide berth, making sure to avoid sitting next to me. Sometimes they even politely turn around as I approach in the cafeteria or stand in the bathroom. Pariah I am. One afternoon, I saw Skip at the smoke-shop and cornered him.

"Why is everyone treating me like I have the plague?" I asked him.

He glanced around to see who was watching us and said, "Some kids know you aren't the innocent boy people say you are. Look, Caddy, I got to go. I'll see you around." He jumped on his bike and took off.

Sometimes this whole thing is too gut-wrenching. I can't describe what this peer pressure has done to what's left of my self-esteem, given the fact that I began this dark trip already struggling with what Freddie likes to call my inferiority complex. Freddie has no problem accepting, even relishing his unpopular status, but facing this ostracism is excruciating for me. Sometimes I just want to forget it and try to move on. I just want to save my skin, get the hell out of Boise and into some obscure college dormitory somewhere, before all this stuff suffocates me.

Sitting in the Superior Court of Ada County has brought those fall days of 1955 back, the whole unraveling love knot: Coach in jail until my dad's firm posted bail; Freddie home schooled away from me the rest of the year, *Tea and Sympathy* canceled, Dir driving across the Nevada desert back to San Fran. There were too many other arrests and trials to think about. Trent's Dad, *por ejemplo*. Off to Tijuana over the weekend. *Ya se fue.* Left the Howdy Pardner to his wife and kids, just up and left without saying a word, leaving his bowl of soggy Wheat Chex. Good old Trent, the homo baiter, discovering a Dad who was going down not on the broads who danced on his roof top, but on the boys who flipped burgers.

Mr. Brown, my boss at the hardware store, pleads guilty, as do most of the others. He is given fifteen years in the pen. He could be out on parole in three or four, but his life is ruined. His store in Chapter 11, his family off to the anonymity of Denver; he'll probably end up selling auto parts in L.A. for the rest of his life. People's lives are being ruined left and right for touching the genitalia of boys aged fourteen to twenty-one, boys walking the dog every morning and evening if my experience was any barometer, boys as horny as hell looking to have some fun—with anything and everything.

I'm not condoning luring kids into dark Dodge Imperials for rides home from school and a copped feel. But at what point do we respect a person's right to say yes, at what point is consent valid? Should a man be put behind bars for ten years because he hand-jobs a Senior high jumper who has a B+ average and stars on the speech and debate team but is tired of being a good boy one sweaty summer?

I've spent six months mulling this stuff over, fed up enough at this point to enter a monastery, though monks are probably less celibate than inmates at the state pen. Maybe I really just long for family life in Provo or Pocatello, places where social mores are strong enough to drive many into righteous damnation of what they unconsciously desire. Dr. Butler knows that. He knows about the craziness of the id, but he is the first to remind me about the necessity and nastiness of social morality. He is teaching me about what he calls the "ramifications" of my love for Coach.

Some of those arrested last fall are, in fact, derelicts. Men who drifted in to town like tumbleweed, some with records, and worked as soda jerks or shoe salesmen. Carl Carlsen got life, believe it or not. Life in prison for blowing Hal Halverson, the biggest greaser that ever walked into a pool hall.

The Fall of '55 turned out to be a free for all. The god-fearing folk went on a rampage, especially after the news broke about Mr. Brown and Coach Williams. Homos were suddenly rearing their ugly heads everywhere, and Emery Bosse and his posse were out to lynch the boy rustlers. A lot of these married suits we learn are what the experts call "bisexuals," curious about making it with guys until they have to go back to live happily ever after with Martha in the suburbs.

Once Emery and his police dogs started their homo-hunt, aided by the help of the Allied Civic Club and *The Statesman*, too much was at stake to shrug it off as just high jinx. The Pink Scare, Dir called it, well before he hightailed it out of our town. Yea, Coach and Garrison and Dir are not just your run-of-the-mill fairies, according to Bosse and company. They're also either Commie puke or at least being blackmailed by the Communist Party, its cells planted all over the great state of Idaho. No one needs John Birch to convince them the Reds are behind the plot to turn our boys into queers. One article mentioned Dir by name, called him a ring leader, reporting that he would be tracked down in the Barbary Coast of North Beach if necessary.

The press has become relentless. Once the story broke at the beginning of November, the mothers of the Junior League were up in arms, with anonymous calls coming into the DA's office in record numbers and respectable men ringing up my Dad all day long, looking for criminal defense lawyers. The City Council was called into emergency session. The DA, my Dad said, had to make lots of arrests in order to survive.

By the time *Time* magazine published its story about the scandal on December 12, though, some of the locals were already backing off a bit, in part because of the spreading news of Frank Jones's attempted suicide at West Point a week earlier. Schleiner had interviewed him over Thanksgiving and the cadet had returned to his dorm and slit his wrists in the middle of the night. He was in a hospital back East, according to my Mom.

Given his father's complicity in the investigation, the official tune suddenly switched from crime to sickness, our leaders realizing how damaging their nasty little cleanup campaign was to the local economy. The capitol of Idaho has an image to uphold and industry to attract, so *The Statesman* cooled its jets and called for an "intelligent plan" to deal with "a serious social problem."

The news desk assured us every community in the country had its homosexuals lurking in the shadows. Most of the victims of this puzzling "physical quirk," as they called it, were themselves infected as young boys and had grown into manhood in order to infect another generation of unsuspecting youth. Tragically, the scourge had multiplied because one adult homosexual usually could "inseminate" several boys. The result of course was the eventual wiping out of entire communities as the homo demons grew in number. I'm not kidding, this stuff was in the papers.

The main concern must be the victimized boys, they insisted. That's where I came in. Once Coach was arrested, all eyes were upon his poor, mixed-up victim, the Cadigan boy, whose liberal upbringing had led to his vulnerability. I've been singled out as one of the poor misguided black sheep in need of psychiatric assistance. Hence my "friendship" with Doc Butler, and our little sessions in those brass-buttoned club chairs.

By the end of the year, the newspaper proposed a town hall meeting to face the challenge of controlling if not crushing the monster. Their whole front-page diatribe came after Thanksgiving. Ten men had been arrested, most of them pleading guilty. Emery Bosse claimed over a hundred boys were involved, and the paper announced a Youth Advisory Committee had already been formed to save the children. They hired a couple of shrinks to come into town and study the mess, which is how Butler got hold of me. Or that's how my Mom got hold of Butler to get hold of me.

A lot of ground to cover, a lot of story to tell. My Dad, you don't even know my Dad. I've barely said a word about him, about his study off the kitchen with its closed glass door, about his office downtown in the old excuse for a highrise—three stories of stucco built in the Thirties. His practice as general as an encyclopedia, but mostly criminal defense, mostly plaintiff's work, taking on the downtrodden in the great tradition of Mr. Darrow. Dad is no Darrow though; he loses a lot of cases, wins some. In Idaho, his percentage isn't bad. But mostly he walks around with his cuffs rolled up, pacing with a butt in his mouth, staring out the window, reading stuff like Aurelius and the great Russian novelists. He subscribes to *The Nation*. He indulges Gloria and her Basque family. Gloria, short and buxom and sexy and . . . *shit*, my mom for crying out loud, but that's the thing, they aren't really like my parents. They're this making-ends-meet scrappy couple drinking too much red on the weekends and spattering olive oil all over while cooking potato pancakes, listening to Lena Horne and getting together with the whomevers for dominoes.

They are fighters, constantly bickering about vacations and un-ironed shirts, about dripping faucets and politics—about my dad's troublemaking social causes like free clinics and social crusades that anger my mother's conservative immigrant family, who are none too pleased with their son-in-law's Indian police brutality cases, his Lawyers' Guild meetings and failed run for City Council.

Kevin Cadigan is by all accounts an embarrassment to the Zubiri clan—sheepherders turned grocers, whose local store somehow still competes with Albertson's for now. The Mormon chain is starting to price Zubiri's out of the market, but local loyalties keep them going.

The Zubiris have never forgiven Kevin for returning Gloria back to her hotel in San Francisco after the silly girl got lost on the cable cars and ended up at the bottom of California Street instead of Ghirardelli Square in the late Thirties. Dad loves to tell the story. Sure, Gloria's parents were happy to see their young whippersnapper show up at the hotel in Northpoint where they were staying on the family summer vacation to the World's Fair, having driven West in their brand-new Pontiac Chieftain listening to Autry sing "Back in the Saddle" every ten minutes between Glenn Miller instrumentals, having just toured through the requisite redwoods and now planning their way east through Tahoe and Sparks back to Boise, probably through Jackpot. Yea, their only daughter showed up all right, but as my drunk parents tell it, Gloria's parents didn't expect to see no freckle-faced freak from Berkeley, California, in his dirty loafers.

Dad says they took one look at him and figured he had *The Communist Manifesto* in the back pocket of his dirty khakis, a rumpled shirt untucked in the back as he brought their baby girl into the lobby. Actually the college boy was just hanging out in North Beach with the Italians when he found Mom lost on a corner with all that black hair blowing around her eyes.

So it went with Gloria in a pickle but no less arrogant for all that. Anyway, they kept writing letters and Dad hitched out to Boise since there was no work, and they got married about the time Hitler was eying Poland and charming Chamberlain. They got married, had me, then Dad went to law school and got drafted and worked in the JAG's office, then got sent to the Pacific, and then wouldn't talk about it anymore. Wouldn't talk about the islands where he was stationed. Wouldn't say a word about the hole in his back, except I got to stick my finger in it when we went swimming.

So anyway, as they tell it, they lived happily ever after, drinking gin and tonics with cocktail onions and green olives. I loved to stick the black ones on my fingers. Why am I telling you all this? All this background a prelude to what happened after Freddie left in a mysterious daze that evening last fall, left speechless over my bomb drop about his own father.

The evening I told Freddie I'd seen his father, I also told my Dad I had to see him in his office before dinner. He was sitting with his feet up reading the *The Quiet American*, looking up from his book at me like I was a Jehovah's Witness or Fuller Brush Man. After a short period of adjustment, he straightens up, takes off his half-moon reading glasses and says, "sure, what's up, Thomas?" He calls me Thomas. It's kind of a joke. He wants someone to address me by my full name other than the Department of Motor Vehicles.

He knew it was serious since I normally never went near his office if I could help it. I had no idea where Mom was, but I didn't want her walking in on us. Hard enough to talk to Dad about my allowance, much less my screwing around with my history teacher. Jesus God. What a mess, what a complete mess. But I had to tell him.

So I go in there and sit down on one of those ribbed wooden armchairs that swivel and tilt back. Dad comes in with his baggy pants and those sheepskin slippers he wears around the house, shuffling mostly, nose in a book half the time.

"Dad, there's some stuff going on. It's kinda getting out of hand, and I didn't want to bother you or anything but I need to get it off my chest, like you say all the time."

He just sits there with his elbow on his cluttered old pine desk, bottom drawer pulled out for his footrest. He flips open the Marlboro box and lights a cig with his Zippo, spreading his fingers over the side of his scalp.

"Tommy, look, I hang out my shingle for just about anybody who walks down the street. There isn't much that hasn't sauntered into my office one time or another, either in Boise or over on the islands during the war.... Good gawd, are you mixed up in this *Statesman* ruckus?"

"Kind of." I'm shaking pretty bad and getting red like always. I am determined not to start cracking up again. Dad tells me about attorney-client privilege, tells me he considers our talk confidential, and not just because of our family connection. Whatever I say will be kept secret, even from Mom.

"Yea so last summer, I was down there in the park. I ran into a bunch of guys and they convinced me to give it a chance, make some money off these older guys that wanted to fool around with us. I was gonna split, but they talked me into it, so I went with McKellar behind the dugout with this older bald guy, but when he started doing it with Kurt I went nuts and started running back to my bike when I bumped into this other guy with a hat and just picked it up and handed it to him and kept going. I was riding home through the park, and I realized the man with the hat was Freddie's dad. And I couldn't tell Freddie because I just couldn't. I know he doesn't like his Dad that much and stuff, but I just didn't feel right about blowing Mr. Udall's cover. But Freddie and I, we are sworn brothers. No secrets allowed, and you know how he reads minds. He knew I was keeping something from him, so tonight I just told him. And Fred looked real funny at me for a few seconds and got up and left. Didn't say anything. Just grabbed his parka and walked out the front door."

At that point, I am starting to tear up, but Dad, he is plenty used to people crying He just sits there with the cig over his head listening, calm, watching the desk, like he knows about everything I am confessing already. He asks a bunch of questions. Do I know the bald guy? No. Did I take any money? No. Who was there beside

McKellar? The Halverson guy, Skip was there and some others I didn't know. Did Mr. Udall recognize you? Yea, I assume. Then the hard questions came. Was that the only time I was down there that summer? The only time at the monkey cages, yes. Then he starts to hone in. Like Joe Friday. Like "where were you on the night of August 15, Mr. Cadigan?"

"Thomas, let's be clear. You will not be arrested for what happened that night, I am quite certain. Only the adults will be subject to prosecution, depending on whom the DA decides to go after. You could be called to testify, however."

I interrupt him, tell him about Schleiner. Tell him I kept my mouth shut. He sits there shaking his head, his dark hair losing its stiff striations from too much Vitalis. It's Sunday. His flannel shirt is untucked. He's in his slippers. He's got a yellow notepad out and an orange pencil in his hand, sharper than a knife point. He doodles, takes notes, grimaces.

"What else were you doing this summer?" he asks me out of the blue, looking me in the eye as I cast mine down like Coco when she's really in trouble.

"You know, swimming, running. I went to the Y to work out." And now that aggressive silence again, the squirm and tick, the eye contact and foot tapping. The cross-examination that crosses the space between father and son, Dad relentless in his refusal to relieve the pressure. All the lectures about truth and honesty and integrity fill the empty space between us as he leans on me with a persuasion greater than any words possibly could.

"There is this thing with Coach Williams, I guess," I tell him. "He helped me out at the gym, taught me to butterfly in the pool. You know, like when he drove me to Lolo last summer and we went swimming together and stayed at a motel when the car broke down."

He sits stolid and expressionless. I only learn later that he had some hunches. He had talked to some people who were looking for a lawyer. He had talked to Dir, talked to Brown, knew the DA. Boise is a small town, abuzz with a queer scandal tearing up the lawns of a lot of Ozzies and Harrietts. My dad the enigma, the sphinx. Solid, unswerving, battle worn.

"So you and Marty Williams? God, Tommy...do you have any idea?"

"It's not like the monkey cages, I swear. It's different. Marty and me, we just clicked. I open up around him, can be myself with him. He's best thing that's ever happened to me. I'm sorry, I can't help it...." I'm crying now. I have no idea what my father is thinking. I assume he thinks I'm delinquent, absurd, fallen under the spell of Coach.

"I'm not in the dark about all this stuff. I knew you might have gotten mixed up with Halverson and McKellar a couple of times last summer. Elly told me as much." He paused as if he had slipped.

It didn't register at first, then I realized he was talking about Elvina. "She left, right?"

"Yea, the whole jazz band has gone back to San Francisco," he says wistfully. He looks down at his notepad as the smoke blows like exhaust out his nostrils. "God, this is not the future I want for you." He sighs again. "You're going to have to lay plenty low because the law is involved in this tangle. His pencil slips through his fingers as he props it against the pad. "If only you had waited...a year from now, when you're in college...everybody experiments. But here and now, sixteen in Boise, Idaho. Jesus, Thomas. This is not...promising."

"What's going to happen?"

"Blaine Hathorne wants names, needs convictions. He has to get guilty pleas to feed the angry mob. And there isn't anybody who is currently safe, except for the victims like you."

"But I'm not a victim, Dad. I started everything between Coach and—"

"In the eyes of the law you are the victim."

3. SUDS

"Mr. McKellar, could you tell the jury your current occupation?"

"I bounce at Bing's right now on the weekends."

"Are you enrolled in school?" Ruth continues her cross examination of the witness. It's late morning, the spring sun streaming through the transom windows lights up the hallowed maple wainscoting.

"I was at Boise State last year, but I guess I'm taking some time off right now."

"So you've dropped out of college, and you have a part-time job throwing people out of Bing's dance hall on the weekends?"

"Objection, your honor," Hathorne interrupts. "Mr. McKellar's employment is irrelevant and her characterization—"

"Overruled. Goes to the witness's credibility. Miss Libby, be careful not to jump to conclusions about Mr. McKellar. Proceed."

"Mr. McKellar, while you played football for Coach Williams at Boise High, did you ever see him physically touch any of the players on the team."

"Yes. Well, he had to."

"Did Coach Williams show members of the team how to block, how to tackle?"

"Yes."

"And that physical contact during football season was the same or greater than what you saw between Coach and Tom Cadigan at the gym in the Y last summer, was it not?"

"It was different."

"Did you ever feel Coach was trying to arouse you when he showed you how to tackle a running back?"

"Well, no but—"

"So when Coach was holding down Tom Cadigan's ankles for sit-ups at the Y, was that physical contact more or less than he made on the field or in the whirlpool in the gym after practice?"

"It was different."

"Was there more contact between bodies during football season than at the Y between Tommy Cadigan and Coach? Yes or no, Mr. McKellar?"

Kurt is looking at the judge and the prosecutor. Hathorne begins to speak but withdraws his objection. The witness admits the contact was less at the Y.

"Mr. McKellar," Ruth proceeds, "you like Tommy Cadigan, don't you?"

"Sure," Kurt says. "I know he likes me, or he used to anyway. He liked me when we were on the team together."

"Is it true you convinced Tommy to watch you have sexual relations with an older man last summer in Julia—"

"Objection, your honor. This line of inquiry is totally irrelevant. Mr. McKellar is not on trial here. He is testifying to what he saw at the Y, nothing more and nothing less."

"Your honor, we believe Mr. McKellar's jealousy may be influencing his version of the truth."

"Jealousy?" Kurt explodes from the witness box. "Are you kidding? Me jealous of that wimp?" The judge tells Kurt to close his mouth while I cringe in the gallery, watching his outburst. Danforth overrules Hathorne's objection but tells Libby he isn't letting her go on a fishing expedition for very long.

"So you did have sex for money on numerous occasions in the park last summer, did you not?"

"Yes. It was just for kicks and they just did me. I never went down on them or anything."

"Thanks for clarifying your position, Mr. McKellar. And you knew the names of many of your clients, did you not?"

"Enough, Miss Libby," the judge says. "Move on."

"Did you meet any of your 'suits' or 'tricks' at the Y last summer?"

"Maybe a couple, I don't know."

The judge is giving Ruth the evil eye.

"Mr. McKellar, let's try another tack. When you saw Coach Williams 'soaping up', as you called it, in a suggestive manner, where were you standing at that point?"

"I don't know. I don't really remember. I guess I was toweling off or whatever outside the shower."

"Did you have your clothes on?"

"Your Honor," Hathorne interjects, "what relevance does Mr. McKellar's state of dress have to do with the accuracy of what he saw?"

"You were staring at Tom Cadigan, weren't you?" Ruth asks, ignoring the objection.

"Well, yea, I was looking at him."

"Trying to get his attention, weren't you? With your towel, drying yourself off. Am I wrong, Mr. McKellar, to state that you were aroused as you stared at Tommy Cadigan during those times?"

"Well, I didn't have a hard—

"*Your honor*," Mr. Hathorne yells.

"Move on, Miss. Libby. You've made your point."

"Do you deny putting your hand on Tom Cadigan's thigh during a mutual masturbation session last summer?"

"He had the hots for me. I was just giving him what he wanted."

"So when Mr. Cadigan treated you like a leper at the gym after you lured him into the monkey cages earlier last summer, you were pretty angry, weren't you, Mr. McKellar?"

"Objection. Counsel is arguing."

"Sustained."

"On the evening you saw Coach Williams soaping up, did you have occasion to take a shower?"

"Probably."

"Was Tom Cadigan in the shower then?"

"I don't remember."

"So, Tom Cadigan could have been aroused by your exhibition, Mr. McKellar?"

"Well, I was sudsing up before Coach started. I was going at it before I saw Tommy. Plus he wouldn't give me the time of day."

"Can you answer the question, Mr. McKellar, please. You don't really know who Tom Cadigan was reacting to, do you?"

"Well, I guess not."

"You can't be sure, can you? Because you were sudsing up in front of Tom Cadigan too, weren't you Mr. McKellar? Trying to get his attention? Am I wrong, Mr. McKellar?"

"Judge, I object—"

"I withdraw the question your honor. I have nothing further," Ruth says. Hathorne lets the witness go. Kurt scrambles out of the box, scowling and glaring at me as he passes through the bar and down the gallery. I'm sure he would have flipped me off if Hathorne hadn't warned him in advance to behave. The jury seems as put off by his body language during his haughty exit as much as by anything he has said.

I'm impressed with the way Ruth questioned McKellar's motive and threw into doubt the idea that Coach had solicited me to commit a lewd and lascivious act. To be honest, I don't even remember where and when and how many times I was getting loose in the gym last summer, how many times I watched Coach or Kurt in the shower. Causation is certainly an issue. The entire male population is guilty under 18.850A at this point in my illustrious career as a budding homosexual. But I'm not the one on trial. Should be, but I'm not. Coach is the culprit under the law, and regardless of how vindictive and unreliable Kurt is, the men and women in the jury box at this point don't seem to be in any mood to acquit their perverted football coach.

When word first got out that Coach was behind bars, I rushed down on my bike to the holding cell when Dad drove me off the road, jumped out, grabbed my bike, and threw it in the back of the De Soto station wagon.

"Get in the car," he ordered me. He took me home and closed the door behind us in his office. "Head over there now," he shouted, "and you will pretty much ruin Coach's chance of even getting out on bail." He grabbed me by the shoulders and looked me in the eye.

"You sarcastic little son of a bitch, wake up for a second. We're not in Ms. Winfrey's literature class anymore, Thomas. You are going to have to listen and listen good if you want Mr. Williams to have a chance here. If you want to send him down river to get buggered by every thug from here to Denver, then go ahead and act like a fool. I can't stop you. But if what you told me last night is true, you pretty damn well better listen to me. Got it?"

"I needed to tell him I was sorry. I got him into this mess."

"You *both* got into this mess. It doesn't look good for Marty Williams right now, son. He'll need an attorney. With you being his primary victim, I can't represent him, but I have some connections. Up north, I have an old friend I went to school with. She lives outside Coeur d'Alene. That is if Williams will pay her. We'll bail him first."

"I want to see him."

"You will keep your butt as far away from the jail house as you possibly can. Do you understand me, young man?"

"Dad, why are you talking to me like this?"

"I'm talking to you like this because you said Marty Williams was the most important person in your life. Except hopefully for your lovely parents and maybe Freddie Udall. If you want to save him from getting locked behind bars in the state pen for fifteen years, you'd better do what I say. This is serious business, and you are in way over your head. You haven't even talked to your mother yet and if you think I'm being adamant, just you wait. We also have your future to worry about, young man, a future I know Marty Williams does not want to hinder. So listen up. I don't have time to police you. You lay low, you shut up, you do your homework. If you don't, it's your own funeral big boy, your own g.d. funeral. And if you are old enough to fall in love, you're old enough to throw your life away. We'll worry about your mother later. That's all partner. Back to *Hamlet*."

"*Merchant of Venice*, actually."

"Perfect. That play will give you a sense of what your friend is up against." He stood up and opened the door to his office, leaving me sitting there I heard him take my bike out, slam the wagon hatch and drive off.

4. YVES

I sit through most of the trial during spring break, stranded on the curved contour of an uncushioned seat, head down between my palms listening to the state of my fate. In fact, I am on the witness list, but because I'm a minor, Ruth has made motions to limit my testimony as to place and time and content.

She has also tried to challenge the constitutionality of the statutes, based on due process and equal protection, but the judge has dismissed those out of hand. Judge Danforth is still wrangling with counsel over me and Freddie getting on the stand. Yes, they've put Freddie on the list and presumably he has also been sent notice, though I haven't heard a single word from him since the day I told him about his dad. He hasn't come back to Boise High at all, apparently being home-schooled for the last half of his senior year. I hear his family has moved to Nampa and are holing up in their new house. My Dad isn't saying anything. Freddie is just one of twenty or so people on the list of witnesses. Hathorne and Company have done their homework, dragging out a string of characters who saw Coach and me together—police, lifeguards, floaters, gas pumpers, drivers, and night managers; our every move has been traced by their blood-hound detectives.

That afternoon in the courtroom, the prosecutor calls the park guard who found me chanting after hours in the cedar grove near Pericles. Ruth asks the judge what that has to do with the defendant, but the prosecution says it has reason to believe the defendant was in the vicinity at the time of the meditation.

Hathorne has already established we were at the Y that evening. What evidence does he have? Officer James heard voices, Hathorne states, but the court gives the prosecution short shrift on this one. James has no knowledge of the persons whose voices he heard other than that of "the boy." According to Danforth, the prosecution is on an "excursion," and he tells the jury to disregard the testimony.

The lifeguard at the Natatorium, Shuck Gerassi, is next. He saw Coach showering beside me after the butterfly lesson, cleaning my back. He says he didn't think much of it at the time. Looked like he was just scrubbing the guy's back. He saw Coach lean over to pick up the soap. Yea, the two of them were alone. Yea the open swim hour was about to close at the time.

"Did you see any genital touching?" Ruth asks on cross.

"No."

"Did you see any arousal?"

"I don't look at that stuff," the lifeguard insists. "I got a girlfriend in Caldwell. I don't check guys out. But after the investigator asked me about it, I kind of remember them being close...."

Ruth is forced to finesse. The witness has provided some eyewitness testimony, but she is able to show Shuck's initial impression of innocence has been tainted by prosecutorial zeal. She succeeds up to a point, but I'm wondering what good all this wrangling might be doing since the jury seems passive, almost comatose at two in the afternoon, their stomachs full of deviled eggs and Mars bars.

One witness perks up some of us. I've never laid eyes on her.

"Do you work for the Forest Service, Ms. Adams?" Hathorne begins with his witness, a thin woman of about forty-five with hair dyed reddish-bronze. She wears a green and gray uniform, a broad-brimmed felt Smokey the Bear hat in her lap.

"Yes."

"And do you patrol the hot springs in that area regularly?"

"Yes, Drummond Springs is included within my territorial jurisdiction, sir."

"Could you tell the jury, Miss Adams, what you encountered there three days after the defendant had been issued a citation on the road to that hot springs while he was traveling with Thomas Cadigan?"

"Yes, I often find rubbish at the hot springs site, since many individuals visit these public premises. On the day in question at approximately ten a.m., I was cleaning up the area at Drummond Springs when I found a piece of torn clothing along with some signs of bear tracks and scat nearby. You may not be unaware, your honor," Miss Adams addresses the judge instead of the jury, "that we often have a rather tawdry element that frequents these more remote bathing areas. So at first blush, I concluded that the abandoned remnant was probably part of the sordid debris from the visits of nudists and other riff raff who sometimes engage in unseemly behavior. Be that as it may, this piece of clothing, together with other evidence, led me to believe there might have been an encounter with a juvenile black bear, aptly named Yves because of his post-sunset visitations. At any rate, I secured the item of clothing in a plastic bag and transported it to headquarters for further inspection."

"What was this article of clothing, Miss Adams?"

"We were able to ascertain, your honor, that these were a pair of male white cotton briefs, size thirty waist. Further inspection uncovered two salient features of this undergarment. One, the elastic band bore the initials T.C. in black marker. Secondly, the officers concluded that the underwear in question was soiled in ways that are not the product of normal bodily excretions. The briefs had a number of starch-like areas consistent with ejaculate."

"Your honor," Ruth is on her feet. "This testimony lacks foundation and is entirely irrelevant to the charges against my client. What possible expertise does the witness have to determine the nature of the residue on the piece of clothing in question?

"Your honor, the prosecution is attempting to prove," Hathorne says, "these briefs were part of a sexual escapade that took place between the defendant and the victim on the night they drove to this area."

"Your honor, this is pure speculation. There is no direct evidence of any illegal conduct in this entire scenario."

"I will overrule the objection at this point, counsel," Danforth states in his pinched voice, squeaky for such a bear of a man. "However, I must also remind the jury that circumstantial evidence alone is not sufficient to prove sodomitical activity beyond a reasonable doubt. The state may proceed."

Hathorne picks up a plastic bag marked Exhibit A. "Miss Adams, does this bag contain the semen-stained briefs in question?" Hathorne holds the plastic bag in front of the witness, then the jury, and then in front of the defendant's table. The Jockeys were entered into evidence in spite of Ruth's protest about facts not in evidence and lack of authentication. I can't believe my dirty laundry is literally being aired in court. It's too much for me to watch. I get up, shoving people's knees out of the way as I head to the high-ceilinged hall. I need to breathe.

"Thank you, Miss Adams. I have nothing further. Your witness, counsel." I hear Hathorne say as I open the door back into the foyer, glancing back. The prosecutor steps lightly back to his table, obviously rather smug with satisfaction at his ability to enter my wank juice into evidence. Good god, don't they know those stains came long before I met Coach in the park, that they were the product of an earlier delightful afternoon indiscretion with William Holden in *Life*?

5. STALLED

Our day is done. I slink out of the courthouse with my head down, my book bag around my shoulder, having been instructed in no uncertain terms to have no public contact with the defendant, Ruth, or my father during the course of the trial. Of course my constant attendance is fooling no one. The jury is made up mostly of old Basque men who hang out at the parks playing bocce ball, a few midlife journeymen, and two canasta-playing grandmothers from Spreckles. Most of the jurors are indeed complete strangers: clerks at Montgomery Ward's, a retired car salesman, and a smattering of Mormons and Catholics, all promising impartiality in spite of their revulsion. I missed jury selection, but I can see their bifocals watching me in the courtroom.

Having skulked down to the bike rack, I make my way back to my garret, giving myself the liberty of stopping at the public library on the edge of the forbidden park in order to pick a few books. *Profiles in Courage* and *Inherit the Wind* are on the recent arrival shelf, so I grab them and proceed down to the men's room after I check them out.

While I slump under that stark porcelain light washing my hands, I hear a door to one of the stalls open and look over to see Kurt McKellar emerge with a smirk of surprise on his face. A sheepish skinny guy I have never laid eyes on before appears behind him and runs out the door. Kurt proceeds to wash his hands beside me, taking out his comb to readjust any of his curly locks that might have gotten mussed up during his interlude with the hapless bookworm.

I wipe my hands and my pants and reaching for my books in an attempt to exit post haste.

He laughs as he puts his hands on the books I have placed on a vacant sink, preventing me from scooping them up. I can't believe he has gone from the halls of justice to the stalls of the public library. I'm scared. How can Kurt show up by some improbable coincidence in the same basement bathroom right after his humiliation on the stand?

Kurt stands between me and my books while I move from side to side, trying to go around him and retrieve them. He pushes my hands away and finally gets me in a bear hug.

"You're not going to get away that easy, Caddy." He cuffs my head. "Little faggot. You think you can just screw me over in front of all those people? I can't believe you'd do that to me. After all we've been through, you mother."

He has me in a headlock at that point, and I'm not resisting. "I didn't tell Coach's lawyer what to do."

He's pushed up against the sink now with his hands on my jacket, staring me wildly in the eye. "You and Coach Williams, huh? You make me sick. Fucking up that guy's life, you little cocksucker. Let's see how much you really like me."

My books have fallen on the floor now and he shoves me toward the stall, but I'm fighting him off, flailing away but not yelling because I'm too scared or stupid. He tells me to shut my mouth and punches me in the stomach hard, taking the wind out of me as I buckle over and he knees me in the ribs. We're in the stall now, and he has slammed me up against the door, my arm jammed up my back as he presses against me, putting his mouth to my ear.

He has his chin on my shoulder. "What you really want...what you've been drooling over forever..." He almost is spitting in my ear as he rams himself against my back pocket. "Now's your chance."

I try to move. He lifts my arm higher up my back, and I groan in pain. He has one free hand to get my belt undone. He twists my arm further and my knees buckle.

"Please. Someone's going to come in..."

"You little snitch. You think you can fuck me over like that." He's dragging my pants down, and I'm in so much pain, I'm almost at the point of giving up. I'm drowning in his force. Kurt fumbles with his own clothes as I try to catch my breath and make one last effort to loosen his grasp. I take my free arm and blindly elbow him in the crotch. He grunts and clenches and bends over, releasing me. We're both entangled in agony for a minute.

I hear the outside door swing open and lurch back to sit on the toilet, rolling Kurt as best I can toward me, coughing as I shove him up against the toilet.

"Excuse me," a voice comes from the sink, a deep voice, thick rubber soles of his black shoes visible from under the stall. "Are these your books on the floor here?"

My voice is hoarse. "They must have fallen. I left them on the sink. Sorry."

"There's not any trouble going on in there? Are you feeling okay? Do you want me to call someone?"

"No, I was feeling a little woozy, but now that I've been able to sit down and go to the bathroom, I think I'll be all right."

"Are you sure I can't help? If you're sick, I need to know." I hear him picking up the books and putting them near the fallen book bag. I put my legs over Kurt's back so the stooping librarian can't detect the other body. I unroll some toilet paper and act like I am doing something necessary behind the green door. There is a long silence and then a sigh.

"Okay, young man. I will let you finish your business, but could you please report to me on the way out so I can make sure you're able to travel safely? I will be back in a few minutes if I don't hear from you."

"I think I'll be fine. Thanks, though." When the door swings closed, I stand up and look at Kurt, still holding his lower stomach as if he has a hernia or something.

"You okay?" He just stares at me and starts to groan. What have I done to him? I open the door and go to the sink to look in the mirror.

My cheekbone is chafed but not bleeding. My right arm feels like it's about to fall off. I pick up my book bag and leave, sneaking out the front door without checking in, hoping the librarian will come back to find Kurt just in case his testicular torsion requires hospitalization.

6. MARIKOI

I manage to hobble into the courtroom the next morning late. When Mom and Dad asked me about my arm and scraped cheek at dinner, I told them I fell off my bike. My father had seen I'd been to the library. He knows my bike wheels have pretty much become part of my anatomy, so crashing—especially when it's dry in spring—is not entirely believable, but he's too tired of my teenage shenanigans to follow up, I figure.

Mom is a different story. *Marikoi*, I have become. Her son the fairy. And my uncles at the grocery store don't want to see me down there ever again. The Zubiris want me gone. They want their nephew the Irish fag to move out to California *inmediatamente*. They can hardly wait for some college to be stupid enough to take my father's money.

It would be easy to throw a couple of sarcastic paragraphs at the Zubiris and chalk them up to yet another hurdle for Tom and Mart to overcome, but it's not that easy. My mom has raised me. She's taught me how to make my bed, do my homework, taught me how to rake the leaves in the fall from Mrs. Hunter's lawn, taught me why it is important to shovel that sidewalk first thing in the morning. She has showed me how to spell, how to proofread, how to bring my nouns and verbs in agreement. She crosses out the unnecessary articles on my essays and puts the *World Book* under my nose. She made sure I was on the ski slope at five, on the tennis court at six, and sweeping the floor of the store at seven. She takes me to catechism, irons my shirts, and drives me downtown to buy school clothes.

In short, she's my mom, and I'm who I am because of her, up to a point. But there comes a time when kids like me become strangers and have to find their way through the world without their parents. I'm trying to understand Mom's reaction. At some place inside me, I want to blame myself as much as her and her family do. I want to be the *verguenza*—the shame—they call me. Only my dad keeps me from drowning in that sea of self-loathing, only his mandate for justice keeps my devotion to Coach alive.

Needless to say, our sit-down after Veteran's Day last November was not, as Freddie would say, "felicitous." Mom had just gotten wind of Coach's arrest, but I don't know what she was thinking. All I know is she wasn't ready for our post left-over lasagna confab in the living room that night. She has her Lipton tea, and Dad has his *dedo* of single malt from Scotland. Glenmorangie. He's a whiskey drinker. Stuff makes me sick.

"Why are you here?" Mom asks me, cupping her steaming brew. She's being her no-nonsense, arch, half-serious self. "You never live in the living room."

"Dad wants me to talk to you about something," I say, looking at his long face. "I need to tell you what's going on."

"Well, *mi amor*, what's up?"

"It's about Coach Williams." She darts a glance at me and splashes a touch of tea on her sweater, managing to put the mug on the side table as she takes her feet off the ottoman, stands up, and goes to the kitchen for a dish towel. I glance at my father, whose head is down, staring at the cadenza. She returns with the rag and sits on the ottoman.

"What about Mr. Williams?" she asks. "He's behind bars, thank god. So what about him?"

"Mom," I say. "He's my friend."

"So, yes, he was a friend of a lot of people. We thought he was a good man. But now he's in jail for molesting boys. So you never know about people. Here's this guy that runs football, this guy everybody loves. Turns out he's a pervert."

"Accused," my dad says. "Innocent until proven guilty."

"Blah, blah, blah. You lawyers. So he didn't do it? Is that it? Is that why we are here?"

"Mom," I insist, looking at Dad, realizing how hard this confession is becoming. "I'm in love with Coach, Mom. I don't know how else to say it. I know it sounds weird to you, but Coach and I—we've been seeing each other." I'm not looking at her as I finally say it. I just feel so relieved to get it out, so flushed and terrified and so real. She sits with her elbows on her thighs for a while after she hears me. She looks up at Dad for a second and realizes he knows already.

"*Marikoi*," she whispers to herself barely audible. "My son. My boy."

"He told me Sunday night," Dad says.

"Who knows about this?" she asks.

"Nobody," I say. "You and Dad. Freddie."

"You must not tell anyone this. No one must know," she states definitively. "Grandma finds out, you will kill her. And my brothers, they will kill you. You think I'm kidding?" She is glaring at me now, uncompromising, direct, honest, and hard. She doesn't raise her voice.

"*Marikoi*," she repeats in disbelief. "You don't know what you're saying. You are a boy, a mixed-up boy. I know my brothers when they were your age. Sex was all they did. In the shower, in the bathroom, in the morning. Sex, sex, sex. You don't know what you're doing. You and your hormones. You have no idea, young man. You cannot be a Zubiri and do these things."

"Gloria," Dad says.

"Don't. I don't need your condescension." She looks at me. "You are grounded. And I am warning all of you. Keep your mouth damn shut. You will say nothing to anyone, do you understand? If you disobey me or your father, I'll turn you out on the street without a moment of hesitation."

"Mom...I love him."

"How could you know anything about love? You think it's found in poetry and novels? It's foundation is the family. And right now I fear you don't want to be part of our family as long as you…. I won't say it. It's sickening. Go to your room. I have to talk to your father."

I begin to protest but realize she won't listen. I head upstairs again for another one of my crying jags. But this time the crying itself is jagged, and I slam the door. I strip the bed and grab the sheets. I kick the mattress and then toss my books against the wall. I throw encyclopedias into sheet rock and kick my chemistry textbook across the floor.

I have a lamp in my hand when Dad comes in and grabs me by the arms and wrestles me to the carpet. He is stronger than I ever imagined. I am flailing madly, yelling and screaming. Dad tries to calm me down and pins my arms to the ground, the dog cowering in the corner, the room in shambles. I finally give up my rage, ashamed and tired. He draws me up by the arms and leans me against the box springs. He holds me and rocks me, saying nothing.

He stands up, and we put the room back together. Once we get the sheets tucked back in and pick up the books, once we straighten the rug and lift the lamp upright, my dad tells me to sleep. I watch him shuffle out in those ragged slippers with their worn-down sheepskin lining.

7. KING JAMES

Hathorne's list of witnesses that March morning five months later reads like an itinerary of our journey to Lochsa. The DA calls the old gas station attendant from outside McCall, who shows up in polyester slacks and a broad-brimmed hat. He knew something was "fishy" that day we filled our tank because that man and his "friend" were in such a hurry to get out of his station. He asked Williams a bunch of questions about where he was going and where he got his 51 Stude, but the defendant was "tight-lipped" and "not real friend-ly-like." When they drove out, the kid put his hand on that slick guy's shoulder. The boy was wearing real short cut offs too, and he had his bare feet up on the dash "real comfy-like."

The Flying A guy is soon dismissed from the witness box, and we are on to an older gentleman I've never laid eyes upon but who has apparently laid his eyes upon us.

"And you came on shift at Cherry Hill approximately 11:00 p.m., is that correct, Mr. Eason?" Hathorne begins.

"Eastman. Yes, Haines Eastman the Third, actually. We are an old Myrtle Beach family. My grandfather homesteaded on the Clearwater in 1888 and traded with the Nez Perce."

"Thank you, Mr. Easeman, but we don't have as much time as we would like to hear your expostulations about family genealogies," the judge says, shaking his head. "We want to know what you saw and heard that night during your security checks around the premises."

"Well, yes, I do understand judge, I just wanted to let you know that in spite of my modest employment, I am a member of a very old and veneered family of Idahoans. Circumstances beyond the Eastmans' control have left our clan rather inseminated but we cling to the land as farmers. We still consider ourselves part of the landed genitalia."

"Thank you, Mr. Eastman," Hathorne says. "So could you describe for the court what you saw and heard on the night of August the 18th at the Cherry Hill?"

"I would be most happy to, Mr. Hathorne. That night I came on duty after the prayer meeting at the First Congregational Church of the Advent of Jesus the Nazarene or what some of us call the First CAGIN. I came on to work around eleven and then 'bout half past did my rounds. Weren't a whole lot of guests staying there that night even though it was the perk of the summer. Maybe four or five cabins were lent. Anyway I remember strolling past number nineteen real steely like, you know not tiptoeing or nothing but just snickering around real mousey and yep, lights were on, and I could hear some strange emissions behind those Phoenician blinds.

"What did you hear, Mr. Eastman?"

"I heard a bunch of talking behind that green door. I heard, I heard, loudly and clear, I heard the word. The A word, Mr. Hathorne, I heard it."

"Could you tell the court what that A word was please?"

"In front of these ladies, I rightly don't know if I shouldn't. This is not a word for tender ears, Mr. Hathorne. I'm not so sure but I may be moving into terror incognito by saying such things out loud."

"Was the word 'abomination,' Mr. Eastman?"

"Objection, your honor. Counsel is leading... Excuse me, under the circumstances I withdraw...." Ruth realizes, I guess, she better stay out of the way at this point.

"I heard it, your honor, I heard them say it. More than one time. One of them was reading from Leviathan. I heard those perverts quoting from the good book, and my heart grew sunken. So sunken. Then I stopped in my tracks. I haltered, Mr. Hathorne, and I felt my duty to see into the darkness of that den of infamy. I felt my duty come forth, Mr. Hathorne. I saw my eyes between the slits of the blinds, and what I saw is not fit for the ears of any woman or child on God's green earth. I heard the word, your honor, and I looked into the darkness of the nineteenth cabin, and my eyes saw what it should never have seen. Your honor, I swear, I saw that man. That man at that desk right there, that table right there. I saw him, your honor. With no pants, in his undergarments in front of that poor child. I saw his thighs, Mr. Hathorne. I saw his naked haunches, your honor. And that poor boy, he had the good book in his hands. There in his fingers he held King James, he did. And it grieves my sorry soul to say that boy too sat there with his panties, naked to all the world, the good book in his white lap."

"His white lap did you say?" the judge asks.

"Yes, the boy was naked as a jailbird, he was, not a stick of clothing on him but for them Jockey shorts those young boys wear nowadays. Nothing else on him. Only the Bible hiding his privates. Your honor, I just feel like I am no longer culpable of speaking about this matter any further. I just can't speak on this subject one more minute."

"Mr. Eastman," Hathorne states quietly, approaching the box. "Let's calm down for a moment. I am going to ask you some quick questions, and then I think Miss Libby will probably not have much more. We do not want to cause you further embarrassment. I ask only that you provide us with the facts. Did you see the defendant make any suggestive signs to the boy that could be construed as sexual overtures?"

"Construed, Mr. Hathorne? Construed? That man had nothing on save for his loin cloth, and he was lain out on that bed like some kind of divan or something. I don't know what else to say."

"And the boy, where was he?"

"He was on the other bed sitting up with skivvies, nothing but, and that sacred tome in his hand. He had King James in the palms of his hands."

"Now you have testified that you saw the defendant and the youth in their underpants. Were you able to detect anything about their anatomy that disturbed you in terms of sexuality?"

"Mr. Hathorne, I am a Christian man. I believe in Revelations. I am a pillar of the church, I am. A pillar of salt of the earth. Born and raised on the Clearwater. I speak the truth before Adam whose fig was more covered by leaves than that man at the table over there with his hairy legs sticking out of those loose—"

The judge interrupts. "Thank you, Mr. Eastman, but we have a very busy docket, and we are trying to ascertain some facts about this case. Tell me, quite simply, were either of the two individuals in question aroused when you saw them through the window?"

"Your honor, I am deeply moved by your question. I believe in Solomon, yes, and you are his successor, judge. Yes, you are the judge of Judges. These men wore white cloth over their gentries, and the folds of this clothing your honor seemed to me to be stretched."

"So in your opinion, these two had erections?"

"There were bumps, your honor. I cannot say more. I know nothing about their elections, but I testify to humps in those loins. Before our lord, I can say lumps. I know of these lustings."

"That is sufficient, Mr. Eastman."

"Thank you, Mr. Eastman," Hathorne continues. "You made another round later that evening, I understand. Could you describe your second visit to nineteen?"

"I saw nothing on that second visitation, your honor. My eyes were averted from the works of Satan. The near vocation of sin. I am contrite, your honor, if nothing else. My prayers are said. But as I approached that room, there came from that sticky den, your honor, sounds that would make a judge blush. There came such gurglings, such breathing, such moans, such groans. Jayzuss, Mr. Hathorne. The light of day should not allow such a travesty. It is not decent. This cannot be said in open court."

"Your honor," Ruth says, "May we approach the bench for a moment?" Counsel and the judge recess into chambers, while the rest of us shake our heads. This guy is a nut job. The jury has come out of its stupor, now perked up with the witness's performance. His circumstantial evidence has suddenly become comic, even though the stakes are serious.

When the questioning of the old geezer resumes, Ruth establishes he is hard of hearing and needs glasses. He thought he'd heard two voices but was not sure, and the sounds included heavy breathing and some groaning, but he did not know what exactly to attribute those sounds to. Within minutes, the bailiff is conducting the confused Mr. Eastman out of the courtroom to the shaking head of his aging wife.

8. RUTHLESS

Ruth is a trial lawyer from Coeur d'Alene who represents plaintiffs in medical malpractice and personal injury cases. She usually doesn't handle criminal law, but Dad coaxed her down here to help Coach. The two attorneys sit up all night drinking whiskey and reminiscing about the Berkeley days. My Mom isn't jealous for some reason, even though Ruth is not married but just living up there on the lake with her mysterious partner. Her "friend" is named Anna LaPlante, a Blackfoot girl from Browning, up east of Glacier, and though I'm plenty naïve about grown-ups and their arrangements, I'm getting the hint Ruth may be on my side.

When I ask her what I'm supposed to say when and if Hathorne puts me under oath, Ruth just advises me to tell the truth.

"Coach," she says, "is a stubborn SOB who is convinced he did nothing wrong even though we both know what you guys were up to is sufficient to convict, regardless of consent or motive or extenuating circumstance. Especially in the atmosphere of this little Boise witch-hunt. Those circumstances could be relevant in sentencing. But we'll be hard-pressed to convince a jury that Coach's relationship with you does not violate the statutes. I've told him a million times to plea down, but he won't listen. I can't knock any sense into him, so I have to do what I can to defend him."

What Ruth doesn't know is that Coach feels no obligation to tell the truth under oath because a law that turns our love into a felony in his mind is itself immoral and unconscionable.

"If the law and the military can lie to me," he told me, "then I don't feel the need to tell the truth under their hypocritical system."

But do I feel that way too? Can I, after swearing on that same King James Bible, lie about what happened because the law is a lie? Can I deny what we did with our tongues that night, deny the proof that would hold us guilty of sodomy as well as lewd and lascivious conduct? I keep facing these questions in my head every night even as Ruth asks me how I'm holding up and reminds me this mess will soon come to an end, telling me that my dad is still trying to convince Coach to plead guilty and mitigate his sentence.

We're all super tense, keyed up. Ruth keeps telling me how worried Coach is about me, how he asks about my mood first thing every morning. Coach and I have only minimal eye contact in court. Rarely, if ever, does he turn around. I have pleaded with Dad and Ruth to remind the DA I don't want to press charges. But Blaine Hathorne is not interested in my protests. He needs a conviction, and Marty Williams is one of his major catches in the dragnet. The other big fish have gone unnamed in the press and uncharged in court. I have said nothing about Mr. U to anyone but Dad, and since November his name has not been fit to print in the news.

Coach is out on bail in an undisclosed location somewhere, and I am determined to find out where. I have to see him, especially if the conviction is as certain as Ruth thinks. I have to get out of the house and follow Ruth somehow or tail Coach after one of the court sessions. I'm even more determined after I see him slumping at the table once Schleiner is called as a witness.

"Mr. Schleiner," Hathorne asks him. "Did you have occasion to interview the defendant?"

"No sir."

"Did you interview the young man the defendant allegedly molested?"

"Your honor," Ruth objects. "This is hearsay. Counsel's choice of language is entirely prejudicial. We have been over this before. My client did not molest anyone."

"The operative term is 'allegedly,'" Blaine Hathorne shoots back. "How long must Miss Libby play this semantic game? Legal pederasty, your honor, is a form of molestation under the law."

"I will overrule your objection, Miss Libby, but I admonish the jury that the prosecutor's use of terminology is purely conjectural unless and until he proves his sodomy case against the defendant."

"Your honor," Schleiner continues, "I did interview the youth, but I cannot report that he provided any information about the defendant in spite of my repeated questioning."

"So why are you here?" the judge asks him, looking at Mr. Hathorne.

"Your honor," the prosecutor states, "our office has become privy to some information concerning the defendant's past military record that may be relevant to the credibility of the plea."

Ruth rises and proceeds to explode when she hears such a suggestive statement in open court, and she gets even more exercised when she sees the witness pull out a set of classified documents from his briefcase. The defendant's military records, she states, have not been previously proffered to the defense and are highly prejudicial even if mentioned in passing.

Counsel storms into chambers again while the rest of us wait in recess for at least an hour, Coach staring at the table. He must know as well as I do what's coming, even if his past military record is only admissible once his line-up of character witnesses testifies for the defense. Ruth must have some knowledge of Coach's past, and her current grandstand will only delay the inevitable. What happened in chambers is still a bit of a mystery, but the lawyers reach some deal about authenticating the military records, or at least portions of them. When they come back in, Schleiner answers a lot of questions about his knowledge and access to the files of government employees.

"Mr. Schleiner, can you please inform the jury what you have discovered about the defendant's past?" Hathorne finally asks. Ruth has not prevailed, and Coach's medical history is about to be dragged out in open court. I am cringing and helpless, thinking about how excruciating it was even for him to tell me his story in private.

"Yes. Luckily, my military background has given me access to Private Williams's blue discharge from the Army a few years ago—neither honorable nor dishonorable. He suffered trauma over the loss of a fellow soldier during a reconnaissance mission in Korea. From the documents I have accessed in my capacity as a governmental official, I have learned—"

"Your honor, this is hearsay," Ruth states.

"But the records are officially unavailable," Blaine retorts. "The witness is testifying to what he discovered from his investigation and reading of this confidential dossier. Your honor, Mr. Schleiner is an investigator working for the government. He has gathered facts from looking over documents only officials like himself have access to. Producing Williams's full psychiatric file from Hawaii is simply impossible and illegal, but the witness has read them."

"There is no evidence of any psychiatric file at this point," Ruth says, "and I find it highly prejudicial that counsel should raise an unproven issue."

"Miss Libby," the testy judge states, "you have agreed to let this investigator testify to what he knows about the defendant as long as you have an opportunity to cross-examine him. I can't see how these objections, which might be technically valid, will further our evidentiary path here. The witness is an officer of the law who has consulted certain discharge documents and medical records. My sense is that he has a right to do so, especially since the records are for the most part not publicly available. I will overrule your objection."

"I would like the record to reflect my exception to this ruling, your honor."

"You have every right to do so, counsel. Proceed, Mr. Hathorne."

"Could you tell the jury what you were able to ascertain about the defendant's military history, Mr. Schleiner."

"Yes," the witness continues. "We know that the defendant received a discharge after a period of rehabilitation, once he was removed from Korea as a result of the death of his companion," Schleiner testifies. "He spent many weeks in hospital at a rehabilitation center in Honolulu and was treated by a very well-known physician, Dr. Hall, who is a disciple of the famous psychiatrist Edmund Bergler. Bergler has written many books on masochism and homosexuality and has worked on techniques of aversion therapy including electromagnetic shock treatments. I have consulted with Dr. Bergler in the past and have a tremendous admiration for his writings.

"Though I was unable to read all of Private Williams's psychiatric records, I do know he was treated by Dr. Hall in Honolulu where much of this rehabilitative therapy with misguided young soldiers takes place. While a letter from Dr. Hall appended to Williams's discharge does not confirm or deny Williams's relationship to sexual deviancy, it does state Private Williams underwent electroshock therapy during his stay in Hawaii, and he hoped the treatment, along with Mr. Williams's new turn toward Catholicism, had cured him of his sexual problem."

"Thank you, Mr. Schleiner. Is it your opinion Mr. Williams had a homosexual relationship with the soldier who was killed?"

"Objection. Calls for speculation. The witness has no way of knowing what transpired between the defendant and his fellow soldiers."

"Sustained."

Hathorne tries again. "Of course, you cannot know exactly what took place in Korea in regard to the defendant's honorable discharge. Only the defendant will be able to provide the jury with that information if and when he testifies." Hathorne casts his eyes over to Coach, whose decision to testify is still, according to Ruth, up in the air. "However," the DA goes on, "from your investigation of this case and your vast experience with these mental disorders in your recent employment, can you say it is highly likely Private

Williams underwent Dr. Bergler's aversion treatment for homosexuality tendencies?"

"What I can say, Mr. Hathorne, is that the vast majority of cases emerging from Dr. Hall's electro therapy practice in Honolulu concern themselves with sexual deviancy and Private Williams's discharge is consistent with those cases."

"Thank you," Hathorne says, on the balls of his feet as he pirouettes toward the defense table. "Your witness, Miss Libby."

"Good afternoon, Mr. Schleiner," Ruth says. "Tell me, have you ever had sex with another man?"

"Your honor," Blaine perks up. "This question is entirely irrelevant and incriminating. Mr. Schleiner is not on trial here."

"Mr. Schleiner claims he is an expert in investigating homosexuality. I am just trying to determine whether he has firsthand knowledge of it."

"Sustained. It is irrelevant, Miss Libby. Police do not have to commit crimes to investigate them."

"Mr. Schleiner, could you tell the court who hired you to come to Boise to conduct this witch-hunt?"

"Objection, your honor. Miss Libby's characterization of this trial is highly prejudicial."

"Sustained," Judge Danforth says. "Miss Libby, be careful. You are an officer of the court. I would remind you not to make a mockery of the process you are a part of."

"My apologies, your honor. I am just thinking about how many families this investigation has disrupted if not destroyed. I suppose we need to take judicial notice of this tragedy, Mr. Schleiner, and move forward. So leaving aside any firsthand knowledge you may have with the experience of homosexual attraction, could you tell the court how you came to arrive in our town?"

"I received a call from a private client who wished to conduct an investigation."

"Could you tell us who paid you to come to Boise and hunt homosexuals?"

"I am not at liberty to disclose my client's name."

"Were you instructed not to divulge the persons who paid you to come from Washington to conduct your investigation?"

"I was asked to keep that information confidential, yes."

"So you feel perfectly justified in reporting on your interpretation of my client's confidential medical records but are entirely unwilling to tell us who paid you to come to our town as a hired gun?"

"I am not at liberty—"

"But you *are* at liberty to conclude that people like my client engaged in conduct you have no firsthand knowledge of?"

"Your honor, Miss Libby, is badgering—"

"Mr. Hathorne, I agreed to allow you to call this witness to testify to information you did not disclose previously to the defense under the condition that I have leeway to ask Mr. Schleiner any questions I might have. Now it seems you are trying to renege on that agreement."

"Counsel," Judge Danforth says. "Let's end this quarrel and proceed. Mr. Schleiner, you are instructed to disclose the name of your private client.

"I was contacted by Emery Bosse on behalf of the Arid Club here in Boise."

"And the Arid Club is a group of wealthy male executives and politicians in town who occasionally meet to discuss civic and business affairs, are they not?"

"I believe so."

"And this power elite hired you to ferret out homosexuals in town, am I correct?"

"Yes, they feel Boise faces a serious underworld problem, a ring of older men who were preying on teenage boys, paying them for sexual favors in parks, the library, and public gymnasiums."

"To your knowledge, did Mr. Williams ever pay for sexual favors in the parks or anywhere else?"

"Not to my knowledge."

"You have told the court you conducted upwards of sixty interviews. Did anyone in those interviews tie Coach Williams to payment of teenagers for sexual favors?"

"Payment, no. His name did come up in relation to the boy in question, however." I cringe at the mention of my new no-name.

"In relation to anyone other than the young man in question?"

"I do not believe so."

"So Mr. Williams was not part of this ring, you spoke of, was he Mr. Schleiner?"

"Well…"

"To your knowledge, he did not pay for sex. Am I wrong, Mr. Schleiner?"

"He did not, Miss Libby. Not to my knowledge."

"Not to your knowledge, I see. Mr. Schleiner, do you have any *knowledge* of the so-called Kinsey scale?"

"I have heard of it, yes, but I—"

"At least you have knowledge of something, Mr. Schleiner. We are happy to know that you have done some study of this field that you are an expert in. The Kinsey scale measures one's proclivity for homosexual behavior, if I am not mistaken. Alfred Kinsey propounded the notion that the proclivity for homosexuality exists in almost every individual, many of whom fall in the middle of the scale between absolute heterosexuality to absolute homosexuality. Where would you put yourself on that scale, Mr. Schleiner?"

"Objection, your honor," Hathorne growls. "We have—"

"I withdraw the question. You stated Dr. Hall reported he hoped Private Williams had been cured of his sexual problem. Did Hall's report state specifically what that problem was?"

"Not in so many words."

"Does the report state Private Williams had experienced shell shock?"

"No."

"Does it state that the twenty-year-old Private Williams had a nervous breakdown as a result of holding a soldier's blown-up brains in his hands?"

"No."

"So you don't really know what happened to the defendant in Korea, do you Mr. Schleiner?"

"Well, I am able to draw a probable conclusion based on my familiarity—"

"But you don't really know for *sure*, do you Mr. Schleiner?"

"Well…"

"Are you married, Mr. Schleiner?"

"Objection. Irrelevant."

"Your honor, I have been given leeway by consent—"

"Overruled. But be careful, Miss Libby. Regardless of the agreement, Mr. Schleiner is not on trial here."

"I am divorced, Miss Libby, though I don't see what business it is of yours."

"And you have been divorced for over five years, yes? And you live alone in Washington D.C., am I wrong? And you do not currently have a fiancée, do you, Mr. Schleiner? And you spend most of your days on Army bases interviewing soldiers about homosexuality, am I wrong Mr. Schleiner?"

"Exactly what is going on, here, your honor? These insinuations by counsel are completely irrelevant," Hathorne states, on his feet now.

"I am trying to establish the credibility, or should I say incredibility of the witness, your honor. Nothing more, nothing less. Mr. Schleiner holds himself as an expert on homosexuality. He feels it his duty to root out deviates from our society, yet he himself spends the better part of his life with these deviates. I withdraw the question, your honor."

She starts again. "Of all the hundreds of interviews you and Mr. Bosse have conducted in your house on 16th Street, of all the boys and men you have interrogated and asked to sign statements in the dark living room with your coffee and cookies, Mr. Schleiner, how many incidents of men paying for sex with teenagers sixteen or under have you uncovered would you say?"

"Well, we can't be sure. Our work is still ongoing."

"You're still weeding out the deviates after eight months of interrogations?"

"I prefer to call them interviews, Miss Libby. No one is under arrest when we chat with them."

"Would you say more than ten cases of paid sex with boys under sixteen have occurred?"

"Not more than ten as of yet."

"Could it be less?"

"It could."

"So this underground homosexual ring that was written up in *Time* magazine may involve less than ten boys under sixteen years of age, am I wrong? And over how long a period of time might these assignations have taken place? All in the summer of 1955, Mr. Schleiner?"

"No. We have uncovered deviates who go back many many years."

"And many of these deviates are convicted felons, are they not?"

"A few."

"And most of the cases of homosexuality you have uncovered are between consenting adults, are they not, Mr. Schleiner?"

"These are still crimes against nature, Mrs. Libby. These perversions are taking place all over our country, and they have now raised their ugly heads here in the Rocky Mountains. I am proud to be part of a team seeking to rid our communities of these sick individuals. We must seek to eradicate this virus wherever it appears, whether in West Point or West Boise."

"Thank you for your work, Mr. Schleiner. You have stated these 'vermin,' as you have called them in the newspaper, appear in all walks of life and every corner of the American fabric, undermining our values as citizens of this great country. Do you believe this disease may exist in the Arid Club?"

"I do not know, Miss Libby. Even the Bar Association might—"

"Could there be homosexuals among the Mormon bishops and elders who have hired you? Is it possible, Mr. Schleiner?" Ruth's questions suddenly raise my hackles. What is she driving at?

"Anything is possible, Miss Libby."

"Thank you for sharing that insight. How many members of the Arid Club have you interro—excuse me—*interviewed* Mr. Schleiner?"

"I don't believe we have had occasion to pull any of those individuals into the house. But you'd have to confirm that with Emery Bosse."

"So the vermin who may exist in the Arid Club have yet to be detected? Why is that, Mr. Schleiner? Why have we convicted one bank officer and arrested a number of transient garment shop workers and now a schoolteacher? And why have most them had sex with boys like McKellar and Halverson who are eighteen or over? Why is that, Mr. Schleiner?"

Counsel objects again, furiously. Ruth withdraws her question. I am waiting for her to mention Freddie's dad, but she says nothing.

"One final question, Mr. Schleiner. You have had so much experience ferreting out these horrible criminals from our country, wiping clean the filth of homosexuality from our otherwise perfect society. In all your vast experiences with these menaces to our society, have you ever come across a murderer, Mr. Schleiner?"

"I may have, but I would have to check my records."

"How many?"

"Well...I am not sure...any—"

"Have any of them been plotting to overturn the government, Mr. Schleiner?"

"I would have to check my records."

"Have you run across in your vast interviews, Mr. Schleiner, two men who were in love with one another?"

"Well—"

"We know, Mr. Schleiner. You'd have to check your records. You'd have to see exactly how many individuals who have found happiness and joy in their lives have been put behind bars because of your wholesome *interviews*. Mr. Schleiner. I think I can say on behalf of most Boiseans, we are glad we could line your pockets for a few months, Mr. Schleiner, but we are not going to be very upset when you get on your flight back East. No one in this town will be too sad to see you head to another peaceful town to wreak havoc. I have nothing further, your honor."

9. JACK BUTLER

I'm sitting Dr. Butler's waiting room reading the *Reader's Digest Condensed* version of *Rob Roy* while I wait for Butler to set his clock on my one-hour drama. Once five thirty rolls around, the Tommy Cadigan show will be over and the next soap opera waiting in Butler's lobby. By then the doc will have ingested the *Reader's Digest* version of my life as a witness in *State of Idaho v. Martin Williams*. His billable hour, yours truly, will be on his bicycle experiencing the magic of psychotherapy.

"How's Tommy today?" the cheerful counselor begins, crossing his legs as he sits in his club chair, steaming cup of instant coffee on the table beside him. "How you holding up with the trial?"

"Coach got raked today. They dredged up his Korea stuff, and I could see him about to lose it. He has these things you know."

"What things?"

"He has these outbreaks, these outbursts left over from the war and stuff and his family. He loses it for a while. And with this jerk Schleiner…"

"The guy you saw in the house on the sixteenth?"

"The same. He was testifying to Coach's thing in Korea."

"His thing?"

"Yea. I told you about it. Coach watched his army buddy get shot, and he flipped out. Schleiner got hold of the records and started talking about his dead friend Desi, about the shock therapy the Army gave Coach to cure his proclivities, about his blue discharge for being a homo. Thank god Ruth kicked butt, showed him up as the *Have Gun Will Travel* guy that he is. But who knows if it makes any difference with this jury? Coach, some are saying, was convicted the minute he was arrested, but maybe Ruth can make some justice. I don't know what I'm going to do if I get called to the stand. That's what driving me crazy right now, doc, if you want to know."

"What *are* you going to say when the DA asks you what happened between you and Coach Williams?"

"I wish I knew." We sit there staring at one another. Butler loves his pregnant pauses, loves to see me squirm. Mom is paying him to squirm me. He's not actually a bad looking guy for his age, forties or whatever. He's in pretty good shape, and I'd say fairly *guapo* for a Mormon. He uses his manly man stuff to suck me in, he does. But I'm on to his tricks. He wants me bawling on the floor talking about my cold and distant father, my overbearing mother, my identification with her need for a penis. Fuck Oedipus in the ass. Some things just fly into my head. I would never say anything like that out loud, especially to Dr. Butler

"Tommy, you're going to get called. I don't think you have a right to take the Fifth Amendment as a juvenile, to be honest. You can try, but the courts haven't extended that right to kids yet. Look, if you don't answer, I am sure Ruth has told you how it will look to the jury."

"But if I do talk, tell them the whole truth and nothing but, then Coach goes to jail even if I can convince the jury that I started it. The truth is not going to set Marty Williams free. It's going to put him behind bars. If I don't say jack, then you're right. They'll probably send him down river anyway. What do you want me to do?"

"I'm not here to tell you what to do."

"Yea sure. I know you're doing a favor for my Mom, your long-lost friend. What kind of favor, might I ask?"

"*Tommy.*" Mr. B finally raises his voice and sits up in his chair, uncrossing his legs. I've hit a minor neuron somewhere. "Look, we've been through this. I am not here to turn you into a happy frat boy next year. I'm not here to straighten you out. That's your decision."

"Why are you here then?"

"That's my question for you, young man." He's getting a little bit pushed out of shape at this point. "You can walk out the door right now, if you wish. I'm not stopping you."

"I need to see Coach," I say, changing the subject. "After what went on down there today, I have to get a hold of him or he's going to go under. I know it."

"You don't know *anything*. Seeing him would be acting against the advice of your friends, counselors, and parents."

"What friends? I don't have any friends anymore. Come on, Doc, let's face it. This sitch sucks. I got you, I got Dad, I got Ruth. Mom is completely wigged out. Freddie is sequestered out in Nampa, and Skip is just as scared shitless as I am. He won't even talk to me."

"And how are you feeling about this situation?" he asks. Here we go, I thought, throwing this whole mess back on me. Isn't that sweet? Let's share our emotions, work through our little problems. So much for the talking cure.

"I'm feeling alone, mad, scared," I pause. "But I'm glad to have you, I guess." That last part comes out of nowhere.

He offers a smile that I can't help but think is rather sad. "I appreciate that. Now tell me what you are mad about, what you are scared of."

"I'm mad at Schleiner, the DA, the entire stupid police state, the Mormons who have locked up Freddie. And scared of them too, scared of their power to send Coach away from me. Scared of a lot of things—the lawyers, McKellar."

"Why McKellar? He's out of the picture now. He's done his damage. Are you still attracted to him?"

I sigh. "Well . . .not to him. But to his body...and maybe to *him* too, even though he roughed me up on Monday in the bathroom of the library." That tidbit slips out.

"He what?"

"He just showed up in the library coming out of a stall in the bathroom with a trick when I was peeing, and he let me have it for ratting on him to Ruth. He got me in a headlock and then started twisting my arm and punched me in the stomach. Luckily, I got away with a random elbow that smashed his balls. I ran for it. Look, don't tell anyone, okay?"

"Tommy, what goes on in here is totally privileged, but I can't permit or condone criminal behavior."

"It wasn't a crime. Kurt was just pissed off that I humiliated him in court." I realize that Kurt was left with nothing now: his star fell long ago, before he had dropped out of Boise State, but he needed company as he plunged to Earth hard.

"What happened in that bathroom?"

I start crying when I hear the panic in Butler's voice. "Nothing." My head remains down as stupid tears well up. "It's over. He just tried to…he had me slammed against the door and had my pants down. He just tried to…I don't know…and my arm, god, it's still sore. But I got away, thank God. My elbow hit a sensitive spot. I got out of there before he could do anything more to me."

"Why didn't you tell anyone? I have to report this to the police."

"Please don't. Please." Weeping and begging, my hands on my head, I'm unable to look at Butler.

"Why are you trying to protect him?"

"Because he's a queer kid. Like me. Like Coach. McKellar's got enough problems without going to jail for screwing with me. I'm tired of being screwed by society. I'm not turning Kurt in no matter what he tries to do to me. I'd rather watch my back until I get out of this place."

"He tried to…to rape you. For the love of god," Butler says, staring at me now with astonishment. "And it's not your duty to protect a thug like McKellar just because of his sexual proclivity."

"You're right." Agreeing with the animated Mr. Butler is a rare occurrence. "I need time to think. Do you promise not to tell anyone until we meet next week?" I realize I've dug myself into a hole. I have told a Mormon elder that a man tried to rape me, throwing an ethical dilemma in his lap that might move him to go public. I need to put my shrink off, let him cool down. I have no intention of ever rat-finking on Kurt, but I want to stave off Mr. B's reaction. Butler doesn't really know what it's like to be queer in Boise, Idaho in 1956. For all his tea and sympathy, he can't understand what we face. He'll never know, no matter how hard he studies the subject. I've hurt Kurt enough, and he's hurt me back. Someone needs to beat the shit out of him and tell him to grow up and fall in love with another football player somewhere. Tell him to go to West Hollywood. He would fit in perfectly with the beautiful people if he just got out of our woods and got his act together.

10. LO

That night, I sneak down to Dad's office and rifle through the Williams file in search of an address. I find the name of a trailer park in Meridian, five miles west of town. It's at least an hour's bike ride across some pretty hairy roads. Memorizing the address on West Amity, I figure I can be there by midnight if I slip out of the house in fifteen minutes and keep the dog quiet.

The waxing moon makes the start of the ride fairly easy, but once I get out of my neighborhood, the roads narrow and there is no shoulder. When headlights come up behind me at forty miles an hour, I have to bail off to the gravel to save my skin, then find my way back to the pavement. In fact, most drivers would jump at the chance to accidentally run one of those anti-Americans cyclists off the road. Another set of headlights seems to interrogate me every other minute. Why so many cars at this time of night? And are they brushing past me at breakneck speed?

I veer down to a less busy east/west road named Victory. It runs through a neighborhood that steadily deteriorates from well-kept clapboard colonials to run-down ranch homes and junkyards guarded by German Shepherds, nurseries, lumber yards, and finally Shady Lanes trailer park. I am looking for 4F through the winding circles of cul-de-sacs in the dark. My hands are numb. I have no gloves, just a hat and parka. Another car comes up behind and passes me as I halt at a corner in the trailer court. Menacing headlights will not leave me alone, even here in this quiet residential area where I spot my trailer at last.

It's after midnight, I knock quietly on the metal screen door, desperate and cold. I'm worried because the Studebaker is nowhere to be found. No one answers. Not wanting to make noise, I walk around to a window and rap on the pane. "Coach, it's me. Let me in," I keep repeating in a throaty whisper until Miss Winfrey pulls the curtain back. Her hair is in curlers, her face aghast and wide-eyed. She motions me toward the front door. My heart sinks. What's she doing in Coach's trailer? Do I have the wrong address?

I'm completely confused as I creep around the trailer to the front door where Miss Winfrey, looking both ways out the door in her pink terry cloth bathrobe and flowered slippers, grabs me. She ushers me in, my head bent as I enter the low-ceilinged kitchenette to a built-in table and bench that passes for a dining room. The feathered tail of her setter Oscar is swishing and knocking into cabinets. Lights from another passing car peer through the windows as Miss Winfrey sits me down and shakes her head.

"What are you doing here at this time of night?"

"Looking for Coach."

"He's not here." She takes out of her purse a pack of Kents and searches for a match. "You need to go home, young man."

I scan the paneled room, its built-in benches and bolted linoleum table, florescent lights overhead and a set of inset shelves strewn with sloppy stacks of binder paper and dog-eared textbooks. Could I have written down the wrong address?

On the table sits a pile of themes, a red pen and the case for her glasses on top of them. Mine on Simon in *Lord of the Flies* is probably in there somewhere. Beside them, I see a copy of *Leaves of Grass* and some legal paper clipped with a black clasp. I see the familiar numbered margins and the formatted heading, *State v. Martinez*. A folded Braves t-shirt rests on a chair above some other clothes.

"I don't believe you." I glance at the laundry, briefs, and white socks under some folded tank tops. "I have to see him."

"You are in way over your head. If they find you…"

And then he appears and my breath catches. He stands barefoot in striped boxers and a white t-shirt. He leans forward, frowning, his hands pressed against the sides of the narrow hallway. His forehead is lined and arched, his boxer flap almost open, his stubble darkened by a day's growth. He looks at me with piercing bloodshot eyes above dark shadows that mark his aspect since his arrest.

Miss Winfrey blows smoke out her nostrils while I sit between them, not knowing what to think. Coach sighs deep, shakes his head and smiles.

"The boy can't be here," she says. "I'm taking him home right now."

"It's okay, Lo. We'll wait for you out here," Coach says.

Winfrey stabs out her cigarette and heads down the hall brushing up against Coach. He shuffles over and sits down on the bench next to me. He rubs his head, pretending to yawn a bit as he puts his palms between his thighs, shaking his head in disbelief. "It's one in the morning." He puts a hand on the top of my knee. "Why are you here?"

"I had to see you. After today, after Schleiner, what they dragged out. I had to make sure you were okay. Sitting there in the courtroom watching you so close, not even able to even say hello. It's so insane. But I guess you're not as bad off as I thought," I continue. "Sorry to break in on your two."

"Lois is putting me up. There are two bedrooms back there." He rubs the back of his neck. "Damn if you aren't jealous. I'm almost glad you are." He puts his arm around me and draws me closer. "I don't want to drag you through this mess any more. Ruth wants me to plead…your Dad does…Lo does. I don't want to give up, but I won't ruin your life over this stupid case, grandstanding on ridiculous principles. I'm probably going to do time whatever I plead. I want to teach them a lesson, but I can't screw up your future any more than I already have. I thought by now you'd be packing your bags and getting on a Greyhound for college, but Hathorne got me on the fast track. He's got me by the *cojones*."

My heart thumps away like a pile driver. "Don't give in. You promised me if we ever got caught, you would stand up for us. Both of us. You promised."

"You're a kid, buddy. You've got your future ahead of you. Maybe Ruth's right, maybe it's not worth jeopardizing your life for a battle we can't win—at least not here and now. Right now, you better get into Lois's car and head back. It's too dangerous."

"I miss you so much. You don't know..." I'm holding back again, there before the nailed-down table with its metal trim, next to Coach in his boxers and me in my jeans with my stupid tears and my penis need, sticking up into my pocket enough so I'd have hide it when Miss Winfrey walks back in. We are holding hands now. "Don't plead guilty. What do you want me to say on the stand when they call me? I could lie, deny I ever touched you."

Coach sighs, and I think it's the loneliest sound I ever heard a soul utter. "Do what your heart tells you. But tomorrow they're calling your friend Freddie. You need to stick to him, one way or another."

Me, I'm so confused, so grateful to find out Coach is not shacking up with Miss Winfrey. I just sit there feeling the dam about to overflow, feeling Coach's leg against mine, waiting for Mrs. Winfrey, who appears in no time, jangling her rabbit's foot. I hug Coach, his thick white shirt covering the dark hair of his solid chest, a chest that holds a hot heart beating against mine.

At least, no-nonsense Miss W is in control. Put the bike in the trunk. Keep your head down and shut up. Don't wake the neighbors. All of these commands come from her expressions without words, and I follow them in a total daze, barely realizing I might never be alone with Coach again. Winfrey raises an eyebrow, points a finger, lifts a white tennis shoe toward the trunk button. I slip into the front seat of the Plymouth.

The trunk stays open until we've driven slowly out of the park. We stop about a half mile down and get out to adjust the bike and shut the lid. We're about to get back in the car when a pair of headlights flashes in front of us, casting eerie blue shadows over us. Miss

Winfrey puts her hands to her eyes, and I stand there blinded, trying to figure out if the police have snuck up on us. The headlights look familiar enough. Turns out they were the same ones that have run me off the road a couple of times, the same red Chevy Bel Air with its round headlights and barracuda grill.

The car comes to a halt and two figures emerge. The silhouettes belong to Kurt and Hal Halverson, the hood from the monkey cages. I should have figured Kurt wouldn't leave me alone after our tangle in the library, but for some reason even now I think I can reason with him. The other guy, though, scares the bejesus out of me. Miss W is already walking toward them, as if to ward off their discovery of me, holding her ground in front of her car, arms folded, seemingly unfazed, a lot cooler than I ever imagined from watching her in the classroom talk about Richard Cory's ennui. I can't believe these guys have followed me out here. If they have. They may be on to Coach's location, waiting for a chance to create trouble. I am standing near the front tire leaning against a fender, wishing Coach were there.

"Hi." Kurt grins above his old letter jacket as he swaggers up, the headlights off now. "You know my friend Hal from the park, remember? Good evening, Miss Winfrey. How are you on this fine night?"

"Kurt, what do you want?" I ask him, exasperated but shaking too. "Why can't you just leave me alone? What did I ever do to you?"

"Well, you ratted on me to Williams's ball-crunching lawyer for starters, then you kicked me in the balls in the library if you recall, Cadigan. There's other shit too, that I'm not ready to go into right now, shit that's ruined my life for good."

"Like what?" I yell. "How did I possibly ruin your life?"

"Just shut up, faggot." Hal's hand rests in his leather jacket, ready to pull out a switchblade or something. "We can talk about that after we beat the shit out of you and empty Miss Priss's purse for starters. I might mention there will also be future payments in store, little woman, if you don't want Boise High to get wind of this rendezvous with one of your prize pupils in the middle of the night."

Hal is a lot more articulate than I suspected, but he's also a thug and I have no doubt he is ready to carry out at least most of his threats. Miss Winfrey looks at me with her gum-chewing jaw and her white Keds, a dubious glance telling me how pleased she is I have gotten her out of bed in the middle of the night.

"So, what do you boys want from us besides cash?" she asks. Everyone at Boise High assumes Miss Winfrey lives in a stucco uptown apartment on the third floor with two Siamese and a leather-bound set of Jane Austin. Instead, here she is leaning against the hood of her Plymouth tapping her foot and chewing gum.

"All your money," Halverson says. "For starters. Let's find out what you got in your purse. You can hand over some more tomorrow if you don't want the school board to pull your license. We can talk about that in a minute."

"And then we're going to ask you to leave tall Tommy behind for us if you don't mind," Kurt sounds sheepish, walking up and putting his arm around me. "Yea Tommy and I haven't quite gone all the way yet, have we big fella? Tonight's the night. Now you've turned me into a queer, I'm going to prove to you how much I enjoy it, Caddy. You're going to carry my clubs big time." He has me in his headlock again.

"Lay off," I plead. "And leave her out of this. As if I could do anything about it at that point. "I can't figure out why you're doing this? You're not facing any charges. Either of you. You've screwed up a lot of people's lives. You've made some money off guys, so big deal. Haven't you done enough damage?"

"Damage? You want to know about damage? After what I went through in that courtroom. You spoiled little mother, with your best fairy friend Freddie Udall and his big homo Daddy."

"Now there's a cash cow," Hal interrupts, "or steer, I should say. A steer, ha, ha. Am I right Kurt? Big Bishop Ed Udall is a fucking jackpot. I can't expect the Cadigans and Winfreys to be quite so flush, but money isn't everything, is it Tommy boy?"

Kurt releases me from his head lock but leaves his arm over my shoulder. I want to take off. I can outrun him in no time, but I can't leave Miss Winfrey behind with Halverson rifling through the car for her purse, which he finds on the front seat. She stands arms folded as he pulls her bag out of the car.

She looks at me and commands, "Tommy run for it." I don't need much convincing, twisting off Kurt's arm and taking off toward the field across the road.

McKellar gives chase. I look back for a second and see Halverson flustered, watching us. I keep running over the plowed field, clomping over dirt clods, as Kurt gains on me. Next thing I hear is a gunshot. We stop in our tracks. Kurt's face looks scared, and he turns to me in the moonlight with a look of dismay.

I run back toward the Plymouth. I'm scared out of my wits too, but have to reach Miss Winfrey. I've gotten her into this mess. Jesus. There's no time to swear, no time to do anything but run and keep my eyes open as the wet dirt goes by underneath my tennis shoes. As I approach the two cars, I look across the road and make out Miss Winfrey's silhouette against the hood of her car. Her arms are raised out toward the Chevy in what seems to be a plea.

Where's Halverson? I am too much of a chicken to do anything but stand frozen for a second before I race across the road to the rear of her Belvedere and then toward Mrs. W. I can't really speak—too fucking scared. I just jump up and run past her toward the Chevy, but as I am ducking down and heading toward the passenger side to find Halverson and face his gun, he jams the car into reverse and heads backward full speed, laying rubber and squeaking the wheel. I see glass on the ground from a broken headlight. I look back at Miss Winfrey gripping a handgun, her arms straight out and locked.

"Get in the car," she says.

Only when Halverson speeds away does she lower her gun and walk over to the driver's side, pick up her purse and wallet, get in, and start the car. We drive away slowly, leaving Kurt, who has come back, standing frozen by the side of the road, as if shocked and defeated. Ms. Winfrey tells me to put the stuff back in her purse.

A half mile down the road, she pulls over, pushes the safety on the revolver, hands it to me, and tells me to put it in the glove compartment and light her a cigarette, which I try to do. After four attempts, I finally get the lighter out of the socket and touch the shaking Kent to its element. I hand her the butt, my hand jittering uncontrollably. She reaches out and takes it, her fingers shaking as well.

"You better have one too," she says as we drive down Amity Lane to Victory and then up to Franklin. She shakes her head at me. I can see those pink rollers sticking out of her flowered scarf.

She wants to drop me off about a half mile from my house. We park and turn off the lights. She smokes another cig and tells me what happened. After I took off, while Hal was rifling through her purse, she jumped in the car and pulled out the gun from her glove compartment. The rest involved convincing that juvie she meant business, which led unfortunately to blowing out one of his headlights. She smiled as she said this.

"It's late. Someone may have called the police."

She talks to me about Coach while we sit in her car. "He lost it earlier that evening," she tells me. "I didn't know what to do but just sat on his bed holding on to him until he calmed down. There's a fight raging inside him, Tommy, between the promise he had made to you, about the advice to break it everybody, including me, is giving him. I have no idea what's going to happen. He's my closest friend, but we both know he has a wild Irish side, black Irish wild. He's on a mission, and is not to be deterred. There is no reasoning with him. Hell, I don't think he can even reason with himself.

"He keeps talking about you, keeps telling me how important you are to him, but he won't let it sink in that his homo crusade may well pull you both down. I keep asking him to come to his senses if he really cares about you. He listens, tells me I'm perfectly right, and then refuses to cop a plea. He's crazed, Tommy. He's crazed, crazed. But so lovable at the same time, he is."

Ms. Winfrey opens the trunk and waits for me to unload my bike. She says nothing. No advice. No reprimand. Just sends me off with another Kent in her hand and tells me she'll see me soon at school. I pedal home, tiptoe up the porch, creak open the door, just in time to shut Coco up after two barks. I take her upstairs for a couple hours of shuteye or un-shuteye—and dog holding.

11. BEST FRIENDS

Freddie refuses to reply to the prosecutor's salutation. His mother arrived early with him in tow. We exchanged glances when he arrived, and ever so lightly he lifted his hand gracefully toward me before he sat down beside his mom in the front row of the gallery. Gazing at his stern modesty, his fine features, and intense quiet reminds me of the comfort of his philosophy I have yearned for since he fled the house almost six months ago. How alone I have been these months without him to tease and tackle, to fret and commiserate with, and now to have him within my sight, but unapproachable, separated by the courtroom bar, not just a railing but a bar that makes our kind of love illegal.

"Mr. Udall. You are currently seventeen years old?"

"Yes."

"And you attend Boise High School?"

Freddie does not reply. He looks at the judge, his arms gripping the sides of the witness box. He appears stolid, unemotional, blinking, but I sense something underneath his veneer, some time bomb ticking

"Well, son?" Judge Danforth asks.

"Is that a question?"

"Yes, it is. Do you attend Boise High School?"

"Oh, I am sorry. I thought it was a statement. No, I do not," he answers.

"Very well," Hathorne states. They're off to a rocky start. It's nine in the morning, but the jury can see that Mr. Udall will not be a cooperative witness.

"Mr. Udall, could you describe for the court your relationship to the defendant?"

"Yes," Freddie answers, pausing on the possibility of being a semantic smart aleck and stopping there, then apparently thinking better of it from what I can tell. "Mr. Williams was my history teacher during junior year."

"Have you had any relations with him during your senior year?"

"I am not sure what you mean by relations."

"Dealings, connections, interactions. Did he act with you in Mel Dir's production of *Tea and Sympathy*?"

"Yes."

"And Mr. Dir's play, which was about a young man accused of homosexuality, closed down shortly before the defendant's arrest?"

"Objection," Ruth starts in. "Assumes facts not in evidence. It is also a multiple question. Is counsel asking for a description of the play or a confirmation of the play's closure?"

"Sustained."

"If you read the script, I think you will find that the play is about a false accusation of homosexuality, actually."

"Thank you for helping us out here, Mr. Udall. We would love to get you off the stand by noon. You were playing the part of that young homosexual in the play, were you not?"

"No, I was playing the role of Tom in Anderson's play."

"And is he not the homosexual?"

"No."

"Who is the source of the accusation in the play, then?"

"Tom is, but your honor," Freddie states, looking at the judge, "Tom is not an avowed homosexual in the script. He is accused of being one by his classmates and certain adults."

"Son," Judge Danforth asks, "could you try to be more cooperative this morning."

"Yes, your honor."

"Do you consider yourself a homosexual, Mr. Udall?" Hathorne asks.

"Your honor," Ruth states, "this question is incriminating and irrelevant. The witness is a minor."

"I do, actually," Fred states, pushing in his black frames and looking at the judge. "I realize many will think me too young to make such a statement, but I do consider myself primarily attracted to men."

The courtroom stirs, Mrs. Udall putting her gloved hand to her mouth, the jury murmuring. Even the newspaper reporters are rustling. I grip the seat of my chair, knuckles white, frantic about what my best friend might say next as he grapples with the truth. The judge quickly calls counsel to his chambers for a short recess. When they return, the judge strikes Freddie's testimony from the record and instructs the press to refrain from publicizing the information because of the witness's status as a minor.

"Mr. Udall," Hathorne continues. "We have called you here today to find out what knowledge you may have of relations between the defendant and Tom Cadigan. I know you are a smart kid, I know you have been instructed to be wary of me—"

"Objection, your honor, assumes facts not—"

"Sustained," the judge states. "Counsel, can we cut to the chase here? Mr. Udall, please tell the court what you know about the relations between Mr. Cadigan and the defendant.?"

Freddie looks directly at me and pauses for a few seconds. We are locked in a truth hug, the two of us, bound by our histories together. "I know Tommy is in love with Mr. Williams," Fred finally states.

"Your honor," Ruth is on her feet. "There is no foundation for this conclusion by the witness. How does Mr. Udall know about this love? On what facts does he base this conclusion?"

"Counsel," Danforth says, "I *do* think it is fair to ask Mr. Udall how he has gained his knowledge on cross-examination, so I will save you the trouble. Mr. Udall, tell us on what you base your knowledge of this love, as you call it."

"Oh, your honor, I have no doubt in calling it love of the deepest kind. I realize that word is thrown around everywhere on television, the radio and church, so I don't want to use it unless I mean it. I have watched Tommy when he talks about Coach, also seen the way he acts when he is around Mr. Williams during play practice and other times. He has also told me—"

"Objection, hearsay."

"The witness has a right to testify to statements made by another in regard to their state of mind or emotions at the time, you honor," Hathorne stated. "I think the law allows such testimony."

"Your objection is overruled, Miss Libby. Mr. Udall, your friend Tommy has stated to you he felt an emotional connection to the defendant?"

"Oh yes, your honor." Freddie turns his shoulders toward the judge. I am proud of him but frightened by his honesty. "There can be no doubt about it. Tommy is a very romantic person. Coach is someone Tommy has told me he can completely open up to, someone who listens to him, really *listens*. Coach has helped him with his workouts, told Tommy his life story. Coach's style—his personality, his body, everything—just sends Tommy into orbit. I've never seen him so happy, so dreamy.

"When Coach Williams came along last summer and they started working out and swimming together, Tommy just lit up. I know that sounds corny. But he is inspired. You can hear it in the way his sarcasm meter has gone down. I know you adults think it's impossible for a teenager to know what love really is, much less know what it is to love a man in his twenties. I know that. I can see it on your faces. I know you think love between a teacher and his student is improper, maybe even repulsive. But it's true. They're deeply in love.

"You ask me how I know Tommy is in love with Mr. Williams. I'm trying to explain what it's like to sit on the bed across from your best friend and have him talk to you about how a swimming lesson in a pool changed his life, how he and Coach had read books about the early fur traders and their Indian companions. I was completely envious and completely happy for him at the same time. I just wish I could be with him now when he's facing the reality that the man of his life may be going to jail because of their love for one another. I just wish we could still be friends."

The courtroom falls silent. Neither of the lawyers can move, and Coach, I can see as the back of my shirtsleeve absorbs tears, is gazing upward in a rare show of emotion. Some of the jurors sit stunned, unable to react to this testimony in light of their need to gather evidence about bodily parts and insertions.

"Thank you, Mr. Udall," the judge says, "the court appreciates honesty."

"Yes, indeed, that was a very moving testimonial," Hathorne states after another long pause, trying desperately to gain control of his witness with condescending sincerity. "And we thank you for it. Tell me, when Tommy Cadigan expressed his excitement about his relationship with Mr. Williams, did he ever discuss his sexual attraction to the defendant?"

Fred sounds more forthright now that he has made his main statement. Is he aware that the prosecutor is back on the body parts track, looking for evidence to convict? "Coach is a kind of a magnet. I think everyone in the school is attracted to him, both girls and boys. Not just the jocks. Mr. Williams is very charismatic. His history class is famous."

"So, Tommy Cadigan is aroused by Mr. Williams?"

"We all are. But Tommy's feelings go beyond infatuation. He's emotionally aroused too. That's the difference. Tommy's relationship has moved beyond the kind of school-girl crush that a lot of the football players have. It's been amazing to witness. I imagine it still is, but I haven't seen Tommy since the day before Mr. Williams was arrested."

"Did Tommy ever tell you he had sex with Mr. Williams?" Hathorne asks.

"Objection, your honor, hearsay. Counsel knows very well that the declarant is available to answer that question."

"Sustained. Mr. Hathorne, be careful. You are dealing with a minor on the stand, so I suggest that you act with propriety," the judge warns.

"Yes, your honor, I was just wondering if Tommy Cadigan ever expressed a feeling of euphoria as a result of a sexual experience with the defendant?"

"You may answer, young man."

Freddie pauses again and pushes in his glasses. I watch him rise up in his chair. I am cringing, almost shivering, my hands glued to my mouth, afraid of my friend's honesty. Freddie pauses, glances at the gallery and then speaks. "I am trying to figure out what you mean by express euphoria. Do you mean did he say, 'I'm euphoric?'"

Hathorne grins slyly. "Not exactly. What I am asking is this. You said Tommy was in—"

"Is."

"You said Tommy is in love with Mr. Williams. I am asking you if Tommy has ever expressed to you his feelings about having sexual relations with Mr. Williams."

"Objection. Assumes facts not in evidence."

"Sustained."

"Did Tommy Cadigan ever explicitly express his joy or excitement about his sexual relations with Mr. Williams?"

"Your honor," Ruth interrupted.

"Sustained. Counsel, I think you may have to wait. While young Udall can testify to Cadigan's expressions of emotion, I am not sure you can ask him to testify to expressions of emotion about the elements of criminal activity in question. We will have to get that evidence from the horse's mouth, I am afraid."

"Mr. Udall, did you ever observe Tommy Cadigan having sexual relations?"

"Well..."

"Your honor, the question is broad and vague. Mr. Cadigan is not on trial here."

The judge intervenes again. "Son, did you ever observe Mr. Cadigan having sex with the defendant?"

"No."

"Mr. Udall," Hathorne proceeds. "You have testified that you have not had any contact with Mr. Cadigan since the day before the defendant's arrest. During your final meeting with Tommy Cadigan, did you ask him about his relations with Mr. Williams?"

"Not specifically, no." Freddie starts to tap his foot nervously. We are both remembering that Sunday evening, both thinking about the way he grabbed his coat from the hook in our hallway and marched deliberately out the heavy wooden door.

"Did you discuss Tommy Cadigan's relations with the defendant during that final conversation?"

"Yes."

"What was the nature of those discussions?"

"What do you mean by nature exactly?"

"Mr. Udall," the perturbed judge says, "please. Describe the content of that conversation."

"We talked about how obvious it was that Tommy was elated when Mr. Williams agreed to take Mr. Garrison's place in the play. It was obvious to me and obvious to Mel Dir, I told him."

"Did you discuss any assignations that the defendant had with Tommy Cadigan? Did you mention any meetings that the two of them had had?"

"Yes," Freddie says hesitantly, not volunteering more than a yes or no as instructed. Hathorne is honing in.

"Describe the meetings that were discussed, please."

Freddie takes a deep breath. "We talked about the play of course. We mentioned the Cherry Hill cabins where they stayed."

"Any other meetings before the night in the motel?"

"I mentioned in passing a meeting they had in the park one night. I may have mentioned their workouts at the Y."

"Mr. Udall, was that meeting at the park you mentioned during your conversation at the monkey cages?"

"No."

"Do you know where it took place?"

"Yes." Freddie looked at the grimacing judge. "In the cedar grove one night in the summer."

"Did Mr. Williams pay Tommy Cadigan for that meeting?"

"Are you kidding? Tommy never took money from Coach."

"What happened in the cedar grove?"

"Objection. The witness has no firsthand knowledge of what happened and those that *were* there are available to testify."

"Sustained."

Hathorne attempts to extract more information about what Fred has learned about our meetings, but the judge continues to sustain Ruth's objections until the prosecutor finally gives the witness over to the defense. Hesitant, Ruth sits at the table for a moment, looking at her notes. I'm slouched in my gallery chair, beside myself with anxious helplessness, my hands still over my face as I watch Freddie blinking, the back of Coach's head unmoved, our fate uncertain.

"Mr. Udall, good morning," she begins. "Just a few follow-up questions. All of the information you've gained about Tom Cadigan's relation to Mr. Williams comes from Tom Cadigan, am I correct?"

"Not all of it. I've watched the two of them during the rehearsals. I saw them in the classroom during junior year."

"When you watched them, did you notice any solicitation by Mr. Williams in terms of sex? Did Mr. Williams make a pass a Tommy?"

"No. Mr. Williams does not make passes at people in school. He would never do that."

"You have no firsthand knowledge of the two of them engaged in any sexual act?"

"What do you mean by firsthand knowledge?"

"Have you ever seen them together kissing or engaging in other sexual conduct."

"No, I have not."

"Thank you, Mr. Udall. So, beyond what you observed at school and what Mr. Cadigan himself has told you, you do not have any knowledge of any sexual conduct between the defendant and Mr. Udall."

"Well, Mr. Dir informed me—"

"Thank you, Mr. Udall, let's move on."

"Your honor," Hathorne stated, "the witness has a right to answer the question."

"Sustained. What did Mr. Dir inform you about, young man?"

"Mel just told me everyone knew how Coach and Tommy were getting close at the gym. They were working out together quite a bit. A lot of the guys knew about it."

"Did Mr. Dir mention any sexual activity?"

"Nothing specific. Just rumors," Fred answers. The judge tells counsel to move on.

"Now you've stated, I believe, it is your impression Mr. Williams and Tommy Cadigan are very much in love, have you not?"

"Oh yes, madly, I would say."

"And you also testified you were envious and excited for Tommy, am I correct?"

"Yes. I believe I said something like that," Freddie answers nervously, pushing in his lenses but also sitting up in the witness chair more attentively.

"Why envious, Mr. Udall?" Ruth asks.

I'm startled by the question, suddenly on edge. What is Ruth driving at? "Because Tommy and I are best friends and I hate to see him—"

"Because you hate to lose him, right?"

"Well, we're best friends."

"But you want to be more than that, am I wrong? You want Tommy to yourself, don't you, Mr. Udall?" Ruth pushes on, raising her voice now, moving away from the defense table toward the witness.

"Well…"

"You want Tommy Cadigan to be madly in love with you, don't you, Mr. Udall?" Why is Ruth turning on Freddie, and why isn't Hathorne, who seems surprised by defense counsel's sudden attack, on his feet objecting?

"I…"

"And is it fair to say your impression of Coach and Tommy's mad love is influenced by your own jealousy? That you really don't know what is going on between them? Is it fair to say that, Mr. Udall?"

"No, it is not fair to say that. I love Tommy, but I want the best for him."

"If you want the best for Tommy, why did you walk out on him the night before Mr. Williams was arrested?"

"I didn't know he would be arrested the next day."

"Mr. Udall, please answer the question," Ruth states, becoming more adversarial. She is attacking my best friend for some reason, and I can't understand why. I want to yell at her to quit it. I am about to jump up from my seat and protest, looking wildly around the gallery. "Why did you walk out on Tommy after he told you... after you got the impression that he liked the defendant?"

"I—"

"Were you angry with him, Mr. Udall? Were you mad because he was not saying you were more important to him than Mr. Williams? Angry because you believed Mr. Williams might steal Tommy away from you?"

"No, I was upset."

"Upset, Mr. Udall? Were you upset or were you jealous? Wasn't it jealousy that made you walk out on your best friend that night? And wasn't it jealousy that made you come in here today with your speech about the defendant and Tommy?"

"No, no, it isn't like that all," Freddie cries. "Your honor, she has it all wrong. I love Tommy. We are best friends, blood brothers. I didn't leave Tommy that night because of his thing for Coach. That's not what happened at all. I left for another reason,"

"Then what was the reason you left?" Judge Danforth finally asks Freddie, his tone more curious, it seems, than anything else. He appears to want to give the witness a chance to explain himself, to gain some relief from Ruth's relentlessness, but the question only increases Freddie's nervous moving of his head from me to the jury to the judge, his glasses turning wildly, his eyes glancing back and forth at Ruth, at his mom, at me on the other side of the gallery, fingers pushing in his black frames almost obsessively now, as he grows more and more self-conscious. It's a moment of truth and Freddie, if anybody, knows what it means to take an oath, to swear to God.

"Well, Mr. Udall?" Ruth continues. "You're telling us you didn't leave your closest friend because he told you he was in love with the defendant. You're asking us to believe you are not motivated by jealousy. How then do you explain your storming off that evening?"

"Miss Libby, please let the boy answer the question."

"My father," Freddie states, almost inaudibly. "I left because of what Tommy told me that my father was doing with Kurt and Skip down at the monkey cages."

If the courtroom were not already in complete silence, no one could have heard him. He is clutching his seat as he speaks, staring at his mother when he finishes his confession.

Hathorne is on his feet. "Objection, objection. This line of questioning is entirely irrelevant. The witness's father has nothing to do with this case. Counsel has been badgering the witness, and Mr. Udall is now engaging in the very hearsay we have objected to for the last day or two."

"Sustained. The witness's final statement will be stricken from the record, and I admonish the jury to disregard it in their deliberations. Miss Libby, you have been arguing. You are presenting multiple questions, and harassing the witness. I am warning you, Miss Libby."

"I still love Tommy, your honor," Freddie blurts out. "I love Tommy, but I can't see him. I miss him every day.... When I went home last November and told my dad how I knew about him down at the cages, he grounded me. We moved to Nampa and I've been home schooled ever since."

Judge Danforth stands up and walks down to the witness box. He puts his hand on Freddie's shoulder, looks him in the eye, and tells him his testimony is over now, and he needs to calm down and return home with his mother. Freddie is angry, flustered, staring wildly at Ruth as he stumbles out of the box and zigzags, almost drunk with shock toward the bar. He stares at me as he approaches his mom, his look full of love and rage. My hands are in front of my wet face as I watch him pass me. Mrs. Udall and her son hurry out of the courtroom. Three or four reporters follow them. I am so mad at Ruth I can barely breathe.

12. AVOCATS

That night in our living room, a stone-cold Ruth apologizes but tells me her job is to discredit every witness who testifies against her client, whether it is Schleiner or Freddie or me. She isn't going to call me to the stand, but Hathorne has a right to. She tells me she had no choice. Freddie's statements established a romantic relationship between her client and me, and she had to try to disestablish it in any way she could. I will face "the same tactics" if, she says, she is still his lawyer by the time I am in the witness box.

'He almost fired me this afternoon and would have if he wasn't in some way heartened to see Mr. Udall get his comeuppance, especially since Freddie's dad has supported this entire reign of terror. But he is furious about what happened. I told him to plead guilty for the umpteenth thousandth time."

Ruth is so cynical. All in a day's work. I can't believe she is sitting on our living room couch with her feet up, sipping her scotch with my complicit father while she boasts about her strategy. What about my friendship, what does Freddie think of me now? She tells me she's sorry, lighting up another Winston. She is an advocate, hired to do whatever it takes to disprove the prosecution's case against her client and that means questioning the credibility of every witness.

"It's not a picnic, Tommy. And Coach knew that when he got into this debacle. I'm afraid it might get a lot messier," she admits, blowing smoke out her nostrils into our dim living room, Coco stretched out on the old braided rug, me standing in front of the fireplace with my hands in my jean pockets.

"The jury has to know they can't put someone behind bars unless there is proof of illegal conduct beyond a reasonable doubt. And my job is to let them know the only way they are going to get that proof in this case is by testimony from either you or Coach because there are no eyewitnesses other than the so-called victim and the so-called perpetrator. That brings this case down to what you are going to say when Blaine and I ask you about erections and ejaculations and the position of body parts at the Cherry Hill, at the hot springs, at the cedar grove or any other venues that you and my client may have conveniently avoided telling me about. It comes down to whether or not you are going to spill the beans. So help you God.

"Sorry, Tommy. Look, I'm on a run with the clichés, hon. It's late, and tomorrow doesn't look very promising, after this morning's drama. Tomorrow, it's going to be you telling the whole g.d. truth, or the prosecutor is going to try to call my mildly demented client. Your testimony may make the difference between one felony and another," she says, pronouncing the crime "fellow knee," slapping the sleeping dog's distended stomach.

Coco is beneath Ruth, half under the table. The dog lets out a long sigh. She is going through Freddie withdrawal. She hears his name, but can't figure out why he won't come when he is called. I can still picture him in the courtroom pushing in those glasses hard and fast about his nose as Ruth drove her nails in. He didn't deserve it. I don't care what her duty is as an advocate. It wasn't fair to Freddie.

"You hurt him," I say to her. "I don't care about your stupid hired-gun philosophy. You hurt Freddie and he's my blood brother. You hurt me, Ruth. I know you came down here as a favor for my Dad and me. I know you want to win. I know Coach and I are gambling, trying to change the world. But what you did to Freddie today after the whole thing with his Dad, with me telling him finally and him racing out of the house. And then getting pulled out of school into the horrible Youth Center and horrible suburb. It's bad news. A raw deal. Freddie is my best friend. I've never seen him so upset in my life.

"I don't care if there is an element of truth in what you were saying. Both of us have known Freddie wants to be tighter with me, but we also know we both have to go to college and make it in the world. That's what we talked about that night. He was happy for me. He was excited Coach and I were together just like he said on the stand. I can't believe you twisted it into some kind of jealousy. That version is just so wrong."

"You might be right," she says distractedly. I'm not even sure she's listening at that point. "But jealousy is rarely conscious of itself. Beware 'the green-eyed monster, that feeds upon itself.' You'll read *Othello* over in Dwinelle Hall since I hear you might be going to Berkeley. A little birdy has whispered. I'm on a couple of advisory boards over there and my sources say," she lowers her voice, and puts her hand to one side of her mouth, my father smiling at her now. "That there might be a chance you will be strolling down Telegraph Avenue pretty soon."

"Now, Ruth," my father says. "Don't get his hopes up."

"You're right, Kevin, my Kevin, *absolutement*. We are a bit premature in our ejaculation, as Haines Easement III would say."

"Thomas," my father says. "You better head upstairs. It's getting late."

"It's later than you think, big boy," Ruth throws in, twirling the sour mash in her tumbler. "It's time for you to hit el sacko and Vanzetti, mister. Tomorrow and tomorrow and tomorrow might be pretty creepy and pretty petty, I'm afraid. You must be ready. 'Readiness,' after all, 'is all.'" She is high now on her Shakespearean tangent, and nothing I can say will penetrate her numbness, the coating she needs to swallow the bitter pill of the law, the profession she has entered to make the world a better not a bitter place. As I am quickly learning, that may well be a distinction without a difference.

13. LIFEBUOY

How can I get to Nampa? It's too far away. I've lost my driving privileges, and I can't see biking fifteen miles. I don't even know Freddie's address and haven't heard from him in months. Whenever I 've tried calling, his mother answers and politely tells me Fred is unavailable and does not wish to speak with me. I've dialed him tons of time and now just hang up when I hear her voice. One time I reach his little sister Sibyl, who gives me the scoop.

"Freddie can't talk to you, Tommy Cadigan, so stop calling this number," she whispers into the receiver.

"Why can't he talk?"

"He's been grounded until he goes on his mission after school. He's going to Africa. But he's not taking me. He's flying to Uganda to make everybody Mormon. He's getting his shots and going to meetings. He already has his ticket, and he doesn't want to spend any more time with bad people like you, Tommy Cadigan. I know what you do in those parks. I'm not stupid,"

I hear her mother's shrill voice in the background. "Young lady what are you doing? Hang that receiver up this instant."

"Goodbye, Tommy Cadigan," she says. "I love you. And Freddie does too." The phone hits the hook.

I know Freddie's plans for college are on hold and he's about to be exiled, presumably because of what he told his dad about my revelation. He's sequestered out there in the flat suburbs with those over-weeded gardens laden with the finest pesticides, and I have no way of getting hold of him, even if I could fabricate some excuse to use the Jeep and head out to those wide lanes of the new subdivision. Freddie is hiding upstairs in one of those vast wall-to-wall carpeted manses, forbidden to read anything but *The Scarlet Letter*.

They've shut him up, and his father, Edward Udall of First National Bank of Idaho, has been spared any indictment because of his status in the community. I have no intention of trying to disrupt that hypocrisy, though I consider it seriously numerous evenings when Coco and I long for our Freddie fix.

Sometimes I feel like calling *The Statesman* and asking some cub reporter new to the beat to meet me in the alley outside the Gamekeeper for a tip that would blow this scandal sky high. Bank Vice President and Mormon Bishop Edward Oren Udall caught with his pants down, or should I say with his mouth open in the dugout. I always wonder whether or not these suits actually get off by giving these blowjobs. I mean, what's in it for them?

I also wonder why someone else has not exposed Mr. Udall, but after the night Winfrey pulled out her piece, I realize Halverson and Kurt have kept silent for a reason. They're keeping Chevys in gas with Udall's hush money, Hal buying pointy shoes and stilettos with his newfound wealth while McKellar—I don't know—is supporting his sick mom or investing in stocks and bonds. McKellar, who knows? I just wish we could sit down and eat a burger together. Somewhere dimly lit, somewhere with a big plate of very thin and very greasy fries, endless refills on Coke, and some plastic squirt bottles full of yellow mustard and red catsup. Just sit down and eat and talk—you know like two blokes—shoot the breeze about Hank Aaron and the Cleveland Browns. Be guys together and stop fighting all the time. McKellar wants to beat the shit out of me, I know that, but I also know that he likes me and that—inexplicably, I still like him. I think about Kurt and me, you know, on a kind of date. A guy date, you know. Maybe a wank in the car on the way home. No biggy. Just two horny teenagers doing it in some abandoned shed somewhere under moonlight one summer. And then just leaning against a log and having a smoke, shoulder to shoulder with our shirts off in August. Just a weird fantasy I have about Kurt, the same guy who wants to strangle me.

Even if I could find Clark Kent in the alley and give him the low down on Ed Udall, the biggest fish in the Boise River, I seriously doubt his byline would ever hit the black and white of *The Statesman*. Hell, for all I know, Hathorne and Danforth already have wind of Mr. U's escapades. No doubt Howard Schleiner, as Ruth proved, has been instructed to leave certain individuals off the list of interviewees. So, when Freddie loses it on the stand and lets it slip, the record needs some serious striking. In fact, the trial is adjourned for a day after Freddie's testimony.

But Freddie's public statement about his father in open court is going reverberate through the community, with or without the stonewalling of *The Statesman*. Mr. Udall and the monkey cages are now linked and the reporters had no choice but to follow Fred out the Hall of Justice and accost Mrs. Udall on her way back to her station wagon that day. Of course, she put her head down and refused to talk to KPAX or KECI.

How do I know this? Hearsay, actually. I wasn't there when she drove off amid the photographers, but I hear about it from just about everybody. I see it on the five o'clock news. I see Freddie's front door in Nampa, the television station's white Ford outside the Udall home. We all do.

And what now? I have no idea what. I want to know what. I want to be on his bedspread next to him, but I can't. They won't let me. I have to go to sleep. I have a big day tomorrow.

14. ON THE STAND

Luckily, I'm called first thing the next morning. I need to get the ordeal over, need to stop thinking about Freddie, if possible. I'm wearing my brown corduroy coat, knit tie and yellow shirt, Oxford cloth, roomy and comfy. But no matter how much I groom for the witness stand, suddenly I am in a twilight zone that scares the living daylights out of me.

I like Blaine Hathorne, actually. After Freddie's ordeal, I assume he wants to go easy on both me and Judge Danforth, especially now after news that the DA's office has conveniently overlooked the eminent Mr. Udall.

"Mr. Cadigan," Hathorne speaks frankly to me. "You have taken an oath in this courtroom today to tell the whole truth. I know you are under an enormous amount of pressure with the alleged perpetrator of these crimes in the same room, but I assure you no harm will come to you for telling the jury what happened to you last summer." Ruth is holding off on objections this morning for some reason, and I am trying to hold my tongue too, as instructed by my dad.

"Do you have a question for the witness, counsel, or will we be listening to your commentary for the next eight hours?" Judge Danforth asks. He must have missed his second cup of coffee.

"Yes, your honor. Mr. Cadigan, how old were you in the summer of 1955?"

"Sixteen."

"On the night of July 28 of that year, did you have occasion to meet the defendant in a cedar grove near the Pericles statue in Julia Davis Park?"

"Yes." I still don't know how far I will go with my answers. 'Just answer the questions. Don't volunteer any information.' Ruth's drilling rings in my ears. Hathorne is starting off slowly, and some of the heart-pounding blush I feel at first starts to lose its hue. I'm ready for him though. I've read the statutes at least ten times. For lewd and lascivious conduct, there has to be manual-genital contact, or genital-genital, oral-genital, anal-genital, manual-anal, etcetera, etcetera. But what strikes me is that such behavior must be done with intent to arouse or gratify the lust or passion of the accused. True, the mere solicitation of such contact is also a crime as is attempted lewd or lascivious contact, but intent has to be there. The sodomy statute (infamous crime against nature) on the other hand does not specifically require intent but does require penetration of the penis into some cavity. Sodomy, unlike lewd and lascivious, has no age requirement.

"Could you describe for the court what happened in the grove, Mr. Cadigan?"

"Yes. After we left the Y, I asked Coach to meet me in the park. He said no, but I pleaded with him. I told him I had something I had to tell him, and it would only take a few minutes. We met at Pericles and then went into the grove where I told him his friendship was more than friendship for me. I can't remember what I said, exactly, except that I started crying, which always happens because of my PBA, my crying disorder, but I told him I had never felt anything like what I felt for him. Told him it was real, driving me crazy. He had to know. I didn't care how he reacted. I did care, but it was burning inside me so I had to get it out. Coach hugged me and told me he understood, but we couldn't be anything but—"

"The defendant hugged you in the cedar grove?"

"Yes."

"Was there any genital to genital contact during that hugging session?"

"I don't know."

"You don't remember if the defendant's genitals touched yours?"

"Mr. Hathorne, I was nervous. I had just told Coach I was in love with him. I was scared stiff. He hugged me, just like you hug your mom or friend when somebody close dies or is in trouble. I have no idea where anyone's genitals were at that point."

"Let's move on. Tell us what happened at the hot springs on the night of August 8."

"Coach and I drove up there for a soak."

"Was there any sexual contact between you and defendant on the night of August 8?"

"What exactly do you mean by sexual?" I'm playing the Freddie game. I know he'd be proud of me if he were in the gallery.

"Was there any genital to genital contact?"

"No."

"Was there any manual to genital contact?"

"Yes."

"Were you naked in the pool?"

"Yes."

"Was there any anal to genital contact?"

"Yes."

"Any penetration?"

"Excuse me?" I say, taken aback by this question, even though I know it's crucial to the case of sodomy.

"Did the defendant's genitals penetrate your anal cavity? The question is quite simple."

"We were in the water. I was upset. I felt him grabbing me from behind. I felt him pressing against me. I can't say, Mr. Hathorne. I don't think he got inside. It didn't hurt in there."

"But did the tip of his penis enter your sphincter?"

"I don't know for sure, but I don't think it did."

"How can you not know something as specific as intercourse?"

"Objection, arguing," Ruth perks up at last.

"Sustained. Move on, counsel. The witness has answered the question to the best of his knowledge."

"Could you describe more completely what happened at Drummond Hot Springs for the jury? I know this is difficult for you, but could you give us a sense of what the defendant did to you?"

"Excuse me, Mr. Hathorne, but you don't know what is or is not difficult for me. It's not difficult for me to talk about how much I love Coach. I don't like talking about what goes on with us sexually any more than you would like talking about what goes on with you and your wife in the bedroom. I don't mean to be disrespectful, but... anyway yes, Coach felt me up, and, in the pool, he tried to hump me, but he never did it to gratify his passion." I am quoting the statute.

"How do you know?"

"He told me, and I could figure it out. He was trying to scare me. He did it to teach me a lesson. He had no interest or intent to screw me for his own lust at all."

"You mean he was rubbing himself against you in the pool without any desire to gratify himself."

"That's right, Mr. Hathorne. Coach was angry with me because he thought I was taking money for sex at the monkey cages like McKellar. That's what Mr. Dir told him. But he didn't know that rumor was untrue until I convinced him, so he wanted to scare me with his aggression. He thought I was one of those guys down at the cages out to have a good time and make some money off married men. Coach thought I was taking him for a major ride in order to get him into trouble or into bed, but once I swore on a stack of Bibles I was not into sex for money, he calmed down."

"Then what happened?" Hathorne asks. He's in a daze over my absurd but oddly plausible story. I'm talking too much again, but it seems to be working. "Once you set the record straight, was there any contact?"

"Almost. We started to hug and then the bear showed up."

"I see. You are telling me the defendant was naked in the hot springs with you and was rubbing his genitals against you and he was not intending to satisfy his lust? Do you really expect us to believe that, Tommy? Can you expect any reasonable—"

"Objection, your honor." Ruth wakes up again. "Argumentative."

"Sustained."

"Mr. Cadigan, how do you know the defendant did not want to satisfy his lust?"

"Sir, how do we know exactly what anyone wants to do? I mean I don't even know what I intend to do half the time." I look up at the judge, who is not happy with my philosophizing. "I guess I figured it out because of the way Coach was acting—so out of character. So ungentle. And then he told me what he was up to once he finally believed me about not trying to deceive him."

"I see. Let's move on, shall we? I understand you were bathing in the Lochsa River with the defendant on the 18th of August, is that correct?"

"Yes, and fishing too. Coach caught a rainbow. Good sized."

"Mr. Cadigan, let's leave the trout fishing aside for a moment and talk about what went on in the water during those swims that afternoon. Tell us, when you were at the river, did your teacher and football coach have occasion to fondle your genitalia manually?"

"Fondle?"

"Yes. Did he touch your genitals with his hands?"

"I'm not sure. My hand might have brushed up against his privates. His hand might have touched mine. Look, Mr. Hathorne, I know what you're driving at. But we were just fooling around. Wrestling and diving and swimming. Coach wasn't up to any sex at the river. We were just having fun." I'm supposed to be shutting up, wary, but I can't help it. I need to tell my story, even though I can see my dad grimacing. I'm just trying to explain, trying to be real.

"You seem to know exactly what the defendant was thinking every time he touched you over and over again last summer even though you just told us you don't know half the time what you yourself are intending,"

"Counsel is arguing again, your honor," Ruth raises her voice. "The witness, need I remind him, is in a sensitive position for a seventeen-year-old, and I expect he is not in need of Mr. Hathorne's sarcasm."

"The objection is sustained, Ms. Libby. Proceed counsel and mind your manners," the judge states with a rare grin.

"My apologies. Tell us, if you can, how you came to know what the defendant intended when he kissed you in the park, when he rubbed your back in the shower, when he pushed his penis into your anus at the hot springs? How do you know what he desired, Mr. Cadigan?"

"Objection you honor. Counsel's statements assume facts not in evidence."

"Sustained." The judge looks down at me. "Mr. Cadigan," he says, "tell the court on what basis you developed your impression about Coach's intended desire during these episodes."

"Well, your honor, I cannot deny that I love the defendant, that's the truth. But to answer your question, I don't know for sure. I know what he told me—in the grove, he was comforting. At the hot springs, he was being mean and angry. At the beach, we were horsing around. I probably was thinking a lot more about lust than he ever was. He kept telling me he liked me but it couldn't work, that we had to wait until I was old enough, that we needed to keep it platonic. He kept telling me that, but I guess I wouldn't take no for an answer. Look, I'm a shy person, but with Coach I just came out of my shell and let him have it. I couldn't help it. And I know he cared about me. I could tell by the way he listened to me, the way he watched me on the bench at practice, the way he took the time to show me how to tackle below the waist. He read my essays and wrote comments. He wasn't going to just turn me away, I figure. But gratify his lust with me? It just doesn't make sense, not the way he treats me with so much care. I just can't see his intent as sex or lust."

Hathorne leans against his table, watching me spin out of control. I am, after all, his witness. He has called me to prove two felonies, and I figure he knows I am trying to keep intent at bay.

But what has this anatomical craziness have to do with justice? Why is the law reducing my attachment to Coach to the mechanics of intercourse? Is this fair, I've asked myself countless times, wishing Freddie were by my side to help me figure it out. Is degrading my love to sexual mechanics justifiable when Hathorne and Danforth are probably exploring fellatio and anal stuff in the privacy of their own bedrooms? If this is the law, then the law *is* an ass.

15. EAST OF EDEN

It's around ten thirty when Judge Danforth, opening a note from his clerk, announces he has been called away on business. We're adjourned until 1 p.m. I have a breather but will be back in the box after lunch. I hate lunch, but Mom and Dad scoop me up quickly and sequester me in the car. They're taking me to the Owyhee for a clubhouse sandwich, my mother behind the wheel of the DeSoto wagon, her silence thick as we head over there. When we get to the entrance, she remains behind the wheel. My dad announces she has to go back to the hospital. I get out of the backseat and walk over to the front window, waiting for her to roll it down so I can give her a kiss the way I always do when she drops me off at practice or Freddie's. This time, the window stays shut. She just grimaces through the pane, raises her hand goodbye and drives off slowly. I can see her eyes glistening, see tears swelling. A snub it is, but I know I have to cut her some slack, since I have been declaring my love for another man in open court all morning

"Your mom's having a hard time with this, Tommy." His eyebrow rises when we enter the hotel and discover glaring, a new reality for Kevin Cadigan at the Owyhee. I suspect Boiseans are conflicted: most of them tolerate, even like my off-beat dad, the scruffy public defender who listens to everybody's problems, but they're thrown for a loop when they hear about his poor boy being molested by that pervert at the high school, looped around again when they hear the poor boy is getting a kick out of being molested, in fact might have been the molester himself.

They do let us into the dining room at any rate, the manager finding us a dark booth in the back, bringing Coke and coffee while we stare at the long, tall menu with specials clipped to the top— Salisbury steak and fish sticks because it's Friday. After we order and get rid of curious Madge with her apron and pencil in her hair, my dad takes out a big fat envelope and hands it to me.

I see the Berkeley logo in the left-hand corner, unglue the flap on the back and find my admission to college. A wonderful moment it is in the midst of all this madness. I hug my Dad and give him a kiss on the cheek, which he accepts rather reluctantly in the public lunchroom. I am hot damn excited to have my ticket out of Idaho but sure as hell don't want to leave Freddie or Coach in the lurch even if one of them is on his way to Africa and the other wishes he could be shipped to Australia.

"So how you holding up on the stand?"

"Okay, I guess. I'm talking too much. I know I'm embarrassing you and Mom, but I'm trying to tell it like it is."

"Well, you are making Hathorne work for his conviction. I'll say that much." He takes a deep breath and then a deep drag off his Marlboro. A big gulp of coffee follows, leaving the shallow white cup almost drained. Our hovering waitress tops it off in no time, anxious to get back to our two-top for some potential gossip. My dad finally thanks her profusely and tells her he can't drink anymore.

"What do you think will happen to Mr. Udall?" I ask him, as I bite into my greasy burger, avoiding the fat fries with their mushy innards. I don't even want lunch, but dad will not hear of it.

"Well, they haven't arrested him yet. I suppose they'll pick him up today or tomorrow. He'll be booked, bailed, and an arraignment will be set. My suspicion is that he will plead guilty and get a suspended sentence or maybe six months for lewd and lascivious. They have to do something now that he's been exposed. By his son, no less. Poor Freddie. Maybe Ruth was being too zealous, but she's a tough one, and let's face it, we wanted to get Coach a good lawyer," he says, forking half a fish stick soaked in lemon and tartar sauce.

"Freddie's going to get into some big trouble."

"Freddie will be rehabilitated by the Mormon community. They take care of their own. I suspect he'll be ushered into some camp where they can re-educate him. The Udalls will be removed from Nampa and probably relocated in Utah—Provo or Orem."

"But I thought Freddie would be free now that his Dad has gotten caught."

"Think twice. Freddie might bolt and end up on our doorstep. But I hope not. I don't want to get on the wrong side of the church around here. And I don't want to get in the business of becoming part of the jack Mormon Protection Plan."

"I've never seen him so panicked."

"He may have been hellbent on telling the truth about the two of you and Coach—"

"You think he wanted to blurt it out and was just looking for an opportunity?"

"Witnesses do weird, unexpected things under pressure."

We eat our cottage cheese in silence after Dad's little round up. I need to get to Freddie somehow. Even hitchhiking, but I'll wait until the trial is over. I will find him if it kills me. I eat a scoop of chocolate ice cream in one of those stainless steel raised dishes they keep in the freezer. I could have eaten the dish too, but we have to get going. We head back through town, walking quickly in hopes of avoiding detection. Dad wants to duck into the smoke shop on the way, and I follow him in. Mr. Toomey behind the counter is surrounded by hanging chips and candy bars, his radio on in the background. He greets my dad as one Irishman to another.

"I guess you heard what happened to the Udall boy, Kev."

"No, I haven't," I hear my Dad say. I'm looking at the magazines while he is chatting up his buddy.

"Oh, it's a crying shame it is. I just can't believe it," Mr. Toomey says. "To have his Dad caught up in this nasty business and then to go and do that to himself. I don't know what in the name of Joseph this world is coming to. It has to stop, Kevin. Got to. They've got to leave us alone. We aren't bad people. We slip up. Sure. We all get into a damn lot of trouble one way or another. But to drag this sex stuff out of everyone and then this bright young kid locks himself in his dad's Cadillac like that and starts the engine and then just lets the exhaust take him. Kevin, you've got to do something about this craziness. This thing is getting way out of hand. You have to stop them, stop this insanity. Go to the mayor, I don't know.

"What a tragedy. That poor boy—and such a brain he was too. I seen him in here, tearing through *Time* and *Life*, page after page, like a photographer. You know I never asked him to buy a darn thing, I didn't. I just watched that boy gobble up every scrap of news with those glasses and that attention, that intense concentration. Seen him down here with your son a couple of times. Never seen anything like him. I know kids that love to read, but that one, that one was smarter than a tree full, I'm telling ya, Kev. I'm telling you, it's got to stop. This stupid lynch mob has gone too far."

I overhear Mr. Toomey, standing there with *Look* in my hands, pretending to read the story about James Dean, hearing but not hearing, taking Mr. Toomey's words in but not their meaning. Dad is looking over at me, the thick envelope sticking out of his suit coat pocket. He takes the magazine out of my hands, puts his arm around me and leads me out of the shop. I can't believe how lucky I am to have a dad like Kevin Cadigan. I'm not even crying right now. I can't bring it into my head.

I used to spend a lot of times walking home from grade school, St Catherine's, trying to avoid the cracks in the concrete sidewalks. I spent so many afternoons with my head down trying to stride over those cracks, but the distance always caught up with me. And then when I came home by myself for the thousandth time and my mom asked me where my friends were, I kept having to make excuses.

Truth is I've never really had any. I don't really know how to make them. I'm better with dogs. When I find Freddie in high school and we become friends, it's a tremendous relief because whenever I get quizzed about my dubious social skills, I can just talk about what Freddie and I are up to. Freddie has bailed me out of a sentence of shyness I'm never allowed to acknowledge. Shy is a disease in 1955, especially for a tall, lanky, good-looking young man like Tommy Cadigan. Shy? Gloria's boy? Impossible. But, yep, I have the shy gene; and yep, Freddie has always been my cure.

When I hear Freddie is the one that stuffs the rags into the exhaust pipe of the Caddy in the Udall's garage and not his father, when I hear that statement of fact again from Dad as we walk past Whitehead Drugs on the corner, I need to sit down. He takes me into the drugstore, and I sit there in a daze. He says he will get me excused from court this afternoon. He asks me why I'm not crying and then withdraws the question. I think he is talking to himself.

I'm drained, dazed, and eerily calm. We both still can't believe Mr. Udall was not the one in that car, but Mr. Toomey has been clear. I don't want to believe it. I tell Dad I have to go back on the stand and finish up. I can't go into the weekend in the middle of this trial with Freddie on my mind. I can't do both, I insist. He is skeptical, worried. He has some of my PBA medicine in his pocket, tells me to take it. I swallow it on condition that he lets me finish up.

16. PENETRATION

"Mr. Cadigan. Here we are again after a long recess," Hathorne begins, assuming his folksy pose. "I realize it's Friday afternoon and you're probably anxious to get this testimony over with, so you can go back home to your friends and the movies or pizza parlor or whatever teenagers are up to these days. I will try to make this quick and painless, but you have to realize how serious this proceeding is just as we know how hard it must be for you—"

"Enough, counsel," Judge Danforth tells Blaine, suppressing a burp. I can hear him from on high over my shoulder. "Ask the young man your questions and spare us the niceties. I appreciate your efforts to make the victim reasonably comfortable, but I have little doubt the son of Kevin Cadigan is quite ready for your examination."

"Mr. Cadigan, could you describe what happened at the Cherry Hill cabins on the night of August 18?" Hathorne starts in. My head is beginning to ache already. I'm holding on to the chair tightly. I can't figure out who has found out about Freddie. It doesn't seem like anybody knows.

"Yes. Coach rented a cabin at the Cherry Hill after the Studebaker broke down and had to be towed to Myrtle Beach. After dinner, we headed over there, took showers, and then sat on our beds and talked about the Bible. Then I went over to Coach's bed and sat down next to him. I can't describe it. I..." The tears are starting all of a sudden, me thinking about that night kissing, thinking about the feel of Coach's muscles pressed into my body. I think of Freddie and shut down suddenly, angrily, schizophrenically, glancing over at Coach's stoic face.

"Your bodies came together on the defendant's bed that night?"

"Yes," I say, determined to be Freddie, determined to steel myself to this homo-hunter.

"I will need to ask you some intimate questions about this encounter. It's my job. Please bear with the court, Mr. Cadigan. Was their manual genital contact?" I can't lie under oath. I can't follow Coach's radical refusal to follow unjust justice. I have to tell the jury what happened.

"Yes." The litany begins. Only oral/anal does not make the cut. There is no question about arousal. Lewd and lascivious is on the table. Hathorne has his case if he can prove intent.

"Would you say that this contact was done for the purposes of satisfying lust?"

"No."

"So, you're telling the court the you two slept together without reaching orgasm?"

"No. I'm not saying that."

"Well, what did happen when you slept together?"

"I don't know, exactly. We made love."

"Did you make love with the intent to gratify your passion?"

"Yes."

"Did the defendant desire to gratify his passion as well?"

"I don't know. You'll have to ask him."

"So, you can tell us he did not intend to satisfy his passionate desire in the other episodes, but in this one you do not know?"

"Yes."

"How can you be so sure about the other times and not about this one?" Hathorne asks. He has cornered me. It's like checkers or chess. I'm trapped. What would Freddie say?

"Mr. Hathorne, at the cabin, I was so wound up with Coach I can only tell you what I felt. I was all over him. It was like I was in another world."

"Did Coach reciprocate your passion?"

"As far as I could tell, yes. But you'll have to ask him for sure. He may have been taking care of me. He may have been feeling overwhelmed. He may—"

"No need to speculate, Mr. Cadigan. We have received your impression."

"Objection, your honor. Counsel is inaccurately restating the witness's testimony," Ruth says.

"Overruled, Miss Libby. The witness has spoken to what he could perceive."

"Let's move on. You and the defendant made love on the night of August 18. We have established that. I have a few more questions about how you made love before Miss Libby will ask you some of her own questions. When you were naked in bed together rubbing against one another in frottage, your erections touching, could you tell the jury whether there was any oral-anal contact?"

"No." The litany again. I tell myself to hold on. No oral genital either way. I have checked my notes. No blowjobs that night.

"Was there any penetration?' Hathorne asks.

"What do you mean by penetration? I told you what happened. We slept together; we didn't screw. I already told you that. But, yes, there *was* penetration! I have never been so penetrated in my life! The entire night was filled with real penetration, Mr. Hathorne. Coach penetrating every cavity I have, the most penetrating time of my life. And now you and your stupid questions are penetrating into my most personal feeling for that man over there.

"Are you happy to be talking about anatomy and proving all the little elements of your ridiculous crime, Mr. Hathorne? Happy to be probing me with your needle, penetrating me with your demeaning questions? Huh? Are you getting some pleasure out of turning the best thing that has ever happened to me into some kind of screw session? It feels good, doesn't Mr. Hathorne?"

"Mr. Cadigan, please."

"Don't Mr. Cadigan me anymore. And keep that bailiff thug away from me for five minutes, then you can call in your men in white coats. Look, judge, I love that guy at that desk over there. You can put his body away for life, but you will never ever destroy what I feel for him and what he feels for me. That is sacred, that is penetrating, that is the truth. Don't you think the two of us thought long and hard about what we did? Don't you think we both knew we were taking a huge risk? But isn't that what love is about?

"Consider the source, you're saying. How can anything I say have any value, especially after the shock of finding out my best friend has committed suicide? No, Tommy Cadigan doesn't know what he's talking about. He's just seventeen. He doesn't know the meaning of justice. He's just a little boy, a little victim. Cart me off to Dr. Butler, cart Coach off to jail. Lock us up, the homos. Put us behind bars. Go ahead. Condemn our hearts, our dreams, our life, liberty, and happiness. Do it in memory of Freddie Udall. And live with it for the rest of your lives."

17. COCO

I want to go to Pioneer Cemetery by myself. With Coco, just with Coco. I convince Mom and Dad to let me take the Jeep out there to the old run-down burial ground where the Udalls have a plot. I haven't been allowed to drive by myself for as long as I can remember, but Dad relents when I beg to visit Freddie and am granted two hours of freedom. I wasn't invited to the church service. I didn't want to face them anyway. I sent Freddie's little sister Sybil a card, but I didn't want to face the rest of them. Not at that point. Not after the hasty, hush-hush burial, all within a week of Freddie's death, before the jury has even reached a verdict in the Williams case.

What a day, that Friday in the Jeep with the windows down, a crazy March day in the fifties, the sunny snowmelt brighter than technicolor. Coco in the back with her head out the window, nostrils against the fresh air, then coming inside to peek through the front windshield, my hand on her head and a quick kiss. Out riding around on those streets out of town looking for that nineteenth-century bone drop with all its rotting angels and eroding poems.

I put her on leash at first, walking down gravel paths, through tilted tombstones and shiny granite slabs carved with dates and middle names no one ever used. It's a big place on a small rise and no one is there to show me where Freddie lies. I start to look for flowers. Surely Freddie's spot will be strewn with them. Surely the wind will die down. I finally let the dog off leash as my search through the rows of graves continues. Creepy. I know he won't have a headstone yet, but his body is somewhere in that dilapidated cemetery. Coco is off sniffing while I walk in circles, Freddie lost in a maze of dead couples.

And then, she barks, sniffing and wagging over the fresh dirt and the endless Udalls.

The lord is my shepherd. I shall not want.
He maketh me to lie down in the green pastures.
He leadeth me beside the still water.
He restoreth my soul.

There on the thick paper beneath the fading roses, the psalm Freddie will lie beneath, his sneakers holding the paper down. Coco paws the earth and smells the soles. She wags her tail, sniffs the dirt. What does she know? What leads her to calm down beside me? In my back pocket I have the note Freddie left for me, the one his little sister secreted in a flowery card and gave to her little brother to give to me at school, which he did with a scowl, telling me to keep my mouth shut about it. The note flaps in the wind as I take it out and read it again. Read it aloud with Coco lying down next to me panting, her mouth open, swallowing the wind, happy now to have found the scent of Freddie, waiting for him to show up. Or not. How much does she know?

> *Dear Tommy,*
> *You know how much I love you, and I know how mad you and Coco are that I have to say goodbye. I wouldn't leave you two if I could find a way to stop blaming myself for what I did to my father. I can't forgive myself for ruining his life, and I don't think he will ever forgive me. I thought of running away to your house, but I don't have the courage that you have. My courage comes in my brain, but I can't find a way out of my family's clutches. Or my own.*
> *I love you so much. You cannot know. Yes, madly jealous but also madly happy for you. I have to get out of the way now. Please keep our dream alive. You are the brave one. You*

will stand up for what we had together, what you and Coach
have now. You will fight for justice, I know it. Bye for now.
Your best friend forever,
Freddie.

There he is underground, the once blued veins of his thin white body, that ribcage sticking out. Is he buried with those thick black rims pushed into his nose, buried with the broken lenses that brought us together in ninth grade?

"Come on, Coco," I say out loud. It's getting dark. She is rolling in the dirt. At least she's not digging. She won't come when I call, though. She is never disobedient and always knows when I'm fed up with her detours. This time she won't have it. She keeps circling the grave, sticking her nose in the shoes, smelling the psalm.

I have to get the leash out and order her to sit, which she finally does reluctantly, defiantly. She's telling me I'm making a mistake to pull her away from Freddie.

I saunter toward the run-down black gate, now darkening in the gloaming, half hidden between swaying cottonwoods. I look up to find the dog has disappeared again. Has she headed back to Freddie, dammit? I should never have let her off leash. Mom will kill me if I don't get back soon. "Coco," I yell into the dead space as wind rustles the heart-shaped leaves. "Coco, come! Cokie, get over here, right now!" Nothing. Then I hear to my relief the crunch of gravel behind the Jones's pillars.

"Hi, Caddy," Kurt says. "I knew you'd come out of that house eventually. And I knew damn well where you'd be headed in that beat-up rig. That Jeep gives you away." My heart sinks as I see him in his faded jeans and Braves sweatshirt, his curly black hair longer now, his freckled tiger face still as striking as it was in the locker room. Everything him about him is as rugged and sexy as ever. But now as threatening. Will he track me down in Berkeley, if I do ever get out of this town?

"Kurt, what the hell? Why are you still following me around?" I ask, already looking for an escape route. It would have to be quick. He isn't going to let me get away this time, and I know he can sprint. He may not be a long-distance runner, but he can spurt. I've seen him on the field with that look in his eye—out for blood, tough as nails. And now I have the ball and he's ready to tackle me.

"I have my spies." he says. "You thought I'd give up now that your pal threw in the towel. Call a spade a spade and leave you to your little college prep BS. 'Fraid not. We still got a score to settle, man. Now that everyone in this town has branded me a queer, you get to run off to your fancy university while I'm stuck in this cow town pumping gas and fending off fat ass drunks coming on to me with their hairy bellies. Yea, let's pay Kurt for a little cash to get some head. Nice work you left for me, Tommy."

"Come on, man. What do I have to do with you and the monkey cages? I didn't make you a—"

"Shut up, you asshole," he says in a growl and grabs my shirt. "Just shut up. Shut the fuck up." He shakes me wildly, tearing the front of my shirt, his head down as his voice falters until he's mumbling into the flannel bundled in the fists of his hand, his shoulder scrunched up as he leans into me, his head down. "Please, just…" He holds desperately on to my shirt, pounding handfuls of cloth at my chest. I try to pull away from him, try to back away, but before I know it, he is on his knees in font me, bawling, holding on to my legs, sobbing.

"Please, please," he keeps saying over and over again as he pulls on the pockets of my pants, his forehead on my belt, weeping uncontrollably in throbs of sorrow and anger, pulling on me, shoving me down to my knees beside him. I am too stunned not to comply with his pleas for help, weirdly mixed with his aggressiveness. He's almost frantic, wrenching the belt, his hands looped to the inside of my jeans, thrashing me back and forth in his wild tantrum.

"Kurt, it's okay, it's okay."

"No, it's *not*. My life is fucking ruined because of you in that stupid locker room, because of you gawking. Why couldn't you leave me

alone? With those stupid eyes, that look, dripping with cum. Cum,
cum, cum. That's all you ever wanted to do with me. And look what
you've turned me into—a flaming faggot. The laughing stock of this
town. All because of you and your fucked-up eyes, which I am going
to get rid of right now." His slump suddenly turns wild, lurching forward to scratch my face, pushing me down on the gravel. I turn over
and try to crawl away from him. He's on top of me now, flattening
me out on the path.

"Kurt, you don't want to do this. You don't..." He's humps me
from behind, his chest on my back, still trying to get his hands
around my arms to my eyes as I crawl out from under him.

Another yelp comes out of him all of sudden, a scream of pain as
he lets go of me and starts hollering and pushing himself across a
flat gravestone. The dog has him by the pant leg, tearing through his
jeans and growling. She loosens her grip and then clomps on again
as Kurt tries to kick her away his hands, but I grab his arms. Coco
growls and bites, tearing his pants off and exposing his underwear.
Kurt slides backwards as I pull the dog off by the collar and scream
at her to stop. She keeps growling madly, barking ferociously, until
I manage to calm her.

We face each on the ground, both bleeding, both dirty, sweating. I
expect Kurt to run away and plan his next attack. Maybe he thinks
I will let the boxer off her leash if he starts to leave. I'm not sure.
We both sit there, knees to chest, shaking and staring at one another.

"Kurt..." I'm shaking. "I'm sorry for everything...sorry for what
happened in the locker room, sorry for telling Ruth what happened
at the cages. But this thing is not my just my fault. It goes two ways.
You didn't need to touch me on the golf course, you know. You didn't
need to take me behind the stands with that bald guy, to flirt with
me all the time. Yea, maybe I started it, but I didn't turn you into a
homo. Come on, man. You like guys, so it sucks because the world
will screw with us forever. What are you going to do about it? Beat
the shit out of me for the rest of your life because I turn you on? This

has got to stop, Kurt. I can't be looking over my shoulder forever because you hate yourself or you hate me because you hate yourself.

"You're better than that, Kurt. You are so cool. You think I'm saying this because I'm trying to get you off my back? Maybe so, but you got me into this shit too. I was going out with Pam until you started undressing in front of me in the locker room. You're just as much to blame."

He smiles a little now, holding his head held up on his elbow as he listens to my tirade. Sulking a little, skeptical but letting it sink in. We are scraped up, pebble marks imprinted on our hands and arms. My flannel shirt is torn and my cheek scratched from his nails, Kurt's jeans are almost in shreds. He is scared of my dog. I can see that. She's still growling as he raises himself up to sit on the lawn beside Frank Jones's uncle, his hand on the shiny flat grave marker. He's wildly desperate in a way I never imagined Kurt could be.

"Can you hug me?" I ask him out of the blue. "Would you scratch my eyes out if I come over there for a hug?"

He's sulking. I know he's sore, but I also know he likes me, and I, in some wannabe, admiring place, also like him. For some reason, I want more than anything else to make him feel good about himself. I want to hold him in my arms. Let him know that he is a cool guy, that he was still wicked, still a star.

We hug long and hard against the Jones mausoleum. He has his head on my chest most of the time and I can feel him shaking a little, sighing even as he presses his chest into mine. We are too tired to do much else than embrace. We try grabbing each other's crotch and getting that part going, but we can't and laugh about it.

I'm still shivering from his aggression, still scared. He says nothing for the longest of minutes before he stands and pulls me up, smiling and grabbing me in a bear hug as he lifts me off the ground. And then he puts me down, running a hand through my hair before he kisses me, turns, and walks away.

The jury deliberates for less than two hours after the judge instructs them the morning after Ruth's closing argument. The foreman rises to announce the verdict. Martin Williams is found guilty of one count of sodomy and three counts of lewd and lascivious conduct with a minor. In spite of what Ruth and Dad told me, in spite of their statements from the start that the case against Coach was open and shut, I can't believe twelve real people, with hearts and minds and consciences, would turn a blind eye to the most beautiful thing that has ever happened to me, just because that beauty comes from the love that two men have shared.

Judge Danforth doesn't take a long time to consider his sentence. He wants to stay in office. Regardless of Coach's otherwise clean record, he decides to throw the book at him. In his remarks from the bench, the Judge calls the defendant "a fox in the chicken coop," a man who has violated the utmost social trust—a teacher charged in confidence to take care of our youth. Martin Williams is sentenced to twenty-five years imprisonment at the Idaho State Penitentiary. The judge's gavel hammers a nail in my heart. I sit stunned in the back of the gallery.

The next thing I know I am being grasped from behind by my father and a couple of khaki police officers, who are trying to pull me off Coach, now in handcuffs. I snapped. I don't remember how I managed to shove my way up to the front or how I hurdled the bar and lurched toward the back of Marty's dark suit. I don't remember how I landed my hands on his shoulders and held on for dear life, screeching his name and yelling "no" at the top of my lungs.

I *do* remember seeing his face turn toward me as I felt them pulling me away from him, felt my dad's arms locked around my chest, there at the defense table while the smug bailiff, with his nightstick and black-beaded belt, attempted to take the defendant down. Coach, unperturbed in the chaos, the eye of the storm, looks me in the eye, smiles. "Chin up, Meriwether."

I watch his blue suit disappear behind the chambers door.

EPILOGUE

To the tune of "We Gotta Get Out of This Place"
by The Animals

I survived Boise, 1955 with the help of Ruth and her partner Ann. With the help of my dad, who is divorced now and lives with El in San Francisco, where I work on civil rights cases when I'm not chasing ambulances. Got to make a buck. I have a couple of gay discrimination cases I work on mostly *pro bono*. I ended up going to law school after studying English at Berkeley. At first, I thought I wanted to be a teacher like Coach, but the Freddie letter became my destiny. His charge to keep our dream alive, to do justice, hounded me through school, stared at me every time I saw a pair of black-rimmed glasses on the street or in class. Plus, what kind of job can a PhD in English get these disco days? Might as well fill out an application at the Yellow Cab Company all my teachers told me.

I went to law school in Montana of all places, the only place I could get in, realizing quickly, in spite of Dad and Ruth's encouragement, that most of the stuff I studied had nothing to do with justice at all. But I finally graduated in the 60s, got into some trouble with the Montana Bar for fooling around in Missoula with a couple of Blackfoot guys, and eventually decided to make the move to the cool grey city of love, San Francisco in 1970, where Mel Dir has since my arrival shown me the ropes, and Elvina and Dad have seen to it that I behave myself, even if the Stud calls every Tuesday during Oldies Night ("You Can't Hurry Love"), even if the Castro is beginning to fill up with beltless faded Levis and white t-shirts like the kind Coach used to wear.

He was still locked up in the early Sixties, even though Ruth had argued twice for his parole. I was not allowed to come near him, and the Zubiris and Udalls kept up a pretty strong front to keep him behind bars. He got out on paper, as they say, in late 1963. I testified at that parole hearing in Boise. So did Mom, Mrs. Udall, and Miss Winfrey. The parole board didn't really have much choice. Coach's record was stellar. He and his priest, Father Aloysius, testified to his renewed faith in Catholicism. Others spoke of the classes he taught in prison. He had spent almost a decade behind bars for the crime of loving me and now would be released under strict surveillance for three more years.

I hadn't seen him since March of 1956. His beard was dark black and trimmed, covering his cheeks and neck. He wore a grey jumpsuit. When he walked by me I could detect a slight grin, saw how sinewy he had become. He had lost weight, but not muscle mass. His arms were thinner but more toned. He looked like a samurai—lean, wiry, meditative, there but not there, almost devotional. Faraway.

I was stunned by his appearance almost a decade after the gavel fell, astonished at my callous sorrow, my impatience with the somber manner of this stranger who had become mysterious and unapproachable, weirdly incongruous with my imaginary Coach. Our eyes met as the guard led him from the hearing, reviving my memory of our blue swims at the same time it placed a river of white water between us.

I spoke to my mother in the parking lot after the hearing. It was December 1, cold and clear at one o'clock in the afternoon. She had to get back to the hospital. She always had to get back there. What did she do there all day long, I wondered as a kid? Why did she always use work as an excuse to avoid me?

"You have a lot of nerve young man, a lot of nerve," she said to me on the move across the white-lined lot that morning. "To show your face out here again after all you have done to us. Maybe you were just a mixed up kid back then, but I thought I taught you to know better. Taught you to be considerate of my family, of the Zubiri name in this community, taught you to be kind to girls, Tommy. I thought I did, anyway."

"Mom, you did teach—"

"Did I make you hate women so much? Is it my fault? Was I not sweet enough, was I too strict?"

"You were a good mother, you are—"

"I know you never liked me. You and your father—on your fishing trips and always with your sarcasm—the two of you. You couldn't stand my brothers, the grocery, our traditions from the old country. How can you call yourself Vasco?" Her eyes began to tear. "Do you have any idea what you've done to our family with your sordid little games, running around with that pederast?"

She began looking for the car keys in her coat, pulling out sticks of gum and glasses and whatnot as she fished for the ring. I had my arms out, one against the roof, one against the open door. She grabbed the handle, trying to pull the door closed.

"Mom, look, I know you're doing what you think is right, but Coach deserves to be free. We weren't trying to hurt anybody when we fell for each other, least of all you" I held the door open even as she tried to pull it shut. "Every day I face what it means to be...the way I am. I can't help this. I'm me. And I love you."

"Do you really, Tommy? And what do you call this mess you've made of our lives? If that's love, then I'm not sure I want to have anything to do with it. Please, I can't talk about this now. Let me go."

She pulled on the door, but I held it open for a few seconds more. It became physical, but I had the leverage, my arm wedged between the open door and the chassis. I was trying to stoop down to kiss her on the cheek, bending my stiff arms, lowering my head toward her profile in the seat while she pulled on the door handle, trying half-hearted to shut me out. We struggled, my head down awkwardly, my arms behind me as I craned to find her cheek at least, but she was crying and cringing and didn't want me near her.

"No, Tommy, not now," she said. "I have to go. I can't handle this, son." She leaned into the middle of the car with her camel hair coat bundled up in the cold, avoiding my eyes. She needed to shut me out and I needed to let her. I brushed her shoulders with my neck, smelled her Arpege, the scent sending me back to the hugs and kisses we shared growing up, back to our shared dog love, back—as I stood there in the cold lot drained and freezing—to the trouble my inescapable love for Coach had brought upon her.

I let go of the metal door and took my freezing hand off the red hood. She wouldn't look at me. She slammed the door shut, tears running down her cheeks, and turned the engine over. She pulled her car toward an exit, the wheels screeching. Six taillights in the back of the Impala Super Sport her new husband had bought her. Six red tail lights, braking and moving on toward some empty intersection with a swinging green light.

Once Coach got out on paper, Ruth found him a job and a place to live in Sandpoint, Idaho, up on the Panhandle working for the Forest Service near Pend Oreille. I wasn't allowed anywhere near him, of course. One of the express conditions of his parole was no contact with Tommy Cadigan. I suspect he was watched closely by his officer and parish, not allowed to travel without permission.

A year later, I answered the phone one afternoon in my office. Ruth told me Coach was gone. "He absconded, broke parole. and took off. He must have headed north to Canada. No one knows where he is." For the next hour, I sat in my chair staring out the window.

I'm going to find him if it's the last thing I ever do. He's got to show up sometime, and when he does, we're going to drive back to that sand bar on the Lochsa, back to that deep green current and those granite boulders. We're going to swim in that river again.

Casey Charles lives in Missoula, Montana, where he teaches queer studies, law in literature, and Shakespeare at the university. His first book, *The Sharon Kowalski Case: Lesbian and Gay Rights on Trial*, was nominated for a Publishing Triangle Award in nonfiction, and a collection of essays, *Critical Queer Studies: Law, Film, and Fiction in Contemporary America* followed. His debut novel, *The Trials of Christopher Mann*, came out in 2013. He has also published two poetry chapbooks, and a full-length poetry collection entitled Zicatela will appear in 2018 from Foothills Press.

For more information on the author and his writing, please visit caseycharles.com.